Other books by L.Z. Smith

Isaac Smith Mysteries

The Bartender Ran Last
Promise to a Dead Man (Part One)

Young Adult Fiction

The Late Show
(My Baby Loves the Western Movies)

Available from Amazon.com
or from
Local4Publishing
localfourpublishing@gmail.com

The Giant Panda

The Giant Panda in considered
China's National
Treasure
There are no Giant Panda bears in private hands. All
Giant Pandas, including those on display at national Zoos
are the property f the Chinese Government and are on loan.
In 1987, the Standing Committee of the National People's
Congress passed an amendment to the Criminal Law, saying
"smugglers of giant pandas shall have a punishment of at least
a 10-year sentence and confiscation of property; under grave
circumstances, life sentence or even death sentence together
with a total confiscation of property shall be applied."
These legislative measures have so far effectively protected
giant pandas and other rare animals from human harm.

`All characters depicted in this book are
creations of the author. Any similarities with people living
or dead are coincidental.
All the events in this book are also the
creation of the author.

Global Talent Agency, LLC
Burbank, California

Local 4 Publishing
1544 Stuart Street
Berkeley. CA. 94703
localfourpublishing@gmail.com

The Last Panda

Promise to a Dead Man

Part two

An Issac Smith Mystery

by L.Z. Smith

Prologue

The bullet smashed through the window. I tackled the attractive Chinese woman, whom I had just met, to the floor, and from that moment, while I lay on top of her protectively, our mutual, inexplicable attraction to each other sprung to life.

It all started out quite routinely; a grievance hearing for an old Chinese Bartender who had been unjustly fired from the Oakland Downtown Hyatt Hotel. I was his union rep and it was my job to defend him. But when gun fire broke out in the basement of the hotel after the hearing, and Peter Wu lay in a puddle of blood, I rashly promised I would watch over his niece. If I had known at the time what I was letting myself in for, I probably would have headed for the hills.

From the moment I met Mai-ling my life took a radical left turn, as if I had been thrown into a demolition derby headed for a brick wall; my career as a union representative for Culinary Local 4 was, for me, over. Negotiating contracts and picking up dues from dead beat cooks and bus boys just wouldn't cut it anymore.

After the gunman fired into her house, I whisked her away to my boat in the Emeryville Marina, and from that point onward my life was wrapped up in a cloak and dagger tale right out of a le Carré novel.

I found I couldn't resist this beautiful Chinese lady, and after saving her life and making love to her, I was hooked. I made a promise to her uncle, and I was in love, an incendiary coupling.

Her attempt to discourage me, insisting she didn't need my protection, *came too late for me. At that point I would have jumped into the fires of hell to protect her from harm.*

So even when I discovered the truth, that her uncle had been on a secret mission for the Red Chinese government—the mission that had gotten him killed—and that she had vowed to take his place, I couldn't back out.

Finally, Mei-ling professed her love, although what that meant to a Chinese Communist I had no idea. I became her accomplice and lover, while not knowing what it was I was an accomplice to, or if she was really in love with me or just playing me. All I knew was that we were on the trail of a group of Chinese smugglers, the same gang that had murdered her uncle, and were now trying to murder her and me, and in between searching and the constant threat of deadly violence, we made abandoned love.

It all came to an abrupt end at 4:30 a.m. on Lakeshore Drive by Oakland's Lake Merritt on a cold early fall morning. The two FBI men in the front seat had pulled us out from a ranch overlooking the small town of Glen Ellen. It was under attack by a helicopter full of commandos. The smugglers who were held up there didn't stand a chance. We too, would have been toast, if the FBI guys hadn't showed up.

And then, sitting in the back seat of the car, with Mei-ling snuggled close, she hit me with the news; she was returning to China. Her mission was over, and I was left standing on the shore of Lake Merritt as Mei-ling Wu swept out of my life as dramatically as she had appeared. When I was told by the same Chinese agent who had tried to kill me, that Mei-ling had left to protect me from the Chinese government, it only compounded my grief knowing she was really in love with me and I would never see her again.

Isaac Smith

December 1991

Fall 1991

Chapter 1

Beijing, China

The 747's jet engines hummed as the flight attendant's soothing voice came over the PA in Mandarin; "We will be arriving in Beijing International Airport in approximately one hour. Thank you for flying with China Air." She repeated the announcement in English, Japanese and French.

Had it been over twenty years since Mei-ling Wu had left her home in Guangzhou City for San Francisco, California? Now she was returning, and wondering what kind of reception she would get. She was no longer the promising young history professor with a guaranteed future in China's academia when she had left. Now, in her late thirties with a Doctorate Degree in ancient Chinese History from the University of California at Berkeley, could she melt back into China, or would she forever be thought of as that woman from America.

She hadn't been eager to leave those many years ago, but her Uncle had insisted. The Cultural Revolution was spreading throughout China and turning ugly. By 1968, it had reached into the University where she was teaching as thousands of young people marched through the campus, waving the Chairman's Little Red Book and chanting its simplistic slogans. They denounced their professors as petite bourgeoisie counter revolutionaries. Anyone attempting to argue with them was beaten to the ground. Mei-ling, like many of her fellow professors, believed the Revolution of 1949 would free them from the constraints of the old China and bring with it a new intellectual and academic freedom. And at first it had, but then everything changed. It wasn't as if they were subversives—in fact many had fought in the Red Army. But Mao had unleashed a storm of anti-intellectualism that was sweeping the vast country and threatening to consume any thought counter to his own in its path. It had been hard for her to believe that she could be threatened. She was a faithful member of the Party, and came from a family of revolutionary heroes.

So she was incredulous when her Uncle told her that her ideas would bring her into direct conflict with Mao's new China. "It won't be long before the purges begin," her Uncle warned her. As head of Internal Security in Guangdong Province he was in a good position to know what was going on, and he feared for the safety of his niece whom he had cared for since his sister died giving birth to her.

Now her Uncle was dead, shot down in cold blood in the basement of an Oakland Hotel where he had worked since exiling himself when the purges extended into the Red Army. It saddened her that her beloved uncle, a hero of the glorious Long March and the War of Liberation, had died so far from home, even though he had ultimately sacrificed his life in the service of his dear People's Republic.

It all seemed a long time ago as she leaned back in her seat and closed her eyes. Her mind drifted back to the cold foggy night in Oakland, California just two days earlier. She lay with her head in her lover's lap in the back seat of the two FBI agents' car, wrapped up in a scratchy blanket against the cold Bay Area night. She didn't know how it had happened, but she had fallen deeply in love with the middle aged union business agent, abandoning everything that she had been taught to believe in China. She had been in America longer than she had lived in China, but she had been trained well in her youth. She was a Chinese Communist through and through, and an intellectual Marxist. But from the moment she laid eyes on him that fateful day after her Uncle had been gunned down she had been drawn to him, as if fate had destined them to walk the same path in life. It was the hardest thing she had ever done; forced to separate from him and unable to tell him why. She could still see the look of confusion and hurt on his face that early morning in front of his apartment on Lake Merritt. "I can't come with you," she said. "It has to be this way." That last kiss lingered on her lips, even here in the jet liner that would land in Beijing in less than an hour.

The man in the uniform of the Red Army sitting across from Mei-ling was flipping through a folder. She recognized the medal from the War to Resist U.S. Aggression and Aid Korea, the same medal her Uncle Peter had worn. She hadn't expected to be interrogated upon her return to China, but since the Tiananmen Square incident it all made perfect sense. She had been in the U.S. for a long time, returning only twice since Mao had died along with his Cultural Revolution.

The man looked up from the file and smiled. His close cropped graying hair gave him a stern look despite his pleasant face.

"So, you are the niece of Comrade Ching-Shu Wu."

"Yes."

"I served under Comrade Wu in Korea. He was a brilliant officer and I had much respect for him. I regret I must ask you some questions before we can clear your re-entry into China."

"I understand Major Huang."

She had to retune her ear as the man spoke Mandarin. She had spoken Cantonese exclusively since she was in America. It was the dialect of her home province of Guangdong in Southern China and the language used by most Chinese immigrants around the world since most of them also came from Guangdong. But Mandarin had always been the official language of China and it had become second nature to her during her studies at Beijing University.

"Why have you returned to China?" the Major said, without taking his eyes off the file in front of him.

Apparently he had no knowledge of the agreement she had made with the Chinese Consulate in San Francisco. It came as no surprise to her; the Chinese Government would want as few people as possible to know what had happened.

"When my uncle was murdered I realized the violent and racist nature of the capitalist country I had been living in. I want to come home to my country where I can serve the people of China."

She saw her answer pleased the officer by the smug smile that crossed his face, as if he was confirming the correctness of her answer.

"Some people take a long time to realize how lucky they are to live in the People's Republic. I see by your file that you where an honored member of the People's Maritime Militia when you where young. Most commendable. I understand your flight to America under the Cultural Revolution. Many mistakes were made. I think you will be pleased by the changes that have happened since you left."

"I am sure I will," Mei-ling managed to smile.

"You have been secured a position at Guangzhou Normal University. But I must warn you Mei-ling, you will be watched closely for the time being."

He slammed his stamp onto her passport with such force it made her jump. Then he handed it to her and gave her another bureaucratic smile. "I am sorry about your uncle. I held him in high esteem. Welcome back to The People's Republic."

She sat there for a moment, not sure what to do next.

"You can go. If you hurry you can catch the train to Guangzhou."

* * *

Chapter 2

Washington, DC

Marshal Lee found his favorite bench in between the Freer and Sakler Galleries of Asian Art on the Capital Mall and sat down. It was where he went when he wanted to think withoutbeing surrounded by the chaos of his office at the National Security Agency.

"So what's so damn important that I had to leave my nice air conditioned office to meet you here?"

Lee looked up as the large man dropped down onto the bench besides him; sweat pouring from his face. It was a hot day in the capital with humidity and temperature vying for top spot in the high nineties. He was shorter than McCraven, but built like a football linebacker. The only thing that had aged was his rutty face, hidden behind dark aviation sunglasses and a mop of graying black hair.

"Mac, old buddy, you've gotten out of shape since the old Company days. Was a time you could have walked for days in the Cambodian jungle without stopping. "

McCraven had risen in the ranks of the State Department quickly after leaving the CIA. They had first met in Vietnam where they had been assigned to the same team. They flew clandestine missions into Cambodia, assassinated suspected Viet Cong agents and whored around Saigon. But after the war they were shifted to Germany. Like Lee, he had grown tired of the spy versus spy game with the KGB. It wasn't like in Nam. There things were simple; you killed the Viet Cong, and if they weren't the Viet Cong it didn't matter, they were gooks and nobody cared. But in Europe the two agencies had grown so used to the Cold War, and the mutual understanding that war between the two super powers would mean mutual destruction, that it had all become a bizarre choreographed dance of one-upmanship. Lee went to the NSA where his particular skills were in demand.

"Looks like you've stayed in shape," the large man said, glancing at his old comrade in arms. "It's the damned humidity," he said, mopping his face and close cropped balding head with a handkerchief. "Didn't like it in Nam. Still don't like it."

"It's that tropical storm coming up from Florida. They say it'll hit sometime this afternoon," Lee answered, as if he was the only one in Washington DC privy to that information.

"That's what they say. So, what's so important that you couldn't tell me over the phone?"

"What do you know about Operation Red Bear?" Lee asked.

McCraven squirmed uncomfortably. He kept mopping his face. His voice dropped a few decimals, as if the trees around them had listening devices. "What do you know about it?"

"Enough to know we've been aiding and abetting the Chinese Reds in carrying out a clandestine operation on U.S. soil," Lee said, not hiding his disapproval. "And that now they've asked us to eliminate a U.S. citizen for them."

McCraven stood up and took off his jacket, loosened his tie and sat back down. He pulled a cigarette from his shirt pocket and fumbled around for his lighter which he finally found in the pocket of his jacket.

Lee recognized it—a Zippo with a Navy Seals logo on it. He had one just like it, but had left it in his desk drawer since he had quit smoking. He watched his friend light up and had a familiar craving.

"This thing has gotten all fucked up," McCraven said. "It was supposed to be top secret, but it seems everyone and their uncle has heard about it. We thought with the Iraqi situation nobody would notice it."

"Well, now they got me involved, and I'm telling you partner, I don't like it," Lee said without changing his stony face. "This entire situation is fucked from top to bottom. Hell, this Isaac Smith is no more than a fucking union bureaucrat."

McCraven laughed. "Since when did you develop a conscience, all the shit you and I have done over the years?"

"We've never murdered a U.S. civilian." Lee said. "Give me one of those cancer sticks."

"Thought you gave them up?"

"Fuck off and give me one," Lee said.

McCraven dug back in his pocket and came out with the pack of Marlboros and the Zippo.

"This has really got you upset," he commented, flipping open the Zippo and lighting the cigarette Lee had stuck between his thin lips.

He took a long drag and two years of abstinence went up in a cloud of blue smoke.

"I'm going to have to know a lot more details before I have a U.S. citizen murdered at the behest of the fucking Chinese Commies," he said.

The two old CIA veterans sat in silence for awhile, watching the few tourists stupid enough to be walking in the blazing noon heat and humidity while trying to visit every Smithsonian museum in their tour guide book. Finally Mc Craven broke the silence:

"I was asked to sit in on the initial meeting with the Chinese when they made their proposal," he said

"Lee looked at his old friend. "Why you?"

"Well, I studied Mandarin when I first joined the Seals."

"What for?" Lee asked.

McCraven shrugged. "Someone checked my file and found out I had learned Chinese at the Foreign Language School; you know the one in Monterey on the West Coast."

"I know where it is," Lee said irritably, wondering if he was telling the truth.

"So I got the call even though it's been years since I learned it."

"Well, this shit is the dumbest idea I ever heard," Lee said, taking another drag off the cigarette.

"I thought the same thing, but these guys that came in with the Bush Administration insisted we support it. Said it was a foreign policy decision. Our people were to stay clear of the operation while the Chinese Consulate in San Francisco conducted a low key investigation, pretty much confining themselves to the Chinatown community. Then this old Chinese bartender was shot down in broad daylight in Oakland. Come to find out he was an officer in the Red Army who had defected to the U.S. during the Cultural Revolution, and the Chinese Consulate had recruited him to infiltrate a gang that was running a smuggling operation. And that's where your Isaac Smith came into the picture."

"Yeah, I read the FBI file," Lee said.

"Then you know he took up with the dead bartender's niece, a Mei-ling Wu. She's been here on a Green Card for over fifteen years. Taught at the University in Berkeley I understand. She went back to China last week and we have reason to believe she was also working with the Consulate. Whatever the Wu woman knew, the Chinese believe Smith also knows. And for whatever reason this particular gang of smugglers was up to something the Chinese Government wants kept quiet."

"The FBI report says they tried to kill him once."

"Well, they missed."

"So we do their dirty work for them?" Lee said.

"No, no," McCraven said. "It's just that…"

"Just that what?"

Lee was growing angry, and his old comrade knew it. He'd have to confide in him even though it was suppose to be classified information.

"Look Lee. I'm going to tell you something, but you have to swear to keep it to yourself."

"Or?"

"Or, I'll have to kill you," McCraven smiled.

Lee knew his old CIA buddy was dead serious despite the good natured smile. It didn't matter how far back they went, or how strong their friendship had been. People in their business did what they had to do and McCraven would have no qualms putting a bullet in his comrade's head.

"You know you can trust me, Mac. But I really have to know what's going on."

McCraven took out another cigarette and lit it off the butt of the old one. He mopped his face with his handkerchief again.

"It's a long story and I'll be damned if I'm going to sit out here in this heat any longer," he said.

"Well, let's go into the Museum. It's cool in there, and there are not many tourists. They seem to favor Natural History and the Aeronautics Museums. Asian Art's not a big draw with tourists."

They entered the Freer museum and were immediately hit by the cool air inside.

McCraven slipped his sports jacket back on.

"That's better," he said. "Let's walk."

They slowly strolled by the collections of Chinese bronzes and jades, paintings and lacquer ware, ancient Near Eastern ceramics, metal ware, and sculpture from South and Southeast Asia.

"An appropriate setting for this story," McCraven said as he glanced at the pieces of ancient art. "This whole thing goes back to the Korean War. A high ranking Red Chinese officer appeared at a UN check point one day seeking political asylum. After a couple of months of interrogation he was convinced to return to the Reds. He was told he could best serve the cause of democracy by becoming a spy. I'm sure he had family in the U.S. and god knows what kind of coercion was used to convince him. Anyway, our people gave him a cover story about being captured and then escaping. They planted the story in the New York Times to be sure the Chinese knew about it. He was welcomed back into the ranks as a hero, and over the years he moved up the hierarchy until he became a member of the inner circles of the Communist Party."

"So, how did he get information to us?"

"You'll love this. He passed information through the Soviet embassy in Beijing. The Russians were as eager to find out what the Chinese leaders were up to as we were. Typical bullshit collaboration and intrigue, but in this instance the Soviet's and our own interests coincided. We did the same thing ourselves if you'll recall."

"But what's all this got to do with Isaac Smith?" Lee asked, as they strolled through the quiet rooms of exhibits.

"Just shut up and listen, will you."

"I'm all ears."

"In the initial meeting with the Chinese we were told that they had arrested our guy. Word was the Soviets gave him up for whatever reason—maybe a trade for one of their own agents. The Chinese said they were prepared to put him on trial for espionage and execute him if we didn't cooperate."

"So fucking what?" Lee said. "You dance with the devil you're bound to get burned."

McCraven stopped in front of a large portrait of a Chinese emperor on loan from the Taipei Museum. He looked at it admiringly.

"Zhu Di, second emperor of the Ming Dynasty," he said. "It's said that he built the largest fleet of ships in history to explore the world long before Columbus was even born. Landed in North America when Europe was just coming out of the Dark Ages. The Chinese had been around the world in ships ten times the size of the Nina, Pinta and Santa Maria. But when Zhu Di was replaced, the new emperor of China thought the expeditions too costly and dangerous to the Chinese way of life. "

"Your point?" Lee said.

"No point. Just history," McCraven said, and started walking again. "History is a strange thing, Lee. Sometimes just a slight change can affect so many things. Take our friend who's being held prisoner in Beijing. He has contacts throughout China with the leaders for democratic reform. You would think after Tiananmen the Chinese Communists would want that information. But they have opted to trade our friend for Isaac Smith's elimination. A nobody. So whatever it is this Smith guy knows, it must be mighty important to them."

He stopped next to an elaborate bronze sculpture of an ancient Chinese soldier on a horse. "So Lee, apparently this gang of smugglers was bringing something in from China that the Chinese Government wanted destroyed along with any knowledge of it wiped away; at least outside the Chinese Government."

"So, what was it?" Lee asked.

"Huh? What was what?" McCraven said, lost in thought as he ran his hand admiringly over the sculptured horse.

"What was so important?" Lee insisted.

"You mean what was it the smugglers where bringing in? Hell, if I know. I'll bet there are no more than maybe two, maybe three people at State who do know."

"Them and Isaac Smith, if we're to believe the Chinese."

"Yes," McCraven said. "Them and Isaac Smith. And that's apparently one person too many as far as the Chinese are concerned."

Then McCraven started to laugh and slapped Lee on his back. "Don't worry, partner. This operation is on hold for now. There are some of us arguing against it. No telling what's going to happen."

"Fuck, what am I suppose to do while you people decide if I murder this dump prick?"

"Play golf."

"I hate golf."

* * *

Chapter 3

San Francisco, Ca.

"What the fuck were you two thinking!"

Agents Feinberg and Berman stood silently in front of the San Francisco Bureau supervisor. Matt Edwards ran his agents by the book and at that moment he was righteously pissed off.

He never did like Gabe Feinberg. The man showed no respect for him or the Bureau. Didn't they have a dress code in the New York office? Edwards couldn't wait for them to be transferred back. Besides the wrinkled white shirt, he wore a bright tie, usually with a half naked girl on it. His thinning hair was always uncombed and he wore a straggly pony tail.

Richard Berman was the direct opposite; always wearing a tailored Armani suit and highly shined Florshiems; far too flashy for an FBI Agent to Edwards mind. Besides that, he had a bad attitude, making it clear he didn't like his assignment, and didn't like San Francisco.

"You were told specifically not to interfere in the investigation around the murder of Major Ching-Shu Wu, the man known as Peter Wu. You deliberately ignored that order, and now I have to explain to my Division

Chief what the fuck happened."

Gabe Feinberg started to speak in their defense, but Edwards cut him off. Berman simply stood there with a straight face and took his medicine like he always did.

"No fucking excuses or explanations. This operation was highly classified, and you were specifically told to stay out of it. Even I don't know what it was about. Why the fuck are you Jewish guys always sticking your fucking noses where they don't belong?"

Feinberg flinched. He was sensitive to anything that sounded anti-Semitic. Berman just stood there stoically. He had told Feinberg on many occasions that he learned not to let those things bother him, not if he was to remain in the FBI.

"It's a damn good thing you guys are going to be transferred back to New York. It won't be my problem after that. Now get the fuck out of my office."

Edwards dismissed them with his hand like he was shooing flies out of the room.

"Oh, and one more thing," Edwards called to them.

They stopped at the door and looked back at the man that had just chewed them out.

"Keep your mouths shut about your little escapade the other night. As far is this office is concerned it never happened. Got it?"

They nodded.

"OK then, get outta here."

Feinberg stared into his coffee cup, as if expecting something to appear in it.

"What's the matter with you," Berman said. "You look like your wife just ran off with the resort crooner or something."

"No such luck," Feinberg said.

"Than what the fuck's eating you?" Berman insisted. "We got off lucky. We could have been kicked out of the Bureau for what we did."

Feinberg looked up at his partner sitting across from him in the cafeteria of the San Francisco Federal Building. They could have been killed on that hot night in the hills surrounding the Valley of the Moon; caught in a full scale military skirmish. It was only luck that they managed to save the lives of Isaac Smith and Mei-ling Wu.

"Something's just not right," he said, as if thinking out loud. "This whole deal stinks."

"Cut the bullshit, Gabe. It's all over. It wasn't our assignment. I know you wanted to protect your boy—what's his face — Smitty. But now it's over. Forget it."

"No Rich, I can't just forget it. We witnessed a federally approved military operation by a foreign country on U.S. soil. Not just any foreign country, but fucking Red China for God's sake. When have you ever heard of something like that?"

Berman looked thoughtful for a moment and then shrugged. "You don't know it was a foreign government that carried out the attack. Shit, with all that fire and smoke—and it was night—for all we know it could have been our guys. Hell, it could have been a rival smuggling gang. We don't know."

"Yeah, then why was that guy from the Chinese Consulate there, the one calling himself Rick? You saw him as well as I did. That was the same asshole that was ready to shoot down that fellow Izzy."

"Izzy?"

"Isaac Smith, the union guy, Smitty. Besides, the U.S. government would never approve that kind of attack. It was totally over the top," Gabe went on, as if confirming his thoughts to himself. "If this thing was sanctioned by some people high up in National Security then the whole democratic structure of our country has been undermined."

Agent Berman sat and thought it over for a moment. This kind of shit could get them into a lot of hot water. What had started out as a routine investigation into Chinese street gangs, his partner was now turning into a international conspiracy.

"Come on, pal. Can't we just go back to New York, make out our reports, and get our new assignments. Your wife and kids should be coming back from the Catskills soon. This ain't none of our business."

"The hell it's not our business," Feinberg said. "We took an oath to uphold the Constitution of the United States. Or have you forgotten that."

Berman looked down into his coffee. He didn't like the accusatory tone of his partner's voice, as if he was his mother guilt tripping him. But he wasn't going to buy in. For all he knew, Gabe just didn't want to go back to New York where his wife and kids would be waiting for him. Gabe seemed to have made a career of staying away from his family. "You want to expose a national conspiracy, go to work for the Washington Post," he said.

"Don't be a shmuck, Rich. We can't let this thing slide and you know it."

Berman took a sip from his coffee. He refused to look at his partner because he knew Gabe was right and that, when it came down to it, he didn't have a choice.

"The NSA you say?" The raspy voice blastedin Fienberg's ear, foring him to move the telephone a few inches from his head. "And that fucking Edwards told you to drop your investigation?"

"Yes sir," Feinberg answered. "And that's not all. We witnessed a full scale military assault on a ranch in the hills overlooking Glen Ellen..."

"Glen Ellen?"

"Yes sir. It's a small town in Northern California."

"A full scale military assault? Are you sure?"

Jack Duggart, Bureau Chief of the New York office of the FBI—Gabe's and Rich's boss—was an old school Bureau man and didn't like the NSA or their meddling in FBI business. He had joined the Bureau in the late thirties when fighting crime was their main work. He had protested when their efforts were turned toward investigating and hunting suspected subversives. Then, when Hoover came out publicly and announced that there was no such thing as Organized Crime in America, he threatened to go to the media and expose Hoover for abandoning the primary purpose of the Bureau. Duggart was old fashioned. He believed in the FBI motto; "Fidelity, Bravery, Integrity." He suspected the crime syndicate had gotten a hold of some damaging evidence against the Bureau Chief—it was rumored that old Herbert had some unusual sexual quirks—and was black mailing him to get the Feds off their backs. In order to keep him quiet, Hoover gave him the Manhattan office to do "what you damn well please, just stay out of my business."

"If what you're telling me is true, than this is serious. It sounds to me like these people are way out of line." Duggart said. "A full scale military assault you said?"

"Huey helicopter and a squad of fully armed commandos from what we saw. We suspect they burned out a Chinese smuggling gang, the same one we were investigating back in New York—The Ghost Shadows if I guess right," Feinberg said.

"This is hard to believe. I want you and Berman to stay on there for a while and do some snooping around. Get me some solid proof of what you're telling me. You'll have to move out of the Frisco office and make them believe you men have returned to New York. I'll cover for you. Keep me informed of anything you find. God damn NSA, think they can go around breaking the laws of the United States of America they got another thing coming. Not on Jack Duggart's watch."

Gabe hung up the phone and stepped out of the phone booth onto Market Street where Berman was waiting. It was four in the afternoon and the hot fall weather was beginning to turn as winter came on. The street reminded him of New York, with crowds of people hurrying to where ever it was people hurry to after work. Street musicians were everywhere; some good, some really bad; homeless people of all ages and genders hustling for spare change alongside the mandatory religious nuts hawking God and salvation.

"The boss wants us to stay on and see what we can find out. We have to move out of the office here and make them think we're going back to New York. We'll relocate to Oakland."

Berman lit a cigarette.

"I thought you gave those things up?" Feinberg said.

"I can't see any good coming from this," Berman muttered, blowing out a cloud of blue smoke as a raggedy dressed woman came up to him.

"Got a spare smoke handsome?" she said through a toothless smile...

* * *

Chapter 4

Dullas Airport

Dark clouds had moved in over Dullas Airport and flashes of lightening streaked the skies as Marshall Lee boarded United Flight 711 bound for San Francisco. His only luggage was a leather briefcase containing a change of underwear, socks and three files. He found his seat next to an elderly woman who was busy knitting.

"I do hope this weather doesn't delay us," she said, as he settled into his seat.

He smiled at her. "I'm sure it will be all right," he said reassuringly.

"Oh, I'm not worried about the storm," she said. "I just don't want to sit in this damn airplane for hours while they decide whether or not it's safe to take off."

He liked this spunky old lady. But he didn't want to engage in meaningless conversation for the whole flight, so he just smiled politely and opened his brief case, removed the folders, and pretended to be busy.

The plane took off right on schedule, rising into the stormy sky. It was rock and roll until the plane leveled off above the clouds. He looked over at the old woman. She hadn't dropped a stitch through the whole thing.

He ordered a scotch and soda from the stewardess and opened a file. The first two he had already gone through; the profile on Isaac Smith and the San Francisco report from Agent Feinberg. Isaac Smith —nickname Smitty—was a union representative for a small culinary union in Oakland, California. He lived in an apartment on Lakeshore Drive, across from Lake Merritt, which he shared with a Black woman and her daughter. According to the Oakland PD the woman had a record of arrests for prostitution, but now was enrolled in college and had a job with the city's Social Service Department counseling hookers on how to turn their lives around.

Isaac Smith was born to Jewish parents in New York in 1945, but the family moved to Los Angeles when he was a boy. They were rank and file members of the Communist Party, but according to FBI records had never been involved in anything important—just working folk trying to get by. After dropping out of City College, Smith bounced around for a number of years until ending up in Oakland where he became involved in his union and was elected Business Agent in 1979. He was credited with exposing a corrupt union president in 1989. Further investigation revealed the union boss was doing time in the Men's Correctional Facility in Lompoc, California, and so was no threat to Smith.

Feinberg's report detailed his and Berman's long investigation into a Chinese gang called the Ghost Shadows, starting in New York's Chinatown and ending in San Francisco. There, for some reason the report abruptly ended, as if the last pages had been purposely removed from it.

They had followed the gang to the San Francisco Bay Area where they suspected it was acting as a front for a powerful Chinese Tong from Guangdong, China.

The third file was marked Classified. He had to pull some strings to get it. It contained the San Francisco FBI Bureau Chief's report on the activities and events during the time Feinberg and his partner, Richard Berman, were attached to his office. Lee glanced through it, but was convinced it wasn't telling the whole truth about what was going on.

The report included mention of the murder of the old bartender Peter Wu at a downtown Oakland hotel, and that it had something to do with Feinberg's and Berman's investigation into the Chinese smugglers, but it didn't elaborate. It noted the sudden return of the bartender's niece, Mei-ling Wu to China, but again was vague as to why she had left. There were too many things that didn't add up, and before he would carry out his assignment there were some questions he wanted answered. He was on his way to San Francisco to get them.

* * *

Chapter 5

Oakland, Ca.

Flight 730 from Little Rock was on time. Smitty hoped seeing Dede and Chanel as they appeared at the Southwest Jetway would help ease the pain he was suffering since Mei-ling left him.. As soon as Chanel spotted him standing there she ran into his arms.

"Uncle Isaac, I've missed you," she squealed.

He lifted the child up and hugged her tightly, remembering how fond he had grown of her since she and Dede had moved into his apartment on Lakeshore Drive, and that he had missed her since she had been away in Arkansas at her Uncle and Aunt's farm.

He let her slip slowly through his arms to the floor when he saw Dede standing n front of him smiling. She was as attractive as ever; all slender, long legged, bronze with high cheekbones, a straight slender nose and shiny straight jet-black hair, but there was a freshness about her, as if being away in the country had finally cleansed her once and for all of her past.

She kissed him warmly on the cheek. But there was no passion, just a sisterly kiss. If anything would have eased the pain of losing Mei-ling it would have been getting lost between her long brown legs.

"Smitty, I'm happy you came to get us," she said.

"Of course I came. Why wouldn't I?"

She gave him her all too familiar stern look. There was no way she could have known he had gotten her phone message, or if he was even alive. The last thing she remembered was him leaving with Mei-ling on some wild goose chase for something only the lovely Chinese lady knew.

"Well, I'm glad you came," she said.

He took the bags and they walked out into the Oakland Indian summer heat, heading for the parking lot across from the airport. Chanel hung onto his arm and it made him smile. Stares of admiration from other men who must have wondered what the gorgeous Black woman saw in this schlumpy middle aged white guy .

The little girl did most of the talking on the ride back downtown to the Apartment on Lake Merritt. She went on about life on the farm; slopping the pigs and feeding the chickens; collecting the eggs every morning; picking cotton with her Uncle and the hired hands.

"I objected to her picking cotton," Dede said. "But Uncle Jonas insisted. Said it was good for her to know what her ancestors were forced to do as slaves."

After the girls had finished unpacking, Smitty took them to the Merritt restaurant for dinner. He listened patiently as they told him about their stay in Arkansas. Dede's aunt had recovered. Dede said she had periodic spells of depression that debilitated her. No one knew what caused it. Smitty envied the simple life they had returned from and wondered how anyone living such an idyllic life could get depressed.

Back at the apartment he went to the kitchen table and lit a Lucky Strike. It made him smile as he watched Dede and Chanel move about the apartment, bringing life back into the lonely place. It took some of the emptiness he was feeling after Mei-ling had left him and returned to China.

But when Chanel ran out of her room hugging her stuffed panda bear, memories flooded back into his mind. Things he had tried to push to the back of his thoughts suddenly flashed back like a bad dream. There was Rick, the Chinese Secret Service guy who had tried to kill him, and then later went out of his way to tell him that Mei-ling had not run out on him as he had thought, but had agreed to return to China as part of a deal to save his miserable life. Mei-ling. He could see the fire of the burning ranch reflecting in her eyes and the smile of satisfaction on her lips as flames destroyed the secluded ranch in the hills overlooking the Valley of the Moon, along with the gang of smugglers and the young pandas that had been the object of so much death and mayhem. When Mei-ling had first told him about them he thought she was joking. That was what her Uncle Peter Wu had been murdered for? That was why he had become a marked man? Pandas. But she was dead serious and gave him some reason why they were so important to the Chinese government; something about national security or some such nonsense. It was all rather silly. Atomic secrets he could understand. He had read all the LeCarre novels. But fucking Pandas? Then he suddenly got a terrifying flash. What if now that Mei-ling was back in China where they could control her, they decided to follow through with their original plan to get rid of the last witness in the U.S. to their little escapade? He could be endangering Dede and Chanel just by being there.

That night, after Chanel had gone to bed, he told Dede all about what had happened since she had been away, omitting the pandas which she probably would have laughed at, sure that Isaac was either joking or had lost his mind. She shrugged off any suggestion that his being there could pose a danger to her or Chanel. She said he was being paranoid and insisted he stay there. He had nowhere else to go anyway since the smugglers had torched his boat that he called home.

He hoped his sad story would be received with the same compassion and comfort he had gotten the last time he had thought he had lost Mei-ling and had confided in Dede about his feelings for the woman. But no such luck.

"I know you'd like me to comfort you, Smitty, and invite you to my bed," she said, as if reading his thoughts. "But now that I have met your Mei-ling I think this time around its better that you tough it out alone. It's not that I don't feel for you my sweet, and I hate to see you suffer, but you're going to have to get over Mei-ling before we can even think about our relationship."

She kissed him on the forehead, and went to her bedroom, closing the door behind her. It looked like the couch for the duration; alone with thoughts of Mei-ling, and it didn't make him happy.

The next morning, after Dede had taken Chanel to register her at school, he contacted his buddy, Ted, at the Oakland Tribune. He made a date to meet him for lunch, and then went into his office at Culinary Local 4 on Nineteenth Avenue in Uptown Oakland. He hadn't been there for a while and thought he'd better show his face. He was the Senior Business Agent after all; he had some responsibilities, despite the fact that they were giving him a free ride ever since he exposed the drug dealing thugs who had taken over the local a few years back, and the beating he took by the union President and his strong arm ex-con pal because they thought he had snitched them out that put him in the hospital for two weeks in a coma. His testimony against them added time to the sentences, and everyone at the Local was glad they were gone and declared him a working class hero.

He was welcomed back with smiles and how-ya-doin. No one asked where he had been or what he had been doing. He had always been a private person and his fellow union reps respected that.

The Local was running smoothly, even without him there. He wasn't sure how he felt about that. The union was the only thing he had cared about until Mei-ling came into his life; he had devoted his life to it and the thought that it could get along without him was somehow depressing.

Gil Martinez, the acting President of the Local, greeted him with a bear hug. Gil was a good guy, and in many ways saved the local from financial catastrophe by stepping in when he had quit after six months as President. Gil had been a longtime Executive Board member and had a good head for business, which was exactly what the local needed; someone who understood money. That wasn't Smitty

He invited him into his office, callingout to the secretary to bring coffee.

"How's everything been going?" he asked.

Smitty lit up a Lucky Strike and offered him one.

"Nah, trying to quit."

"I'm ready to come back to work," he lied.

"Look Smitty," Gil said. "To be honest, you look like shit."

"Thanks pal."

"No, really; I don't know what you've been up to, but I can see you haven't been resting."

Smitty took a drag from his cigarette, but didn't say anything.

The secretary came in with two steaming Styrofoam cups, accompanied by the remark: "I ain't paid to serve coffee. It's not in my contract."

She was a decent looking woman in her med thirties, a bit overweight, with pitch black hair pulled back into a tight bun.

Gil said something in Spanish to her, and it seemed to appease her. He had been a bartender for many years and was good with people. Marta forced a smile and then left the office.

"She's a tough cookie that one is. Sometimes I'm sorry we hired her. But she's efficient and can translate Spanish to English like a pro."

Gil sat back in the leather chair that had been occupied by every President of the Local since the waitresses first opened the hall in the fifties when the union was in its heyday.

"You kinda like the job as President," Smitty smiled.

"It's a big headache. I can see why you quit. But you're indispensable as the Senor BA, and I hope you come back to work soon. When you're ready. But first you need to get over whatever it is you're dealing with," he said.

"I'm that easy to read?"

"I've know you what, twenty years at least. I can read people pretty well, just as I assume you can."

It was a talent bartenders gained over years pouring drinks and listening to people's problems.

"Well, most of the time. Some people are impossible to understand what makes them tick," Smitty replied.

"Get the hell out of here and don't come back until you're ready. See Marta. She has your pay check."

Smitty smashed his cigarette out in the ash tray on the big desk. "Thanks Gil. And if you need me for anything you can call me." He took out his business card and jotted down the number at the apartment. "Just don't give it out to anyone."

He dropped the card on the desk.

"Sure thing."

"Oh, I've used the union credit card on a couple of occasions. I'll pay the union back when you get the bill."

"Don't sweat it, Smitty. Now get the hell outta here."

He walked by the large business agents' office. There were eight desks, but only three had signs of being used. Loss of members had reduced the staff at the Local to a minimum.

He picked up his check from Marta who mumbled something about people getting paid for not working. Smitty ignored her and left the union hall. He headed downtown for the Ringside bar on Fourteenth Street where he had arranged to hook up with Ted.

"So, I thought you'd run off with that Chinese gal of yours and I'd seen the last of you," Eddy the bartender and owner of the Ringside, remarked with a smirk as he pulled the tap on the Guinness. He was an ex-fighter and one time contender for the light middle weight title. He bought the Ringside in the Fifties after suffering a brutal knockout. The bar was next to the Tribune Building and he had done a big business with the newspaper guys until the paper moved to smaller digs in Jack London Square. He had been threatening to sell the place over Smitty's objections.

"Who told you about Mei-ling?" Smitty asked

"Jasmine. Came by a couple of times looking for you. Damn, she's changed. Says her real name's Dede like you told me. I always said the girl was too smart to be a hooker. She looked great. First time I ever seen her without the tight dresses and makeup. She was a knock out then, but now she's just a really good looking young woman. What she sees in you I'll never know."

He set the glass of dark Irish ale in front of Smitty.

"Order you the usual pastrami on rye?"

"Nah, I'm waiting for Ted to go out to lunch."

"That's another guy come by looking for you. Didn't say nothing 'bout no Chinese gal though. Just said you'd gotten yourself in some hot water and he was worried 'bout ya. Don't see those boys from the Trib now they moved their offices down to the Square."

"Damn, you know more about me than I do," I laughed.

"People talk to bartenders like they know everything 'bout everything."

"Yeah, seems that way."

The phone rang and Eddy moved down the bar to get it. Smitty picked up the copy of the Tribune that was sitting on the bar. There was a story on the front page saying how the Russian government had restored the old name Saint Petersburg from what had been Leningrad. He was glad his parents hadn't lived to see the collapse of their beloved Soviet Union. President Bush's nominee for the Supreme Court, Clarence Thomas, was being accused of sexual harassment by a woman named Anita Hill. Thomas was a Black man so he was bound to be confirmed even though Hill was also Black, but that didn't seem to matter. The Dems didn't have the backbone to vote against a Black man, even if he was a right wing Christian fundamentalist and a womanizer. The whole world was changing rapidly, and not for the better as far as he was concerned.

"Hey Smitty," Eddy called from the end of the bar. "That was Ted. Said he'd meet you at the Grotto at one"

Lazy bastard. Now that the Tribune has moved he's too lazy to walk up to the Ringside, Smitty thought. He was about to finish off his Guinness and head for Jack London Square at the end of Broadway when he spotted an article in the paper that sent a chill down his spine:

Suspect in UC Prof Murder Released
For Lack Of Evidence
by Ted Harlin
Tribune Police Reporter

Oakland – The suspect in the murder of UC Berkeley professor Idira Banerjii was released yesterday for lack of evidence police said.

Rav Banerjii had been arrested more than three weeks ago in connection with the murder of the young woman whose body had been found in her apartment with a gunshot wound.

Police had originally believed that Mister Banerjii was the brother of Ms. Banerjii, and that the motive had been called an honor killing, a practice prevalent in India and some other countries, but relatively unheard of here.

Further investigation showed that Mister Banerjii was not related to the dead woman, and had been on his way back to India after working in Silicon Valley for two years. Banerjii is a common name in India

"This was a pure case of overzealous police work," Jerry Robinson, Banerjii's attorney said. "They had claimed to have had a confession, but Mister Banerjii said he had never signed the statement that the police had given him. I am pleased to say Mister Banerjii is now on his way home where he was expected over three weeks ago," Robinson said.

Police sources say they are now looking for a Chinese woman named Mei-ling Wu. The murder victim had contacted police the night before her murder wanting to file a missing persons report on Wu who had been staying with her in the North Oakland Apartment.

Ms. Wu was the niece of Peter Wu of Oakland who was murdered last year in the basement of the Hyatt hotel where he worked. She was a lecturer at UC Berkeley where she had known the murdered woman.

The police have no motive in the murder of Ms. Banerjii and said they were seeking Wu for questioning.

Smitty had originally suspected Rick, the Chinese Consulate agent, of murdering Idira because she may have had knowledge of the pandas. And while he was sorry that the beautiful Indian woman had been killed, he was somewhat relieved when he read about Rav Banerjii's arrest. Rick had denied killing her the night he had come to tell Smitty he had been reprieved thanks to Mei-ling's sacrifice. But Rick was perfectly capable of lying and he may have killed Indira after all in which case no one was safe.

"You alright, Smitty," Eddy asked. "You look like someone's stepped on your grave. It's going on one. Ain't you meeting your buddy?"

He found Ted at his usual spot at the long bar with his usual martini in front of him. The restaurant was half empty. The Grotto had been struggling along for years, but it was the last unionized joint in the Square. So they kept going even though the food had gone on a steep decline, as if the chefs saw the writing on the wall and just didn't give a shit any more. But the bar still served generous drinks, and Ted said he liked the way they prepared calamari; sautéed in olive oil and garlic.

"So, you're still alive," he said as Smitty slid onto the bar stool next to him.

"Last time I looked."

"Well, I won't ask you what happened because you aren't going to tell me even though I'm your professed best friend and you're sitting on a story that could get me a Pulitzer Prize."

Smitty ordered a JD over. "Listen Ted. I promised I wouldn't tell anyone. Your buddy Feinberg has probably told you everything I could tell you."

"Gabe, hell. He's mum, wouldn't say anything. Only that they got you and your lady friend out of a jam in Glen Ellen. It's a damn good thing I called him after talking to you. You owe me, Smitty."

Smitty remembered that night like it was yesterday—the helicopter hovering over head; the two FBI agents breaking in the door of the storage shed where he and Mei-ling were being held captive; the escape as a squad of commandoes set fire to the ranch house with the gang of smugglers burning everything in sight including the out buildings. Smitty assumed the contraband pandas went up in flames with everything else.

"Yeah," he said, as the bartender set his drink down. "But for now I can't tell you anything."

They sat there for a few minutes in silence, sipping their drinks. Ted seemed preoccupied. Finally Smitty broke the silence.

"So, how's the wife doing? Still attending those sensitivity training classes?"

Ted looked up. "No, said they were bullshit. Now she wants to bring her mother and auntie from Vietnam to live with us."

"Christ, Ted, what did you say?"

"Doesn't matter what I say. When you marry a Vietnamese you marry the whole damn family. That's just the way it is."

"That oughta put a damper on your sex life."

"Well, at this point that won't be much of a loss."

Suddenly the waitress came up behind us, startling Ted. She was in her fifties and looked it. It was easy to see she expected the restaurant to close up any time."

"What you fellas having?"

A quick glance at the menu as Ted ordered his usual, sautéed squid.

"I guess I'll have a bowl of clam chowder," Smitty said, thinking they couldn't screw clam chowder up too bad."

The waitress jotted down the orders and walked away without a word or a smile.

Once again they sat there; Ted staring into his martini and Smitty wondering what the fuck was going on with him. Was his marriage so bad that he was really depressed? It was unlike the Ted he had known for over twenty years, until finally...

"I don't give a shit what you or fucking Gabe say, I'm going to find out what the hell this thing is all about."

That was the Ted, Smitty knew, the intrepid reporter who had earned a reputation for always getting the hard story. He had been a reporter during the war in Vietnam and broke open a story on US officers raping and killing Vietnamese girls. That was when he first met Gabe Feinberg who was in the military police at the time.

"But you said your editor won't run a story even if you did find out."

"Fuck him. If he won't run the biggest scoop of his pathetic little career, than the New York Times, or the Washington Post will. And if they refuse, there's always Nation Magazine. This is just the kinda story they would eat up."

Smitty was stunned and lamely asked; "How do you know there's a story here?"

"Because my best friend won't tell me anything, that's how I know. Besides, if the FBI is covering this up, it's got to be big."

He went back to staring into his martini glass when the waitress slipped in between them and unceremoniously set their food down. She mixed up the orders and placed the calamari in front of Smitty and the chowder in front of Ted and didn't wait for them to correct her.

They switched plates without a word. Ted squeezed two slices of lemon over the squid and started to eat. Smitty looked into his bowl. Little hunks of potatoes, celery and what were obviously canned clams swamming around in a thick milky soup.

"Must be a Chinese cook," Smitty mumbled, more to himself than Ted."

"Huh?"

"The chowder is thickened with corn starch. Chinese cook, without a doubt." He dumped a packet of oyster crackers and a lot of pepper on top and sipped at it without interest.

They ate in silence, until Smitty couldn't take it anymore.

"Look Ted. You know how you were constantly warning me to walk away from this thing, telling me I'd end up in some alley in Chinatown with my throat slit? You remember.?

He nodded without looking up from his plate.

"Well, I'm warning you now. You start probing into this you're going to end up dead, and you are my best friend and I'd hate to see that happen."

Ted scooped the last morsel of squid into his mouth, wiped up the plate with a piece of sour dough, and then wiped his face with a napkin.

"I'm a fucking reporter, Smitty. What do you expect me to do? The fact is, if it wasn't for you I would never have happened onto this story. But now that I have, well, buddy or no buddy, I'm going after it."

There was nothing more to say. Smitty had already lost the only woman he had ever really loved, and now he could lose his best friend. If Ted ended up dead it would be his fault. He felt like shit and ordered another drink.

* * *

Chapter 6

Valley of the Moon, Northern California

Agents Feinberg and Berman drove into the small town of Glen Ellen. It was the second time in two weeks that they had been to the scenic little community renowned only because it claimed Jack London's famed Wolf House in it boundaries. Berman, who was a fan of London, explained to his partner how the famous author had sunk all his money into what was to have been his dream house, only to have it mysteriously catch on fire the day of its completion and burn to the ground. London was never to recover from the tragedy, living out the last years of his life in a small house near the burnt out remains of his dreams. Thousands of people from all over the world now came to pay homage to the famous author.

"That's a fucking sad tale," Feinberg said, half listening to his partner while deciding how he was going to go about their investigation without raising suspicion.

Berman had relaxed since Jack Duggart, their boss in New York, instructed them to continue with the investigation. They had the cover they needed, but it didn't stop the uneasy feeling he had about the whole operation. He was lonely for familiar New York, and now here he was, driving around in the Northern California countryside.

Gabe stopped in front of the Jack London Inn. He wanted to confirm that Smith and Mei-ling Wu had been there. He needed to trace their movements and return to the Stover ranch to get some solid evidence that what they saw there that night really happened. Without proof Duggart wouldn't move on it, and the biggest violation of U.S. sovereignty since Pancho Villa and two hundred of his men raided the small New Mexico town of Columbus in 1916 would go unnoticed.

"The guy with the cute Asian chick, sure I remember them," the girl behind the counter said after Feinberg and Berman both flashed their FBI identifications. "They stayed two nights. No problem. Seemed like nice people."

"You don't remember anything unusual?" Feinberg asked.

"Well, now that you ask, I remember the guy on the night shift said they had checked out late. He remembered because the Asian girl was dressed in these sexy camo shorts. Bill —that's the guy on the night desk—he'd remember something like that. And besides, that was the night of the strange lights up in the hills. Everyone was talking about it the next day. The old timers claimed it was Indian spirits."

"Yeah," Berman said. "This valley was an Indian spiritual place. According to Miwok Indian legends the moon rose from the valley, or was "nestled" in the valley, or may have even sprung up multiple times in one night. It's all rather vague."

Gabe shot Berman a disapproving look.

"Yeah," the girl said. "Anyway, a lot of folks believe that Indian spirits still live in the hills. It even got a write up in the Press Democrat."

"You have a copy of that?" Feinberg asked.

"Yeah," the girl said. "I cut the article out." She reached into her purse, which was more like a small suitcase; rummaged around for a minute and finally produced the clipping. She started to hand it to Gabe.

"Make me a copy," he said.

"Sure."

The two agents watched as the girl went to a copy machine behind the counter. Berman admired the young woman's backside as she intentionally leaned over the machine. She ran the copy and handed it to Feinberg.

"Thanks."

"Say, those folks didn't do nothing wrong, did they?" the girl asked.

"No, nothing like that. Just a routine investigation," Feinberg said.

"Oh good. I wouldn't want to think I got them in any trouble."

"Just routine," Berman reassured her.

"You want any more information stop by the General Store up the street. You can't miss it. Old man Toliver knows everything that goes on around here."

The Glen Ellen Country store was like a hundred rural stores Feinberg had seen throughout upstate New York and the New Jersey countryside; American flag in the front, 50 pound bags of feed stacked up, small farm implements: Inside; dry goods. It looked like is hadn't changed in fifty years, except for the bank of modern glass door refrigerator units in the back displaying dozens of brands of beer, sodas, juice, milk, ice tea, and various dairy products.

The old man standing behind the counter was clean shaven with a close cropped haircut and a tuft of gray hair sticking out from his half buttoned flannel shirt. Ex–military type Gabe thought.

"Morning gentlemen. Can I help you?"

Gabe walked to the counter and flashed his ID while Berman went to the rear and inspected the cold drinks.

"Hmmm. FBI eh? Looking for Reds you come to the right neck of the woods. Hundreds around here, but they're all retired...or dead."

"Yeah, bunch of radicals from San Francisco moved up here in the fifties," Berman added, putting a couple of bottles of Perrier mineral water on the counter. "Raised chickens and provided eggs to most of Northern California ... red eggs." He laughed at his little joke.

"Forgive my partner," Gabe said. "He's a walking encyclopedia of trivia."

"Quite accurate, however. Except for the eggs. They aren't red. Kinda of a deep orange. That'll be three bucks. Next time try our Calistoga water. It's local and cheaper."

"Give the man three dollars," Gabe said to Berman. "We're interested in some Asian men who may have come through here about fifteen days ago. You didn't happen to notice anyone like that?"

"Well, as a matter of fact, an Asian man came in to get some supplies. He was accompanied by a big white guy."

"Could you identity him if you saw him?" Gabe asked.

"Maybe."

Berman produced a stack of photos and laid them on top of the three dollar bills on the counter.

"Are any of these him?" Rich asked.

The old man thumbed through the pictures, and then stopped at one.

"This one. He's the one who came in. I'm sure of it. See," he pointed to the picture. "That scar on his cheek. Made him look real mean. He and the white fella got out of a black Lincoln. There were some other guys in it, but I couldn't make them out. It was dusk outside. There were a couple of panel trucks too. They didn't get out either."

"Did they mention where they were going?" Feinberg asked.

"Sure did. Asked for directions to the Stover place. The old man had died a while back, and I heard someone bought it. I figured these

guys were going to set up a temple or some such thing. Lot of that sort
of thing been happening around here since the sixties, you know. I didn't
think he seemed like the religious type though."

"Well," Rich said. "You were right about that."

"You looking for these guys? I suspect they're still up there."

"Can you think of anything else that might help us?" Gabe asked.

"Well, there was this couple came in a few days later. She didn't come
in, but I could see through the door she was Asian. From what I could see
she was a cute little thing. The guy was a white fella."

Berman pulled a couple of new photos from his pocket and laid them
on the counter. "These them?"

"That's them all right. The white guy seemed kind of edgy, if you
know what I mean. I thought they might be going up to the Stover place
too, so I asked him. Well, you would have thought I told him he won the
lottery when I told him how to get there."

"Say," Berman said, as he collected the pictures. "You ever run into
Tommy Smothers? I hear he bought a place around here..."

"Come on Rich, we're done here," Feinberg said, coaxing his partner
toward the door. "Thanks pal. You've been a big help," he said to the old
man.

"Always glad to help the FBI. Say, you don't think those folks were
terrorists or something like that?"

"Couldn't say," Feinberg said. "Thanks again."

"Where to now?" Rich asked as they got back in their car.

"Back to Stover's ranch..."

"Winery," Berman corrected.

"Ranch, Winery. You know what I mean."

*

The road up into the hills Northeast of Glen Ellen was much different
in the hot afternoon sunlight than the last time they had taken it. Then

it was early morning, under the light of a full moon. They had turned in their Agency car and rented a new Ford Crown Victoria with operational air conditioning much to their relief. Gabe wasn't sure what they would find at the Stover Ranch. The commandos, or mercenaries, were doing a pretty good job of burning everything in sight while they got away after saving Isaac Smith and Ms. Wu from sure death. But they were both trained investigators, and Berman—a pain in the ass for the most part—was a specialist in forensic evidence.

Gabe slowed down near a gravel road leading into the hills. "I think this is it," he said.

"Say, wasn't there a sign in front? Rich said.

"Yeah, but I'll swear this is it."

He pulled onto the gravel road and drove up the hill until they reached the gated entrance. The Lincoln Towncar was gone along with the body of the guard they had killed the last time they were there.

"Seemed to have cleaned the place up pretty well," Rich said as Gabe braked to a stop.

Berman jumped out and swung the gate open and then got back into the car.

"Damn it's hot out there," he said.

One day in an air conditioned car and you're spoiled already," Gabe laughed.

"Never did like the heat," Berman mumbled.

There wasn't much left of the house and outbuildings of old man Stover's ranch, or what he had sarcastically called a winery. The burnt out hulks of several vehicles dotted the gravel road in front of what used to be a house.

"Shit, I haven't seen nothing like this since I was in Nam," Berman said. "Reminds me of a village I was sent in to investigate after it had be napalmed."

"What were you suppose to investigate?" Feinberg asked.

"They wanted a body count. We were supposed to determine how many people had been killed there, so they sent in a team of investigators. I headed up the investigation."

"Great job you had in the Army," Feinberg said sarcastically.

"Better than the infantry," Berman said. "Let's do this thing."

"Let's check the house first; see if there are any remains," Feinberg said.

They both stepped out of the Crown Victoria. There was an uncanny silence; no birds chirping or insects buzzing; nothing but the hot autumn sun beating down on them. Berman grabbed a small black satchel from the back seat. Feinberg checked his camera. They both pulled on rubber gloves.

They walked over to where the house had once been, but was now just a black outline on the ground with a stone fireplace crumbling into it.

Berman gave it a once over. "Looks like they've sanitized the place pretty well." He sifted through the ashes with a rack he found nearby, stirring up small clouds of the black ash. "Usually there would be burnt corpses. Even after napalm there's usually charred remains. But there's nothing here, not even bones."

Feinberg walked around the building searching the grounds and snapping pictures.

"No evidence of the fire fight we saw. No shell casings that I can see."

Berman scooped some of the ashes up and put them in a small plastic bag and marked it.

"Let's check out what's left of the vehicles," Feinberg said.

"You go on," Berman said. "I'm not through here."

Gabe walked over to the shells of the three vehicles. He could still identify them; the smell of burnt rubber permeated the air. The Lincoln Towncar, which must have been moved from the front gate where they had left it, and the two panel trucks, at least what was left of them. He photographed the Towncar and then moved on to the first truck. The cargo compartment was still in tack with a huge hole in one side and the other side completely blown out. He could identify dozens of holes left by high powered rifles. He looked inside the truck. There were charred remains of what appeared to have been large wooden crates. He took a couple of shots and then called Berman over from the ranch house.

"What do you make of this?" Feinberg said.

Berman stuck his head inside the cargo compartment. He didn't say anything. He pulled out a small flashlight from his pocket, took off his jacket, and crawled into the remains of the truck.

"They didn't bother to clean out whatever was in these crates," he said.

"What is it?" Berman asked.

"Can't tell. Everything's burned up. I'll take some samples and we can send them to the lab." He took out another couple of evidence bags and scooped up some charred material from what was left of the crates.

As they walked back to the car they noticed the large smoothed out spot in the area about a hundred yards from where the ranch house was.

"Must be where the helicopter landed," Berman noted, slapping the black ashes from his pants where he had crawled into the truck. "Damn. I'll have to get my clothes cleaned now."

Gabe took more pictures and they got back into the Ford Victoria. They were both covered in sweat. Feinberg started the car and the AC blew relieving cold air onto them.

Just as he started to back out they heard a pop and the rear door window shattering.

"Shit, someone's shooting at us!" Berman shouted. "Get the hell outta here!"

Feinberg stepped on the gas and for a moment the wheels just spun in the gravel. Another pop and the rear window blew up. The tires finally grabbed hold and the Crown Victoria headed for the gate, kicking up a cloud of dust.

"I think I'm hit, Gabe," Berman said as Feinberg sped down the gravel driveway heading for where it let out on to Wall Road.

"Rich. You all right?" Feinberg said, as he swung the car onto the paved road.

Berman was inspecting his side. He pulled his hand out from under his coat. It was covered in blood. "I think the bullet passed through the seat and creased my side. It's just a scratch."

"Scratch, hell," Feinberg said as he pulled over to the side of the road. "You're bleeding like a stuffed pig. He pulled out the Glock 9mm he kept in a holster on his belt and placed it on the seat."

"It's OK I tell you. Just drive."

It was almost three i when Feinberg pulled up in front of the Glen Ellen Country Store. The afternoon heat semed to be keeping must people off the streets. He glanced over at his partner who was slumped in his seat holding the tee shirt he had taken out of his canvas suitcase against his side. The once white garment was now soaked in red.

"How you doing, Rich?" he said.

"I'll live," Berman mumbled back.

"Hang in there. I'll see if there's a doctor in this berg."

The old proprietor, Mister Toliver, was standing in his usual spot behind the counter.

"Well, the FBI man. You have some more questions for me?"

"My partner's been hurt. Is there a doctor in town?"

"How bad is he? If it's bad you'll have to go into Santa Rosa to the Community Hospital. If it's not there's old Doc Fisher, but he's on vacation," Toliver said. "If he just needs some first aid I can help you. Was a medic in Korea."

"You'll have to do then," Feinberg said.

"Well, let's get your partner in here."

Toliver trailed behind Feinberg into the hot sun. He took a look at the dusty Crown Victoria with the shattered windows, and then the man in the front seat with blood all over his side.

"Damn, them people up at Stover's do this?"

'Never mind," Feinberg said. "Let's get him inside."

Toliver went over to the passenger door where Feinberg was already helping Berman out.

"How you doin' son?" Toliver said, lending a hand.

"I'll live," Berman muttered, still clutching the blood soaked tee shirt to his side.

"Bullet wound," Toliver said, after he cut the bloody shirt off Berman. "Didn't think those fellas looked like the religious types."

They had taken Berman through the store to the back where Toliver had a small apartment and sat him down at the kitchen table.

"How bad is it?" Berman asked.

"Superficial," Toliver answered. "I could clean it and bandage it, but it could use some stitches."

"Can you do it?" Feinberg asked. "Stitch it up."

"Sure, but it will leave a scar. Real Doctor has the new technology. Let this thing heal clean with no scarring."

"I'd rather not go to a doctor. Not if you can do it." Berman said. "They'll have to report it to the police. You do the best you can."

"You know who they were...the people that bought Stover's?" Feinberg asked, as the old man went to a cupboard and pulled out a small brown canvas back pack with the U.S. Army insignia and a red cross on it.

"Couldn't tell you," Toliver said, as he opened the back pack and started pulling out medical instruments and supplies.

"This going to hurt?" Berman said.

"Don't worry, I got some local anesthetic."

"Say, that's not left over from the Korean War is it?" Feinberg said.

"Don't be silly, pal. I replenish my supplies every couple of years."

"Anyone know who bought the Stover's place," Feinberg insisted.

"They can probably help you over at the Glen Ellen Real Estate office. Just down the street," Toliver said. "Now get out of the way so I can work. I should be finished here by the time you get back."

The middle aged woman with the platinum bouffant hairdo went to the filing cabinet. Feinberg watched as she thumbed through it wondering why the Glenn Ellen Real Estate office hadn't converted to computers. But looking around it was understandable. He felt like he had stepped through a time warp and been transported back to the 1950's, the woman proprietor with it. At least they had an air conditioner, noisy, but pumping out wecomed cold air.

"Here we are," she said, bringing a file over to the counter. "Stover Vineyards." She laughed. "Vineyards, that's a laugh. Wasn't a grape vine on the place."

"Who bought it?" Feinberg asked.

"Let me see. Oh yes, I remember now. It wasn't a who, it was a what." She giggled at her own joke. "The Far East Investment Company in New York."

Feinberg jotted the name down on a pad and wrote himself a note to check on the Far East Investment Company. "Who was the seller?"

"The county. Old man Toliver didn't have no relatives. The county took it for back taxes. Sold it for a song."

No help there. Feinberg thanked the woman and headed back to the Country Store.

"Always glad to help the FBI," the woman said, as he walked back into the glaring sun light and 1991.

It was the second time he had heard that. Feinberg was beginning to think FBI agents visited the town often.

Berman was sitting up by the time Gabe returned to the store. He had on a new shirt with a stag deer imprinted on red flannel.

"Thanks Toliver. You've been very helpful," Feinberg said, handing him his card. "How much we owe you?"

"No charge for the doctoring," Toliver said. "Give me five bucks for the shirt. It's new."

Feinberg pulled out his wallet and dug out a ten spot. "Listen, you'd be doing us a big favor if you don't mention anything about this to anyone," he said.

"Glad to help the FBI," Toliver said.

"If there's anything the FBI can ever do for you, give me a call," he said, handing Toliver his card.

"Thanks," Toliver said, taking the card. "Hope I never need to. And go see a doctor in a couple weeks," he said to Berman. "By then it should have healed up enough they won't be able to tell it was a gunshot wound. But you have to get those stitches out." He turned to Feinberg. "I gave Agent Berman some bandages, antibiotics and pain killers. Now you be sure and keep the wound clean."

"Will do," Berman said.

"Oh, is there an auto glass place in town?" Feinberg asked, as they went to the door.

"Got to go into Sonoma for that," Toliver said, as he stepped behind the counter. "Hold on while I get your change."

"That's okay, keep it," Feinberg said.

"No," Toliver said, ringing open the cash register, "I said five bucks and five bucks it is."

Feinberg took the five dollar bill and thanked the old man again.

Berman slept most of the way back to the Bay Area from Sonoma where they had stopped to have the windows replaced. The man at the glass place said they were lucky because he had the windows in stock. He didn't ask how they had been shattered. He just shouted at a couple of Mexican men to get to work and the windows were replaced in a half an hour.

By the time Berman opened his eyes, the sky was grey and fog was rolling across the low hills to the east. The Bay was on his right with the setting sun peeking out in the horizon below the Golden Gate Bridge.

Feinberg turned off at the University Avenue off ramp, headed out toward the Berkeley Marina and pulled into the Mariott Hotel parking lot, passing an old man sitting in a lounge chair holding up an UNFAIR sign.

"Where are we?" Berman said.

"Hey how ya doing partner?" Feinberg said, noticing for the first time that Berman was awake.

"I'm good. Those Vicodin the old man gave me work just fine. Where are we?"

*

Feinberg woke up early and went to the hotel window that looked out onto the marina. The sky was gray. Berman was still asleep. He had taken two more Vicodin before he went to bed and would probably sleep late.

He showered, shaved and dressed as quietly as he could and was out the door. It would be nine in New York and he wanted to talk to his boss, and give him a report.

The hotel restaurant hadn't opened yet, so he grabbed a cup of complimentary coffee in the lobby and found a public phone. He dialed the New York Bureau Chief's direct number. Duggart answered.

"Did you find any evidence on the site?" he asked.

"We took some samples of what we could find in the ashes. Whoever those guys were they were pros. They didn't leave any trace of what had happened except for some bullet casings – M-16s, and what was left of several vehicles. I would have expected to find at least some charred bones, but they must have taken everything. The little we could find we bagged up."

"You haven't taken them to a lab yet I hope."

"No Sir."

"Good. I want you to send them to me directly overnight. I don't want any outside labs used. We'll use our own people for this."

"Yes sir," Feinberg said.

"Do you have anything else to report at this time?" Duggart said.

Feinberg had wrestled over whether or not to tell his boss about Berman getting shot and had decided against it. But now that he was confronted by his Chief, he felt he had to report it.

"I'd like to go back and get the son-of-a bitch.," Feinberg said.

"Listen Gabe, I can understand your wanting to get this guy, but I don't want whoever it was arrested. The NSA people will find out about it and snatch him, sure as shit. It's obviously too dangerous for you men to stay out there and I want you to return to New York,"

"But..."

"Don't argue with me Feinberg. You two get on the first plane you can catch and get back here. And bring me those samples. I'll check some things out on my end. This thing stinks."

"Yes, sir."

The restaurant was opening. He was their first customer. He ordered what was called the Marina Special, an omelet with spinach, ham and a bunch of other things. He sipped his coffee waiting for his order and brooded over the fact that he wouldn't be able to go back and kill the bastard that shot his partner

* * *

Chapter 7

San Francisco

Headwinds blowing down from Canada had caused Fight 711 to arrive at SFO thirty-minutes late. Marshal Lee had managed to keep his conversation with the old woman to a minimum. It helped that after two gin and tonics she had dropped off to sleep for nearly the entire flight.

With no luggage but his overnight bag, he went straight to Hertz and picked out a Cadillac Sedan de Ville. After all the shit he had done for his country he had decided a long time ago that he would always travel first class.

He checked in at the stately Fairmont Hotel and went up to his room that overlooked Union Square, the heart of downtown San Francisco. He ordered dinner from room service—New York Strip rare, baked potato, and a spring salad with blue cheese dressing. He was a strictly meat and potatoes man. The new fad that proclaimed red meat unhealthy made him laugh, and the so-called new cuisine that flowed out of Alice Water's Chez Panisse Restaurant in Berkeley was finding its way into too many restaurants in Washington and New York as far as he was concerned.

After dinner he sat at the desk and took out the complimentary pad and pen from the drawer and drew up a list of who he wanted to see while he was there. First stop would be the FBI office in the Federal Building where he expected to find agents Feinberg and Berman. Lee suspected there were holes in the reports he had read and he wanted to fill them in. Next, the Chinese Consulate: he was eager to question the man Rick, whose real name was Huang Xiabo. Huang appeared to be playing a pivotal role in this little drama. Next on his list; Ted Harlin, Isaac Smith's pal and a crime reporter for the Oakland Tribune. And lastly, Isaac Smith, the man he was ordered to have eliminated.

But first he made a call to his old friend, Malcolm Stanford. Stanford had been head of national and international surveillance at the CIA for thirty years and coordinated all surveillance work with the NSA and FBI. Five years ago he had been forced into retirement. No one knew where he disappeared to, except Lee. Lee suspected his friend went into hiding. After he retired the FBI and NSA set up their own surveillance units, and separated national and international, so four units replaced Stanford. Malcolm Stanford was a threat. He knew too much. They would never again allow that to happen.

Lee hadn't seen him since he retired to the West Coast. But shortly after he disappeared, Stanford had contacted him and gave him a phone number where he could be reached. They agreed to meet for dinner the following night.

Supervising FBI Agent Matt Edwards looked up from his desk at the large man who had walked into his office unannounced.

Marshal Lee had never liked the Bureau; they had a habit of interfering with affairs of National Security which they had no business doing. Like the CIA, the Bureau had become too beauracratic and he could tell right off the man sitting behind the desk was a perfect example.

"The name is Lee; that's L-E-E like the Civil War general. I'm with the National Security Service." He pulled out his ID badge and dropped it on the desk.

Edwards picked it up and looked it over. "Have a seat Mister Lee.

What can I do for you?"

"I'm here to interview agents Feinberg and Berman."

Edwards kept holding Lee's ID badge, unconsciously flipping it over and over. He had had his fill of the NSA during the Chinese Consulate Affair and thought they were finally out of his hair. Apparently he was wrong.

"Feinberg and Berman ... I sent those two back to New York couple of days ago and good riddance as far as I'm concerned."

"You had a problem with Agents Feinberg and Berman?" Lee asked, surprised a Bureau officer would complain about fellow agents to an outsider.

"Look Lee, I run a tight ship here. Those two refused to obey instructions, especially that Agent Feinberg. I don't know if you have this problem in the Service, but I find Jews to be undisciplined when it comes to following orders. I've sent a complete report to their Chef in New York on their failure to cooperate with this office, but I doubt if anything will be done about it."

"Well, I can't help you there pal," Lee said, reaching across the desk and taking back his ID. "Maybe you can be of assistance?"

"I don't know what I can tell you that I didn't put in my report which I assume you've seen."

"Well, let's just assume I didn't see your report Agent...Edwards was it?"

Edwards leaned back in his chair. He didn't like the condescending tone of Lee's voice. He didn't like Lee at all. He just wanted to get him out of his office. "There's nothing to tell," he said. "You people made sure the Bureau was cut out of this operation. The fact is, if anyone should be mad about Feinberg and Berman it should be you people—it was your operation they stuck their noses into. Now that I think of it, I can't blame them much when you consider it was the reason they were here in San

Francisco, now, wasn't it."

"I read Agent Feinberg's report. Is there anything he omitted from it?" Lee noticed a drip of perspiration run down Edwards's forehead. "Anything that might indicate they were more involved in our operation?"

There was a moment of silence. Lee could tell the man sitting across from him was running something through his mind.

"Well," Edwards finally said. "When that old Chinese bartender was gunned down in Oakland Feinberg started going directly against my implicit instructions to stay out of the case. But as far as I know, what he wrote in his report was as far as he went."

"He and Agent Berman didn't make a trip up to Sonoma County?"

"Sonoma County?" Edwards took out his handkerchief and mopped his forehead. "Not that I know of."

"Are you sure of that, Agent Edwards?"

"Well, now that you mention it, Agent Berman was dispatched to Sonoma County to investigate something or other ... I can't recall now what it was. I'd have to look back at the assignment roster."

"That's all?" Lee said, looking Edwards straight in the eyes. "To your knowledge, Agent Feinberg didn't join him in Sonoma?"

"Look Lee, I said I told you what I know." He stood up. "Now, if there isn't anything else, I have a busy schedule today."

Lee could see he wasn't going to get any more out of Edwards. He stood up and offered his hand.

"Well thank you for your time, Agent Edwards."

Edwards wiped his sweaty hands with the handkerchief and accepted Lee's outstretched hand.

"If there's anything else this office can do to be of assistance to the Service, I would appreciate a call first."

"Sure thing," Lee said with a smile and walked out, leaving the door open behind him.

The Chinese Consul, Mister Xiang Zhongfa, looked at the man sitting across from him. "I'm sorry Mr...." He looked at the business card again, "Marshall Lee. As much as we desire to cooperate with the American government I'm afraid I cannot help you."

"Well, maybe your attaché, the man who calls himself Rick —Huang Xiabo I believe his name is. Maybe he can answer some questions,'" Lee said

"Oh, once again I must apologize, but Mister Huang has returned to China."

The Consul was smiling. Lee wanted to beat his smug face to a pulp.

"Well perhaps you can fill me in on what you know about Operation Red Bear," he said.

That wiped the smile off the Consul's face. He looked down at his desk for a moment, and then back to Lee, avoiding eye contact.

"I have no idea what you are talking about, Mister Lee. This sounds to me like something better taken up with our Embassy in Washington."

More evasion.

"Perhaps you can tell me something about a Ms. Mei-ling Wu."

"Mei-ling Wu," the Consul repeated. "Hmmmm, yes, I believe I still have her file."

He hunted through a stack of manila folders that were neatly piled on the corner of the large desk.

"Ahhh. Here it is." He opened the file. "Mei-ling Wu. Yes, I recall now. She came to us several weeks ago requesting to be repatriated back to China. Apparently her uncle, Mister Peter Wu, was murdered must brutally in Oakland, across the Bay where he worked as a barman or some such thing"

"Bartender?"

"Bartender, yes. You Americans are a very violent people. This sort of thing could never happen in China. Your authorities have not solved this senseless murder of this poor Chinese national. We have filed a complaint with your government."

"Come now, you know there's more to it than that," Lee said. "Peter Wu was in reality an expatriate by the name of Major Ching–Shu Wu who had been recruited by this Consulate to spy on a group of Traid smugglers."

"Really Mister Lee," Xaing said after laughing. "You've been reading too many spy novels. As far as I know all we did was grant Ms. Wu's request and arrange a flight for her back to her home in Guangdong. Now, if that is all, I have some pressing matters that require my presence." He stood and offered his hand.

Lee knew a brush off when he heard one. He turned and walked out, leaving Consul Xiang with his hand dangling in the air.

He grabbed a cab outside the Consulate on Laguna and went back to Union Square and the hotel. He had learned no more than he thought he would from the Consulate. But the mere fact that the attaché, who was probably in the *Guóānbù*, the Chinese Secret Service, had been sent home meant the guy calling himself Rick was either in trouble or was just laying low for awhile. He smiled thinking how the phone to the Chinese Embassy in Washington was probably burning up by now. Word that he was snooping around would quickly get back to the State Department.

"Fuck it," he said. He had done a lot of dubious things for his country, but he had never been asked to violate the Constitution by assassinating a U.S. citizen. Lee was a ruthless man but he liked to think he had his principles.

The doorman at the Fairmont greeted him and he went up to his room.

He pulled out his list and glanced at it. He knew who was next, but it was habit. FBI Agent Feinberg. The little prick at the San Francisco office had said the two agents returned to New York, but he wanted to check. He called the New York Bureau of the FBI. The woman on the other end of the line said Berman had returned to the office that morning, but Feinberg wasn't with him—probably took a few days off, he was told. Lee asked if he could talk with Agent Berman. He waited on the phone for a few minutes until it picked up.

"Agent Berman."

"Hi, I am looking for Agent Gabriel Feinberg. I believe he is your partner."

"Yes."

"I was wondering if you could tell me where he's staying in the San Francisco Area," Lee said, on the outside chance Berman would tell him.

"Who the fuck is this?" Berman said.

"Just a man looking for Agent Feinberg."

"And why the hell should I tell you?"

"Look this is a matter of life and death and I have to make contact with Agent Feinberg as soon as possible."

"Well pal, I won't give you the time of day unless you identify yourself," Berman said.

Lee thought quickly. If he couldn't get Berman to talk he'd have to check every hotel and motel in the San Francisco Bay Area. "I am Lieutenant Shane Flynn of the San Francisco Police Department. I spoke with agent Edwards at the San Francisco Bureau office, and he told me you and Agent Feinberg were investigating a Chinese smuggling ring here. They told me Agent Feinberg was still in the Bay Area."

"So, what's your interest?" Berman asked.

"I'm on the organized gang unit and I have acquired some information I think you people could use."

"So why pass it on to us?"

"Because I was told by my superiors to discontinue our investigation, that's why. I've put a lot of time and effort into this case and I'd hate for it to be a waste."

He sounded convincing enough, but Bermaan would need more information before he gave up his partner's whereabouts..

"Sorry pal, but I'm not at liberty to give out that kind of information, especially over the phone."

"Thanks," Lee said and hung up.

Berman looked at the phone for a moment. Then he dialed the San Francisco Police Department and asked for Lieutenant Flynn. There was no one in the department by that name.

Malcolm Stanford sat across the red naughahyde booth from Lee. His full head of thinning white hair was pulled back into a scraggly ponytail, and a matching thin white beard and wire rim spectacles gave him the appearance of an eccentric college professor.

Original Joes: the long bar was two deep; the counter in front of the open kitchen was full; classy women and men in silk suits and ties mingled with longshoremen, construction workers, city employees of both sexes and politicians of every strip. The lights were low and the noise level was four bells. Original Joe's was an authentic part of San Francisco.

"I just love the sweet breads here," he said. "Make a practice of coming to the City at least once a month to catch the symphony and satisfy my cravings. You should really try them."

Lee sipped his scotch and soda. "Never could stomach offal. I'll stick to meat and potatoes if you don't mind. But I'll say this about the place. Reminds me of the old days. Good choice."

"Suit yourself, but you don't know what you're missing. Damn it's good seeing you Lee. I've missed our lunches.

"Well, you moved all the way across the country, and as far as every-one else is concerned dropped off the map entirely."

"Yes, as far away from those pricks that I could. I'm surprised they haven't hunted me down. You're not here to kill me I hope?"

Lee laughed. "You're a dangerous man, old friend, and what makes you think they're not looking?"

Stanford took a sip of his red wine. "Dangerous? I suppose so. You don't think I would retire without setting up a little insurance. You know me better than that, Lee. Got me a nice little ranch on top of a mountain in Santa Cruz where I can keep tabs on everything that's going on. Nice little setup. Anything happens to me and the world will know about their shenanigans. You ever need to know something, a little insurance of your own, you let me know."

Lee laughed. "That's the old Malcolm I know."

"Well, when you've been doing a thing all your life, it's hard to stop, if you know what I mean."

The waiter came with their food and set it down. The sweet breads cooked in a red sauce with pasta and a salad on the side. Lee looked down at his own plate; a hunk of prime rib an inch thick and still bleeding.

"You remember what I said, Lee. You need anything you call me."

After that the conversation fell into old times as they savored their dinners.

* * *

Spring 1992

Chapter 8

Guangzhou, China

Mei-ling sat at the outside table sipping tea at the expansive outdoor café. She looked up at the buildings of the University across the wide bicycle filled boulevard. The cafe was a favorite hangout for students, but since Tiananmen, gatherings of students were scrutinized closely by government informers and she was surrounded by empty tables. She had been fighting depression. Not so much because she was unhappy with her classes — they were in great demand, but not because students sought to learn about their own country's history, but because they wanted to know what it had been like living in America. This only made her more suspect and she knew she was under close surveillance, making her life intolerable. Thoughts of Isaac Smith and Oakland increasingly occupied her mind, and at the moment she was deep in thought wondering how she could return to America. It wasn't just that she missed Isaac and longed to be held by him, but more so because she now believed her government would renege on their agreement with her and that his life was in danger.

She was so wrapped up in her thoughts that she failed to notice the man with a cane walk up to her.

"Mei-ling? You are Mei-ling Wu aren't you?"

She looked up. "Johnny Wong?"

"It is you," he said. "I heard that you had returned to China. What a coincidence. Out of the millions of people in Guangzhou we should run into each other."

"Johnny, what are you doing here?" she said, still unable to believe her eyes.

He started to sit down. Then hesitated. "May I?"

"Please," Mei-ling said, still unable to believe that of all people she should run into, Johnny Wong was not high on the list. Johnny was a bartender back in Oakland and a good friend of Isaac's. He had been attacked outside his apartment building after helping Isaac translate her uncle's journal. He was badly beaten and suffered a concussion and a shattered leg. She saw he was walking with a cane. He leaned against the small table to hold himself up.

"The leg hasn't healed?" she said, as he worked his way into the metal framed chair.

A waiter hurried over. Johnny ordered tea and sweet buns.

"Well, that's part of the reason I'm here. My old man knows a Master of Qigong. I never had much faith in the ancient Chinese healing methods, but I figured, what the hell, I'll give it a try. Kaiser hadn't helped me none. Said it would take multiple operations and there were no guarantees. We still have a lot of family here and he wanted me to pay respects to our ancestors. I've seen the herbalists and acupuncture specialists too. And I must admit, I am walking much better. So maybe there's something to be said about the old ways."

"That was terrible what happened," Mei-ling said. "Isaac should never have gotten you involved."

Johnny laughed. "Smitty was in love. He needed my help to find you, and I'm a sucker for love. Besides, I always had a thing for you, Mei-ling."

"You like all the women," she laughed. It was the first time she had found humor in anything since returning to China. Then she looked around, leaned across the table and lowered her voice. "How is Isaac, have you seen him?"

"No," Johnny said. "I've been here in China for the last month."

Mei-ling sat back as the waiter came and put a tea pot, cup and a plate of small sweet buns on the table. She waited until he was gone. "I must get a message to him," she said. "It is of great importance."

"Sure," Johnny said. "I can do that, but why don't you just write him?"

"This is China, Johnny. They read any letter going to America from anyone, but especially people like me."

"Really?" Johnny said, noticing for the first time her unease. "I never thought about that, but now that you mention it, I suppose you're right. What do you want me to tell him?"

"Please Johnny, lower your voice."

"What? What's the matter?"

"There are eyes and ears everywhere; I don't want to make trouble for you," she said in a hushed voice. "I can't talk here. Can you meet me tomorrow at my uncle's grave in Sihui? Its not far. We can talk there."

"Sure, no problem. I know the place. But what's the matter?"

"I'll tell you about it tomorrow. I'll be there sometime in the morning. If you don't see me, please wait. Now I'd better get back. I have a class soon."

"Sure Mei-ling. Tomorrow. I'll be there."

She got up, walked behind Johnny and put her hands on his shoulders. She leaned down and whispered in his ear, "Be very careful Johnny.

Make sure you're not followed." She kissed him on the cheek and was gone.

Johnny watched as she hurried across the boulevard, dodging the bike traffic like an expert, admiring her sexy athletic body when he felt a tap on his shoulder. He turned to see a nondescript young man staring sternly down at him. He wore a plain white shirt open in front and sported Ray-Ban sunglasses—or knock offs of Ray-Bans. "Do I know you?" he asked.

"What business did you have with the woman? Do you know her?"

Johnny's mind raced. "Huh, oh no. Just a pretty lady. Thought I'd try to get a date, but no luck."

The man's face showed no emotion, like it was etched in stone . "May I see your papers."

If he had been in Oakland he would have demanded to see some sort of ID from the man. But this was China and he quickly decided not to challenge him. He dug into his pocket and pulled out his visa. The man inspected it.

"American."

"Yes. Visiting relatives."

"Wong. There are maybe a million Wongs in Quanzhou."

"We're a big family," Johnny laughed.

The man obviously had no sense of humor. He stared at the visa for what seemed like a long time.

"Is there some problem?" Johnny said

The man handed the visa back to him: "Be careful who you speak to next time, Mister Wong."

All Johnny could think was that Russians must have iron asses, because the beat up Lada he borrowed from a cousin had no apperant suspension.

He bumped up the dirt road to the hillside cemetery just outside the town of Sihua. Johnny wasn't impressed with the Russian car, pure utility with no comfort, but it got him to where he was going and now he hoped it wasn't too late to find Mei-ling.

He asked the unformed woman at the cemetery entrance where the grave of Peter Wu was. She just looked at him with a puzzled expression.

"Oh, I'm sorry. Major Ching Shu Wu."

The woman smiled. "Comrade Major Wu. Yes"

* * *

Chapter 9

Sihui, Guangdong Province

Johnny followed the path up the side of the hill as instructed; passing the thousands of stone monuments that marked probably millions of family grave sites. He was hot and sweaty as he had to struggle with his cane, taking care not to fall. The dust was thick; filling his nose and eyes, and the place had an eerie feeling as if he was being watched. Then he saw a lone figure standing at a large monument. It had to be Mei-ling. He looked around. There was no one else in sight. He figured it was safe to approach her. After his encounter with the Chinese man at the outdoor cafe he had gotten extremely cautious.

"Mei-ling?"

The woman turned to him. She wore a scarf over her head that she wrapped around her lower face so that only her eyes were uncovered, giving her an exotic and mysterious look. There were fresh flowers next to the grave stone with a picture of Peter Wu in a military uniform.

"You weren't followed?"

He looked into her eyes; the shining black ovals that seemed to embrace anyone she looked at. It was no wonder Isaac had fallen for her. There in the emptiness of the cemetery he was half tempted to make a play himself. He dismissed the idea as soon as it occurred to him. Unethical and kinky. Not his style..

"So, what's all the cloak and dagger shit?" he said instead.

"It had to be fate that we met yesterday. There is no other way to explain it."

Johnny smiled as she took his hand in hers. They were cool and soft. He didn't believe in fate, but it did seem pretty amazing that they meet in a city of millions of people.

Did anyone approach you after we talked?" she asked, letting go of his hand and turning toward the grave.

"Well, yes. But I blew him off."

"Perhaps. But as you can see, I am being watched pretty closely. It's because I lived in America so long. After the student uprising in Beijing the government has been super paranoid. It's not surprising that they're watching me."

"But wait a minute, Mei-ling. You're the niece of a highly respected Major in the Red Army. Doesn't that count for anything?"

"Johnny. Don't be a naive American. This is Red China. The rest of the Communist world is crumbling and you think they're going to let that happen here?" .

She had first got a hint that her deal with the Consulate was known only to a few people—probably in the Intelligence Agency— when the officer at the airport had no knowledge of the agreement. As far as the Internal Security Agency was concerned she was just an expat who had returned home after nearly twenty years in America.

"You, of all people, know what Isaac and I were doing. God knows you paid a high price for that knowledge."

"Forget all that Mei. What message do you want me to take to Isaac?" He put his hands on her shoulders. She folded in against his chest and he let his arms fall around her and held her. He heard her quietly crying, something totally unexpected. After a minute she pulled back from him.

"I'm sorry, Johnny. I didn't mean to do that. She dug into her hand bag and pulled out a red handkerchief and wiped her eyes. Then she put her hand into her blouse and pulled out a small brown envelope and handed it to him. "I want you to take this to him. It's very important. But be sure and put it somewhere safe where it won't be found."

"Don't worry, Mei." he took his cane and screwed off the silver handle. Then he rolled the envelope into a cylinder and shoved it down into the cane and screwed the top back on. "Pretty cool, huh."

"You'd better go now. I want to spend some time with Uncle Peter."

"Are you going to be all right?"

She kissed him on his cheek. "Don't worry about me. Just make sure Isaac gets the letter."

She turned back to the grave stone. He looked at her for a moment, and then made his way back down the hill to the Lada.

* * *

Chapter 10

Washington, DC

Marshal Lee stood at his window overlooking the Capital. He had been confined to his office for over three months, with nothing to do. He was supposedly waiting to hear if any decision had been made on the assassination of Isaac Smith.. That was his job; to eliminate enemies of the United States. But this one still troubled him. He couldn't figure out how this innocuous union guy could be a threat to the United States. It wouldn't be an assassination; it would be murder. He hoped that since so much time had passed they had decided not to carry it out.

Lee had come from a long line of military men, including his famous great grandfather General Robert E. Lee. His father had wanted him to go to West Point, but he had opted for the Naval Academy and then went into the Navy Seals where he gained a reputation for his skill at killing. From there it was an easy move into the Central Intelligence Agency, and then NSA where his particular set of skills elevated his career quickly.

But for all the dirty things he had done for his country, he believed he had always maintained his honor. There was nothing honorable in this assignment.

He walked back to his desk, picked up the file on Isaac Smith and thumbed through it for the hundredth time. "A fucking union official," he said to himself. "How in God's name did this guy get mixed up in this thing?"

His earlier trip to San Francisco had yielded zip. He gave up after being unable to contact FBI Agent Isaac Feinberg and returned to Washington.

The file didn't tell him much. If it had been twenty years earlier, Smith's parent's politics might have drawn some suspicion on him. They had been typical New York Jewish rank and file members of the Communist Party. But now, in 1993, no one gave a shit about the Communist Party. The Party never had been very large, but now it had shrunk down to no more than maybe 3,000 members. There was nothing else in his file other than his union activity, and having participated in a number of peace marches and rallies during the Vietnam War.

He dropped the Smith file on his desk and picked up another file stamped "Classified." It was FBI Agents Feinberg and Berman's report on the Ghost Shadows Gang activities in San Francisco. Agent Feinberg had put Smith under surveillance soon after the murder of Major Ching Shu Wu, aka Peter Wu. According to Agent Feinberg's report, Smith's only fault was falling in love with Wu's niece, Mei-ling Wu.

He looked at her file photo and could see how Smith had been attracted. There was one incident that caught his attention. Feinberg had interceded in what he described as the attempted murder of Smith on the night of the Oakland Hills fire. There was no explanation as to why he had gone to the home of Mei-ling Wu on that particular night, only that he had stopped an agent from the Chinese Consulate from shooting

Smith and possibly Ms. Wu as well. No report was filed with the OPD. Apparently the Chinese believed Smith was some kind of threat to them then, but Feinberg made no reference to it in the report; only that the incident had occurred.

The phone rang. It was Mac MacCraven, his buddy at State. He hadn't heard from Mac since their last meeting back in October. He wanted to meet at the Lincoln Memorial. Was Mac the one pulling the strings? He had never been quite sure how high up his old comrade was at the State Department, only that he seemed to know a lot about the Smith case.

McCraven was sitting on the bench in front of the Memorial smoking a cigarette and looking up at the majestic statue. It was a bright, warm Spring day, the kind that made living and working in Washington D.C. bearable, unlike the last time they had met when a tropical storm was moving up the coast and the weather was hot and humid.

"Mac." he said, as he sat down on the bench.

"There you are," McCraven answered, looking at his watch. "Right on time as usual."

"So, what's on your mind?"

"Lincoln," he said, looking back up at the statue. "A lot of people consider him our greatest president."

"Yeah. Did you bring me out here to discuss history"

"You ever study Civil War history, Lee. Of course you have. Your great grandfather was Robert E. Lee."

"It was required at the Academy. But you know that."

"Yes, I was just making conversation."

"You want to tell me something?" Lee said, getting impatient.

"You know that Pesident Lincoln suspended habeas corpus during the Civil War? Violated the very Constitution he took this country to war over, and he violated it himself."

"Okay, thanks for the history lesson, Mac. Now you want to tell me what you dragged me out here for?"

"Well, I'm just saying that sometimes government has to bend a little when it comes to national security," McCraven said, dropping his cigarette on the ground and stepped on it. "Listen Lee, we know all about your little trip to the West Coast three months ago. The Secretary got an irate call from the Chinese Ambassador claiming that you went in and harassed the Chinese Consul in San Francisco. He was going to file a formal protest. I had to go out on a limb to smooth that one over and save your ass from the guillotine."

"I didn't like his attitude," Lee said.

"Well, what the fuck were you doing there anyway?"

"Come on Mac. I thought I was getting an assignment and I wanted to check on some things; make some contacts. Just routine."

"It's customary to report to someone and apparently you didn't make any friends with the local FBI either. I suppose you didn't like their attitude either?"

"Look Mac, this all happened nearly four months ago. I never got the go ahead so I thought the operation was scrubbed, which to my mind would have been the best way to go. Now, out of the blue, you're telling me I upset some folks at State?"

"Well, I cooled things down, but there's still people after your butt.'"

"Fuckem. What do you want from me, a thank you for saving my job...?"

"Oh don't get so defensive, Lee. You're far too valuable to us to let something this stupid end your career. Come on, let's walk. It's such a lovely day."

They stood up. A soft breeze blew through the budding leaves on the

Elms, and white and pink blossoms floated down from the cherry trees like snow, covering the walkway on the Capital Mall.

"I know you were against this operation from the git go, Lee, and I don't blame you. I spoke against it, as I told you, but we got our orders."

"So, now after all this time you want me to carry it out. Is that it?"

"Well, to be blunt, yes we do."

"That don't make sense," Lee said, pulling a cigarette from the pack in his pocket. Ever since he had first heard about the operation he had taken up smoking again after a two year abstention. "Smith obviously hasn't said anything to anyone or we'd surely have heard about it by now. So we're still doing the fucking Chinese Government's bidding?"

"Hell, Lee, the Chinese never did tell us they wanted Smith dead. I doubt if they care one way or the other about him now. They got what they wanted and we got our guy in China off the hook and safely into the arms of Uncle Sam."

"So, if that's the truth and I was lied to all along, who does want him silenced? Or are you telling me our own people want him gone."

McCraven stopped and turned to Lee. He pulled out his zippo lighter with the insignia of the Navy Seals and lit Lee's cigarette. "Look my old friend, everything has changed. The President of the United States was once head of the CIA. You remember how things were when we were with the outfit, or the Seals for that matter. No questions asked. You got your assignment and you carried it out. We're all soldiers in a war for the security of our nation. It's still CIA rules. They still want Smith silenced, and you got the job. I told them we could count on you."

"No Mac. When I went out there I was checking up on this Smith guy, and I'm convinced he doesn't know anything, or at least, hasn't told anyone. His best friend's a reporter for god's sake. If he was going to tell anyone, it would be him, and there haven't been any stories about it anywhere. Any reporter worth his salt would have taken it and run. This guy, Harlin, is no slouch. But nothing."

"Harlin, I seem to remember something about him."

"You should. He exposed that case when several officers were accused of murdering Vietnamese prostitutes in Saigon. Harlin reported the story in the left wing Pacific News Service. That would have been okay, but the New York Times picked it up, and there was a lot of hair pulling at the White House over it. So, I don't think he'd pass this story up. Do you?"

"No, but we're taking no chances. Smith got to go."

"Okay boss. But I still don't like it. It could be just the thing that will make Harlin start digging. So, don't say I didn't warn you."

"Look buddy, if it's any consolation, I recommended they find someone else to do the job. But they want you. Get one of your assets to do it if it's such a problem for you."

"No, if I'm going to do this thing, I'll take care of it myself," Lee said.

"Suit yourself. Just make sure it gets done! We want him gone."

With that McCraven turned and walked back down the mall toward the Capital Building. Lee watched him as a small wind devil swept up the cherry blossoms and covered him in a pink and white cloud.

* * *

Chapter 11

New York

Gabe waited at the Stamford station for the train to New York after a long weekend with the wife and kids. He hated Connecticut with its upper middle class pretentiousness; its big houses and swimming pools and tidy streets and pure bred dogs. He had never wanted to move out of New York. He had a comfortable walkup in the East Village when he meet Miriam who was going to NYU studying—he never was sure what—but she was a beautiful raven haired Sephardic fox and when he got her to his bed she was a wild woman.

When she announced she was pregnant and wasn't getting an abortion, his whole life changed; big Jewish wedding bought and paid for by her parents, thank goodness—his mother and father were happy. Then his new father-in-law announced that he was buying them a house in the burbs—New York is no place to bring up a child—he refused to give up the apartment.

That was ten years and two kids ago. Miriam was no longer the hot raven haired chick, but had morphed into a nagging middle-aged Jewish mama. Now, he found himself spending more time at work and using the flat when he had to spend the night in the City, which over the past few years was becoming more often than not, especially after being assigned to cover organized crime in the city's large Chinatown.

He settled back in his seat. The Connecticut countryside rushed past the window as the train sped to New York. Everything was turning green with the beginning of Spring and a light rain spattered against the glass. He opened his brief case and took out the old file on Isaac Smith, the Oakland, California union official who had gotten himself tangled up in Chinatown intrigue after witnessing the murder of an old Chinese bartender. He wondered if Smith—Smitty as he liked to be called even though he insisted on calling him Izzy, because what kind of name was Smitty for a Jew—would have gotten involved if he had known at the time that the old bartender was, in reality, an exiled officer in the Chinese Red Army and involved in spying on Chinese smugglers.

He assumed he had been taken off the case after returning to the New York office from San Francisco, until he got a call from his boss at home that morning telling him to review the file when he got into the office, and then to come see him. Luckily he had kept a copy of it in his brief case, probably because he never considered the case closed. He remembered saving Smith's life on two occasions; his and the old bartender's niece who had gottenthe union man involved in the first place. Mei-ling Wu, a classic Chinese beauty. If he had been in Smitty's shoes, he probably would have done anything she wanted too.

Now something was up. It had seemed odd to him that he hadn't heard anything about it since he and his partner, Rich Berman, had returned to New York. They had been on the case for over a year investigating the New York Chinese Tongs. It had been a priority, and they had

been sent to San Francisco when their informant in New York's Chinatown told them the Ghost Shadows had expanded to the West Coast
and were working for one of China's largest Triads, smuggling drugs and
immigrants into the U.S. Their investigation ended when Berman was
nearly killed in an ambush on a deserted ranch in Northern California's
wine county.

Jake Duggart, head of the New York Bureau office rarely called him by
his first name, but this seemed to be an occasion. He was a small man
with thinning gray hair and wire spectacles that made it appear time had
stopped for him in the 1940's. But Duggart was nobody's fool, and he
was a Bureau man 100 percent despite his vocal disapproval of head hon-
cho Hoover..

"Gabriel, I want you to return to the West Coast."

"What's up?"

"You reviewed the file like I asked?"

"You told me to."

"Don't be a wise ass, Feinberg. I assume you're up to speed on the
case then."

"To tell you the truth, I never forgot the details. I wanted to stay on
the case in the first place."

"Yeah, but it's not in my jurisdiction and there were higher ups that
wanted the thing dropped."

Gabe remembered the last orders he and Berman had gotten from
the San Francisco office District Supervisor to shitcan all knowledge of
the affair, particularly the clandestine military type assault on a ranch
house in the hills overlooking the Northern California town of Glen Ellen. Anyone reading the classified report from the Frisco office would
never have known it happened.

"So, what's changed?" Gabe asked, knowing his boss wasn't the go-along-get-along type, and had wondered why he had seemed to forget about the case after getting irate when Gabe had reported what he and Berman, along with Isaac Smith and the woman, Mei-ling Wu, had witnessed.

"What's changed is that my contact in the State Department tipped me off that there has been a contract put out on your friend Isaac Smith. That's what's changed."

"I don't get it," Gabe said. "It's been nearly four months since this thing went down. Ms. Wu is back in China and I thought the whole thing's been buried."

"Well, apparently someone wants this guy Smith silenced and I'm not going to let that happen. The military assault was bad enough, but this is straight out murder. Gabe, this is America and we can't let this happen if we can help it. You agree?"

Gabe sat down in the chair in front of Duggart's desk. "They'd do that?"

"Look Gabriel, I've been around for a long time. I've seen some people in government agencies starting to operate like the goddamn KGB. That's okay by me as long as it's the CIA operating outside our borders. But now they think they're above the goddamn law and can do anything they want right here in the USofA."

"So, what can we do?"

"I want you to go back to Oakland and take Smith under your wing. I want you to protect him. I don't care what it takes, but I won't allow these bastards to kill an American citizen. But before you agree, I want you to know this is totally unauthorized and we can both get into a lot of trouble. So..." he stared into Gabe's eyes "...are you in or out?"

"What about Rich?"

"I'm asking you."

"How long will this be?"

"As long as it takes."

"I'm in."

"Good. You'll report to me alone. Understood?' He pulled an enve-lope out from his desk drawer and tossed it to Feinberg. "That ought to be enough to keep you going. Anything you need you contact me."

Feinberg took the envelope and was about to leave.

"Say, did they ever figure out what those samples we brought back were?"

Duggart laughed. "Some kind of animal fur," he said. "One of the techs claimed it was from a bear."

"A bear? That doesn't make any sense."

"That's what I said."

* * *

Chapter 12

Alameda, Ca.

It had been nearly four months since Mei-ling had returned to China. Winter had come and gone, but Smitty's love for the beautiful Chinese lady remained, consuming his every moment. No matter how much he tried to convince himself that he was over her he knew he was lying.

It all seemed like a dream, but it was all too real. He would close his eyes and her image would come back to him, haunting him by day and filling his dreams at night.

He knew it wasn't over. There was something missing, something undone. He found himself reading her last note to him over and over—he had found it in his coat pocket several days after she left him standing in the early morning cold on Lakeshore Drive after telling him she was returning to China. It was written on a sheet of note paper from the Jack London Inn where they had spent a couple of nights. Some how I will return to you. She must have slipped it into his pocket before they had headed out to Stover's Ranch that night on the hunt for her precious panda bears. He knew when they set out that it was a suicide mission, but it hadn't mattered. He had nearly been killed twice before; once locked up in a shed with the blazing Oakland Hills fire roaring down on them; then again, after being rescued from the fire by the guy from the Chinese Consulate calling himself Rick, only to have the same guy turn around and threaten to shot him in cold blood that same day, and would have succeeded if not for the intervention of FBI agent, Gabe Feinberg. He remained at Mei-ling's side, protecting her in his feeble way, even though at times, it seemed it was she who was protecting him; all for some contraband pandas that the Chinese government believed were so important that all trace of them had to be wiped from the face of the earth. None of it made sense to him; only the promise he had made to the dying Peter Wu to protect Mei-ling. And then he had fallen deeply and hopelessly in love with her.

The funny thing about it was, he had never actually seen the panda bears that had created so many problems. The closest he had come to them were the two narrow escapes from death when Mei-ling and he had gone to find them. If they had ever existed, all evidence was in the ashes of the Stover Ranch. All he had was Mei-ling's word.

Indira Banerjii, the pretty young Indian professor of Far East studies, had probably been murdered because of her association with Mei-ling. Now he believed everyone who might have knowledge of the bears was in danger. He had tried to warn Dede, but she wouldn't hear it. Ted? Forget about it. The fearless reporter was now more determined than ever to uncover the story that lay behind Peter Wu's murder. Nothing would stand in his way of a good story. Smitty felt responsible. If anything happened to either one of them it would be on him and there was nothing he could do about it.

Living with Dede had become unbearable. She told him he'd receive no comfort from her and she meant it. He slept on the couch, and aside from enjoying being with Chanel, it was no substitute for the comfort of a woman's arms. Any woman.

He had started going into the union office, going about his duties half heartily, and found himself hanging around at his pal Eddy's bar more and more. At least there he could drink, and Eddy was a good listener, but that only made things worse, and he found himself drinking more and talking less. A shrink would have diagnosed him as clinically depressed. He needed a change. He needed to escape from everything.

The days were getting longer and warmer. He found himself drawn to the Alameda Marina. He missed the sound of the clanking halyards as the wind blew them into the masts of hundreds of sailboats He missed the cool ocean breezes in the evenings and the peace that came from sleeping in a cabin with only the soft lapping of the water against the hull.

Trish, owner and sole proprietor of Alameda Yacht Sales, was tall, blond and tan. Middle-aged, she had maintained her good looks and must have exercised religiously because she had the shapely body of a movie star when women had voluptuous figures. She had sold him his first two boats and had always been friendly and helpful. He boarded her fifty foot motor yacht where she had turned a corner of the large salon into an office. It was one of those older yachts with teak decks, varnished trim and polished brass. The name on the stern was Sexy Lady. It had been built for Rita Hayward by Howard Hughes. At least that was the story. As far as Smitty was concerned, the present owner was no less sexy.

"I was wondering when I'd see you. Have a seat," she said in greeting. "You must be either the most unlucky sailor around or the most careless."

"I guess it would look like that," he said, dropping into the wooden captain's chair in front of her desk.

"And now you're looking for another one I'll bet. I could make a living off you, Smitty," Trish laughed.

"If the insurance company pays off this time. Two claims in as many years for fire; they got to be wondering 'cause they're still investigating and it's been over three months since I filed a claim," Smitty said. "You wouldn't have a drink?"

She smiled warmly showing a mouth full of perfect white teeth that must have been well tended by a professional.

"Sure honey. You look like you really could use one," she said, getting up and opening a cabinet. "Scotch?"

"Bourbon, if you have it."

"Knob Hill okay with you?"

"Expensive."

"Nothing's too good for my favorite customer," she smiled.

He took the bourbon from her tan manicured hand, and took out a Lucky. She picked up a lighter and leaned across the desk exposing the deep cleavage between her ample bosoms. He wondered how many boats she had sold with the pose.

"I wouldn't worry about the insurance," she said. "They'll pay eventually."

"Not for awhile, I'm afraid. In the meantime, to be quite honest, I need a place to stay," he said, not knowing why she would do something about it or even care for that matter. "I thought maybe you might have a boat—a perspective sale—I might bunk in for a while … until my insurance money comes through."

She sat back in her chair, her mind working, her eyes sizing him up.

. "Can you cook?" she finally said.

"Actually I'm a pretty good cook," he said, omitting the fact that Dede did most of the cooking at the apartment, and he usually had breakfast at the Merritt Bakery, or stuffed down a pastrami on rye at the Ringside with a glass of Guinness.

"Well, I'm a terrible cook, and eating out every day is getting expensive. Boat sales are down this year. I can put you up for a few days. I live on this boat by myself since my old man ran out on me and there are a couple of empty cabins."

I couldn't believe my luck; shacked up with a beautiful blonde on a luxury yacht.

"But don't get any ideas," she added with a smile.

"I appreciate it," he said, hoping that she didn't mean what she said. Dede had told him he'd have to work out his pain from the loss of Meiling alone, but he needed the sympathy of a woman's warm body to lean on; a personality weakness he supposed. A shrink once told him it was because his mother had breast fed him too long.

He drove back to the apartment to pick up some things. Dede and Chanel weren't at home. Chanel had started school and Dede was probably at the UC Berkeley Law Library studying.

He grabbed up his things, threw them in an overnight bag and sat down at the kitchen table to write a note.

My Dearest Dede,

I need to be alone and am going away for a while. You are probably right about me working out my loneliness by myself. I can't expect you to take care of me every time I have woman problems. You have your own life to lead.

I know you didn't believe me when I told you that you could be in grave danger. I can't tell you everything that has happened to me, or why I am so worried, but believe what I told you and be very careful. I love you and Chanel very much. You are like family to me. I'll stay in touch.

Much love,

Smitty.

He went down to Lakeshore and crossed the street to where he had parked his car. When he opened the trunk to throw the bag in, he noticed a man leaning against a tree staring at him. He looked like he didn't belong, dressed in a gray suit and tie with a fedora hat pulled down over his eyes and smoking a cigarette. People who hang out at the Lake were dressed casually. This guy stuck out like a sore thumb. Smitty stared back. The man simple tipped his hat, smiled and walked down toward the lake where the usual suspects were jogging or walking dogs. Smitty shrugged it off. Perhaps he was being overly paranoid.

Trish wasn't kidding about not cooking. The refrigerator and cupboards were practically bare, unlike her well stocked liquor cabinet. He stopped at the large Safeway on Bayshore Island, the southern extension of Alameda. By the time he got out of there, he was a couple of hundred bucks poorer. Sautéd shrimp and garlic in brown butter, roasted red potatoes with rosemary and asparagus tips for dinner ought to impress her. He picked a good California white sparkling wine to go with it.

Trish sat at her desk working on the computer while he cooked. She had a cigarette dangling from her full red lips and sipped at a scotch and soda that Smitty had mixed for her. She still had on the shorts she had been wearing earlier. He glanced at her, admiring her long shapely tan legs. Apparently she wasn't used to being catered to by a man, and she seemed to be digging it. The red potatoes were in the small oven and he was trimming the asparagus and peeling shrimp.

"Smells good," she said, smiling as he threw the asparagus into the hot olive oil and garlic, poured some white wine over it and put a lid on. He had taken a series of cooking classes, thinking it would be a good back up if he ever left his union job. Bartending was out of the question. The job had changed too much since he pulled beer and filled shot glasses of whiskey and tequila. He didn't know the difference between a Long Island Ice Tea and a Sex on the Rocks without a rolodex.

Trish came over and placed her hand on his shoulder and leaned over the stove to take in the aroma. He got a whiff of her lightly perfumed hair and longed for more.

"If it tastes half as good as it smells, you can stay as long as you like," she said, and then kissed him on the cheek. Her lips were soft and warm on his half shaven face.

He set the saloon dinette with some good china and silverware he found in the cupboard, and lit a couple of candles in an effort to make it romantic.

Over dinner she told him she had opened the Yacht brokerage with her husband. At first, things had gone well and she thought they were happy. But then things began to change. Their marriage had started going downhill and he was becoming abusive. Being in business together only increased the slide. Then, a year ago, he had told her he was going to crew on a yacht to the South Seas in order to get some space and think. She later learned that the yacht belonged to a wealthy divorcée and he was the only crew member. She had filed for divorce and was waiting for the papers to come through. It occurred to Smitty that she was in need of love and comfort as much as he was.

After dinner she switched off the radio and put on a tape of Johnny Hartman and John Coltrane —very romantic—and they sat side by side finishing off the wine. He told her the story of his own lost love, leaving out the details. She asked him to dance as Johnny Hartman sang My One and Only Love. From there it was a short step to her master cabin.

She was shy at fist; undressing in the dark. But the little light that flowed through the port windows silhouetted her supple body. It was as perfect as it had been with her clothes on. She said she hadn't made love to a man since her husband ran off with the rich divorcee, and six months before that. He asked if she was afraid he'd come back, at which point she reached into the drawer next to her bed and pulled out a .38 police special.

"It keeps me company at night," she said, putting the gun back and smiling. "It seems I have a new pistol now to keep me company."

They cuddled for awhile, kissing and touching like two teenagers in the back seat of a car. She slowly grew more excited and from then on it was as if all the time she had gone without came bursting out in a storm of passion.

When they finally came up for air they lay side by side breathing heavy from the work out. She held his hand on her breast and then said something he had never heard from a woman after making love to her:

"Thank you, Smitty." She kissed him softly on his lips and then rolled over and was sound asleep in seconds.

Smitty lay in the dark with his eyes open. He looked over at her. She was breathing softly. He admired her white statuesque back which reminded him of a Greek goddess. But he knew he wouldn't be able to sleep. He thought if he closed his eyes he would see Mei-ling and feel guilty, but what he saw instead was the man in grey standing next to the tree at Lake Merritt. Fear gripped him and the vision of the man going up to the apartment in the dark and attacking Dede while Chenel looked on forced his eyes open. Maybe he would kill her too so as not to leave a witness. Fear seemed to blow out of proportion in the stillness of the night.

He got out of bed and made his way up to the salon where there was a phone on Trish's desk. He called the apartment. The phone rang for what seemed like forever until she finally answered.

"It's me, Smitty. Are you all right?"

"Fuck Smitty, it's the middle of the night."

"I know," he said. "I was just worried about you."

"Well, I'm fine. Where the fuck are you?"

"Never mind that. Just take down this phone number and call me if you notice any strangers hanging around."

"If you're so worried about us you shouldn't have left," she said.

"Just take down the number, Dede."

"Well, OK. Let me find a pencil."

He gave her the number and she hung up without saying goodbye.

"Smitty, what are you doing up here."

Trish stood in front of him in a sheer robe that hung open in front, with her blonde hair flowing over her full breasts. The color matched her pubic hair. He wondered if she dyed that too. It was too perfect to be natural.

"Come back to bed, baby. I want you to make love to me again...."

All thoughts of the man in grey vanished from his mind.

* * *

Chapter 13

Guangzhou, China

General Angúo Wang had the same fatherly smile as her Uncle Peter. He was always a big man, but now he was so fat that he barely fit into his chair. His face was puffy, but his eyes were as alert as ever. Despite his weight his uniform was tailored perfectly. He had been her uncle's closest friend in the Red Army. They had fought side by side as young men against the nationalists and had risen in the ranks together. She had known him all her life and recalled how he would always bring her a small gift whenever he visited. She called him Uncle Wang when she was small. Mei-ling hoped he would help her. They spoke in Cantonese. It was comfortable for them both.

"I was saddened at the news of your uncle's death. I had arranged to have him flown back here. I visit his grave often. I will do anything I can to help you, but as you know, Beijing is very nervous since the unfortunate events there two years ago."

"I understand, but all I want is permission to attend an educational conference in Hong Kong," Mei-ling said.

"And what is this conference about. It's not some subversive gathering cooked up by those dissidents in Hong Kong?"

"No Uncle, it is on the early Ming Dynasty."

The old General laughed. "Hmmmm, Hong Kong, eh. That would be suspect in some quarters these days. As you know, we will be taking Hong Kong back from the British Imperialist in a few years, and there are many people there who oppose it."

"I understand, Uncle, and I have to tell you that I have been watched since my return from the United States.

"Yes, I know. It is very unfortunate. Many of us do not approve of this crack down, but the leaders in Beijing see it differently. The whole affair has been handled very badly."

"I know I am asking a lot, Uncle, and I wouldn't want to cause you any trouble."

The General laughed again. "Trouble? Let me worry about that. You meet me at the Dong Jiang Haixian Da Jiulou this evening, and I'll see what I can do. You know this restaurant?"

"The one by Haizhu Square. Yes Uncle. This evening."

"I will be there around seven. I will be on the fifth floor. Ask for me. We can eat together."

The old General couldn't have picked a better place to meet. Dong Jiang was one of the most popular restaurants in Guangzhou. It was five stories tall, and could serve nearly a thousand diners at one time, and it was usually over-crowded. It would be impossible for anyone to overhear their conversation.

Mei-ling made her way to the fifth floor. The noise level was deafening. She knew the old General read her like a book, and knew exactly what she was up to. Would he help her? She'd soon find out. She would have to take her chances.

She got to the fifth floor. The place was packed with large families crowded around tables. Everyone seemed to be talking at the same time as waiters slipped between the tables with trays piled high with steaming platters of food. A woman with the look of someone in charge directed her to a table in the back. She walked past a long row of tanks teaming with live fish, crabs, lobsters.

Mei-ling had expected an intimate dinner with her General Uncle, but instead found him at one of the large round tables surrounded by members of his family. Great heaps of seafood in large ornate bowls crowded the table. She knew many of the people at the table; the General's matronly wife, four of the General's grown children, several unfamiliar faces she suspected were spouses along with five small children.

"Ah, Mei-ling," the General said. "You all know Mei-ling, my good friend Ching-Shu Wu's niece."

Everyone smiled and nodded.

"I invited Mei-ling to eat with us tonight. Make room."

Mei-ling politely ate, while evading questions about her time in the United States, and graciously acknowledging expressions of sympathy over her uncle's tragic death. Her hopes that the General would help her began to fade as the night wore on.

After the diners had finished cleaning off thier plates, enjoying the last of their beverages and slices of fresh oranges, they began to get up to leave as the General accepted the check. The woman who had directed Mei-ling to the table took it from him, smiling. It was clear the General wasn't expected to pay.

As they gathered up their coats and started for the exit, Mei- ling had all but given up hope that her uncle the General was not, or could not, help. But just then one of the children, a boy of around eight, pushed a fat red envelope at her. It was the kind money was put into for children at New Year.

"Here auntie Mei. This is for you."

So, the General was going to buy her off, she thought. She stuffed the envelope into her bag and followed the General's entourage.

Outside, waiters were busily setting up tables on the walkway for the overflow crowds. She was saying her goodbyes to everyone, when the General came up to her and pulled her to the side. He took her hands and smiled.

"I hope you like my little gift to you. It is in honor of your Uncle."

Then he leaned over, kissed her on the check and whispered. "Be very careful, Mei-ling." And then he was gone.

She stood there for a minute as crowds of people pushed past her. A soft warm breeze blew through her hair.

She went to find her bicycle and peddled through the crowded boulevards to her small apartment near the University.

Looking out over the view of the University and the lights of the sprawling city of millions from her small balcony, Mei-ling was still thinking how her Uncle Peter's good friend General Wang had tried to buy her off with money. She had thrown her bag down on the kitchen table without turning on the lights. She lit a cigarette. Her life in China was becoming intolerable. The sudden outpouring of students demanding reforms had caught the members of the government off guard and they reacted violently. Now every student, every college professor, was suspect of holding subversive ideas, and she had sensed she would be high on the list after her interrogation upon returning from many years of living in America. It had seemed like a miracle running into Johnny Wong over two weeks before. She wondered if he had been able to get her message out of China. It had brought back all her memories of her brief time with Isaac Smith, and she realized how much she missed him; he who had only wanted to fulfill his promise to her Uncle to protect her from harm. At the time she believed she was protecting him by leaving America, but now it seemed the promises of the Chinese authorities had been expedient, just to make her cooperate with them and reveal the hideout of the smugglers. She feared for him, and had written him that she would return. Now it seemed her hopes were dashed; that even the powerful General Wang was incapable, or unwilling to help her.

She put out her cigarette and went back into the small apartment, turned on the lights and sat at the kitchen table. The fat red envelope was sticking out from her bag. She pulled it out and stared at it for a while, resisting an urge to tear it up and throw it in the garbage. But she finally opened it; if nothing other than to see how much money the General felt it would take to appease her. There was a large stack of bills, but surprisingly they weren't Yuan but Hong Kong dollars mixed with U.S dollars. She looked further and found a ferry ticket to Hong Kong with a British/Hong Kong Passport. She stared at it for a couple of minutes, trying to convince herself it was real. Then she opened it and saw that it was made out to her and had her picture. Was it possible? Soon she would be back in Oakland, California and in the arms of her lover where she could protect him from harm. But even with the passport, it would be extremely dangerous. She remembered the General's last words to her; "be very careful." It would be risky, but she knew she had to go, no matter what the risk.

* * *

Chapter 14

Alameda, Ca

Three days and nights passed. Making Trish happy had become an obsession and Smitty realized that in that time he hadn't thought about Mei-ling while Trish was making up for the time she had gone without sex. During the day she would sit at her desk while he fooled around in the galley until she summoned him to her and they would make love, in her desk chair, on the carpeted floor, on her desk, on the table. When he asked if she shouldn't do some work, she just shrugged and said the yacht business was slow.

In the evening she would hover over him while he prepared dinner, kissing him on the neck and playfully feeling him up. Then after dinner she would take his hand and lead him back to bed. He was exhausted and began to feel used; a prisoner of love.

Finally one morning after breakfast and a quickie, she told him she had to go and meet with her attorney about her divorce. It was his chance to make a jail break.

He had wanted to look in on Johnny Wong, the bartender at the Oaks Card Club in Emeryville. Johnny had been beaten up pretty bad by some Chinese hoods on his account. He had helped Smitty out, mainly by translating a journal Mei-ling had left with him. It was Peter Wu's, and he had hoped it would help him find out where Mei-ling had gone after disappearing from his boat. It all seemed so long ago.

Johnny was a good friend. His father was a big shot in Chinatown, and some day Johnny would take his place as head of the Wong wholesale Market and President of the Oakland Chinese Merchants Association. But in the meantime, he liked being a bartender, and he was good at it.

It was a quick drive through the Alameda-Oakland Tube under the estuary, and then up San Pablo Avenue to Emeryville where the Oaks Card Club was open twenty-four hours a day. Smitty thought he'd find Johnny back behind the bar where he always was. It was months since he got out of the hospital. But instead of Johnny, a young Asian woman was tending bar instead.

"Johnny, oh, he can't work no more," she said.

"What happened?"

"Don't ask me. You can go to the office and they will tell you."

Megan, the book keeper, was in her usual place behind a big desk stacked with papers and receipts as she stared into a computer screen. Megan was a good looker, but more than that, she was smart and would have done well at anything she did. She practically ran the Club.

"Well, look who's here," she said, pulling her eyes away from the computer screen. "Haven't seen you around lately."

"I'm looking for Johnny," Smitty said.

"Gee Smitty, Johnny's out on extended medical leave. We don't know if he's coming back. Left me in a bind; you guys won't let me fire him, and I can't hire a permanent replacement until I know what's going on with him."

"That's what the contract says," he smiled. "I'll see if he's at home."

"If you see him, tell him to give me a call. I haven't been able to reach him."

"Will do."

He left the Oaks, missing the shot of Jack Daniels that Johnny had always poured him when he came in, and refused to let him pay. The Oaks wouldn't be the same without Johnny Wong.

He went to Johnny's apartment. He had been there a couple of times before—a 1950's style complex off of Grand Avenue near Lake Merritt. But when he went to ring the buzzer to Johnny's apartment to open the front gate, he couldn't find his name on the list of tenants. Thinking his memory had failed him he thought he was at the wrong place. A lot of the apartment buildings on the low hills overlooking the Lake looked the same. But just as he was about to give up an older black man came to the gate and opened it.

"Excuse me," Smitty said. "Do you happen to know Johnny Wong. I believe he lives here."

"Johnny? He moved out over two months ago, I'm sorry to say. He was a great guy, Johnny was ... used to invite me in for a drink. Shame what happened to him. Couldn't get around with that busted knee of his, and the damn elevator in this joint keeps breaking down. We complain to management, but that don't do shit. Yeah, I know Johnny. I miss his smiling face around here."

"You know where he went?"

"Said he was going to stay at his old man's house for awhile. That's the last I see'd of him."

*

Smitty had no idea where Johnny's family lived, but he did know where the Wong's Wholesale Market was, so he headed for the produce district on the west side of Highway 80 just off of Broadway and Jack London Square. He stopped by a phone booth to call Trish and let her know he would be back later that afternoon. The phone rang about five times. He figured she was still at her lawyers when someone picked it up.

"Trish, is that you?"

There was silence on the other end, and then a click and a dial tone. Smitty shrugged it off.

It was already after one o'clock and the markets were getting ready to close up for the day. Wong's was on Third Street between Franklin and Webster, a large warehouse with three loading docks. A couple of older Chinese guys were sweeping up. They looked at him with blank stares when he asked for Johnny and then went about their work, so he walked into the warehouse. The place smelled like sour cabbage and old lettuce. A young Chinese guy came up to him: "We're closing up, Mister."

"I'm looking for Johnny Wong," he said.

The man laughed. "I didn't think you were looking for bok choy. What you want with Johnny?"

Smitty handed him his business card. "I'm a friend of his."

The man looked at the card. "Isaac Smith. You're Johnny's union man, Smitty. I seen you at the hospital after Johnny got attacked."

Smitty nodded.

"Johnny talks about you all the time," the man said. "He's in the office. I'll get him for you."

He watched as the man climbed a metal stair case to a bank of offices overlooking the warehouse, and disappear through a door. It wasn't long before he came out with Johnny trailing behind him, hobbling along with the help of a cane.

"Smitty," he yelled down. "Come on up. I been looking all over for you."

He climbed the stair case and was surprised as Johnny grabbed him in a bear hug. "Where the hell you been?"

Johnny led him into his office. He instructed the young guy to get some coffee. "Sorry, I don't have any liquor here. My old man doesn't allow any drinking on the job."

"That's OK," Smitty said. "I went to the Oaks and they said you were out on medical leave. You plan on going back?"

Johnny frowned. "Don't think it's in the cards, Smitty. The old man wants me to run the business, and I don't know about this fucking leg of mine. Seems my bartending days are over." He hesitated for a moment as if watching a large portion of his life float away. Then he recovered and smiled. "Gee I'm glad you showed up. I got something for you. I tried to get you at the office, but some rude woman there said you was out on leave yourself. "

Smitty sat in the metal folding chair across from the desk. "Well, I'm here now. I wanted to see how you're doing. I went to the apartment, but they said you'd moved back in with your family."

"Yeah, I got tired of fending for myself, what with this bum leg, and the damn elevator at the apartment building kept breaking down. Now my mother and auntie hover over me like mother hens. But that's not what I have to tell you."

"So what's this all about?" I asked.

"Well, when I was released from the hospital, they said my leg wasn't healing right. They told me I'd be in a wheel chair unless I got an operation, and even that wouldn't guarantee I wouldn't be crippled for the rest of my life."

"Damn Johnny. I'm really sorry. This whole thing is my fault." Smitty said, remembering back to the night when Johnny left his boat after helping him translate Peter Wu's journal. Smitty knew the Chinese gangsters were hanging around the marina and was afraid they had snatched Mei-ling, but he didn't think they'd bother Johnny. They must have followed him home, and that's when he got jumped. Johnny told Smitty after it happened that it was a signal to anyone in the Chinese community what would happen if they were caught helping an outsider.

"Forget it, Smitty. I knew the chances I was taking. But anyway, my old man said he wanted to send me to China, to Guangdong where he's from. He wanted me to meet our family and to pay respect to our ancestors. But he also wanted me to see some old guy who practices Qigong and this acupuncture guy. Well Smitty, I was always a little skeptical about these old Chinese Voodoo things but I have never been to China. So I figured, what the hell, can't hurt. And as you see, I'm out of the wheel chair."

"You were in China ... Guangdong?

"Yeah."

I lump formed in Smitty's throat. "Guangzhou City?"

"Yeah, you know Guangzhou?"

"That's the city Mei-ling's from."

"Damn Smitty, that's what I been trying to tell you all along. I was having tea at a café near the Normal University after a treatment and I look up, and who do I see."

"Mei-ling?" Smitty said, not believing his ears.

"Mei-ling, sitting two tables away. Seventeen million people in Guangzhou and we run into each other. It's like ... I don't know ... karma or something."

Just then the young guy came in with two styrofoam cups and set them down on the desk.

"Did you get sugar and cream?" Johnny said.

"Oh yeah," and he dug into his jacket pocket producing some sugar packets and powdered creamers.

"Go on and finish up closing," Johnny instructed like he had been giving orders all his life. "My kid brother."

All the feelings Smitty had for Mei-ling and had tried to bury in Trish's arms came rushing back. "Come on Johnny, did you talk to Mei-ling? Did she say anything about me?"

"I got up and sat down across from her," Johnny said, as he dumped four sugar packets in his coffee. She looked up from the book she was reading. She seemed really nervous, like she was being watched or something. But I could tell she was happy to see me. I didn't want to get her in any kind of trouble, but shit, Smitty, it was Mei-ling, right there sitting across from me; five thousand miles from Oakland. What's the odds? She extended her hand to me to shake and smiled. She asked what I was doing there, in Guangzhou, and I explained to her about seeing my family and getting treatments on my leg. Then she lowered her voice and covered her mouth with her hand and asked how you were doing. Smitty, I didn't even know you two had split up."

Smitty briefly explained what had happened since they had visited him in the hospital in the summer, omitting a lot of details that he didn't have to know.

"Well, anyway, it was pretty obvious that she didn't want to talk openly there. She asked me to drive to Suhui ..." and he proceeded to tell Smitty about his trip in the Lada and his encounter with Mei-ling at Peter Wu's grave, and how she slipped him the envelope for Smitty, and he hid it in his cane. He omitted the part about his sudden desire to jump her bones there in the silence of the graveyard. Johnny reached into his desk drawer, pulled out a crumpled up envelope and slid it across the desk. Smitty stared at it for a minute, not really believing what he had just heard, and that the proof of Johnny's incredible story lay in front of him.

"Go ahead, Smitty. Aren't you going to read it?"

He could tell Johnny was curious about what was in the letter after carrying it half way around the world. Smitty took it and slid it into his pocket.

"I'll read it later,"

Johnny's face dropped a little in disappointment, but he didn't say anything. Didn't press him.

"Whatever you say, brother. I know it's personal."

Smitty suddenly was not interested in going back to Alameda and Trish. Somehow he felt like he would be cheating on Mei-ling. He just wanted to go somewhere, have a drink and read the letter alone. But he figured he should call Trish and let her know he wasn't coming. He owed her that much.

"Can I use your phone, Johnny?"

"Sure, no problem," he said and turned the phone on the desk around for Smitty. "If it's private I can wait outside."

"If it's no trouble."

"Walkin's trouble, Smitty. But I got to get up and stretch this leg every fifteen minute. That's what that Chinese doctor told me."

He watched his friend as he stood up and grabbed his cane, noticing the carved Dragon that climbed up the shaft to a silver handle that had carried Mei-ling's message five thousand miles. Johnny limped to the door with the Styrofoam cup in his hand. Smitty got up and opened it for him.

"You got one of those cigarettes of yours?" he asked.

Smitty pulled out his pack of Luckys and gave Johnny one, then snapped open his Zippo and lit it. Johnny took a long drag and walked out onto the metal walkway.

Smitty dialed Trish's number and went over in his head what he was going to say to her.

"Trish, it's Smitty..."

"Where the hell are you?" she said.

"I had some business I had to take care of..."

"Well I need you here, Smitty." He could hear the urgency in her voice. "My attorney told me my ex is back in town and I'm afraid he'll come here. Smitty, he has a violent temper."

"Well, you should get a restraining order."

"My lawyer said he was taking care of that, but it will take at least a day or two for it to go through. I need you to be here. I'm frightened."

"All right babe. I'll be there as soon as I can."

"Hurry Smitty. I'm scared."

Unfortunately he decided to jump on the freeway and get off on Park Street. He figured it would be faster than going back through the tube and working his way through Alameda. He was wrong. He got caught up in stop and go traffic all the way to the exit. He thought about the letter that was burning a hole in his pocket, but figured he'd have to get to it later.

His thoughts drifted to Trish—how their relationship reminded him of the woman he had lived with at the Lake Marritt apartment before she had left him for an old boy friend in the Valley. The only thing they had in common—in fact, the only thing he had in common with most of his girlfriends—was sex; pure unemotional sex. They were middle aged women in the service industry who were too old for partying, and all they wanted after long hours of hard work was relaxation, and sex was their way of relaxing. He liked Trish, but he couldn't remember being in love with any of the women he had been with. Mei-ling was a whole new experience for him. But he owed Trish, and he would help her in any way he could.

He finally got off the freeway, only to get stopped again because the Park street draw bridge was up to let a sail boat pass down the estuary. As he sat in the line of cars waiting for the bridge to come down, he wondered how one small sailboat could cause so much mess. But it was Alameda where life moved slowly.

He hadn't realized how late it was when he pulled into the marina parking lot until he noticed the sun was setting over the estuary. What should have been a ten minute drive from the produce district had turned into nearly an hour and he imagined Trish panicking by this time. He thought she was probably overreacting, and his head was filled with thoughts of Mei-ling. He would have stopped right there at the marina gate to read the letter, but wanted to save it for when he was alone so he could savor every word.

He climbed the steps up to the boat and looked through the large windows. The blinds were open. The inside was cast in shadow as the sun disappeared and the sky turned a brilliant pink and gold. He sensed something was wrong as soon as he entered the salon because it was deathly quiet. Trish always had KJAZ on the radio, twenty-four hours a day. Then he saw that her desk chair was on its side and papers were scattered over the floor. The telephone was in the middle of the cabin. He could hear the dial tone buzzing. He made his way to the door leading into the narrow passage way leading to the forward cabins. The door to the master's stateroom where he had spent the last several nights was ajar. He cautiously opened it. It was dark inside the cabin. He felt along the cabin wall and found the light switch. The lamp gave off a dim light. Trish was sprawled out on the bed, her blonde hair streaming in front of her face. He softly called her name thinking she was asleep—hoping she was asleep. When she didn't respond he knelt down alongside her, and then he saw the blood soaking the pillows, forming a halo around her head. There was a hole in her temple and he pulled back at the terrifying realization that someone had shot her.

He caught a shadow in the corner of his eye and then, out of no-where, he saw a dark figure, and then something heavy hit him in the face, and another blow to the side of his head, and he seemed to be falling into an empty black void floating down ... down ... down into a dark hole.

* * *

Chapter 15

Alameda Marina

Smitty slowly opened his eyes and found himself resting on Trish's soft blood stained breasts. A jack hammer was pounding inside his skull. He didn't know if he had been out for an hour, five hours or five minutes. He forced himself off the bed. Trish's .38 lay next to her. Bruises marred what had been her lovely high cheek bones.

All he could recall was a shadow coming up behind him before the proverbial lights went out. Whoever it was must have killed Trish, and he remembered her panic on the phone over her estranged husband being back.

He tried to stand up but his head started to spin so he sat back down until it stopped. He felt like he was being watched and then caught a glimpse of a stranger looking back at him. Then he realized he was looking into the full length mirror Trish had on her wall. Only it was a stranger he saw there and it sent a chill down his spin until he realized the stranger was him, only now he resembled Quasimodo with a huge purple lump on his left temple, and another on the side of his face.

He tried to get up again, this time with some success, and managed to stumble to the cabin door, into the narrow passageway and up the stairs to the salon. The lights from the dock lit up the room in an eerie orange haze. The desk phone was on the floor, a million miles away. He wasn't sure his legs would get him there so he dropped down on all fours and slowly crawled to it.

After more than ten rings, the 9-1-1 operator answered.

"Get someone down here. Trish is dead."

"I'm sorry sir; you'll have to be more specific. Are you in any danger?" He reassured the operator he was OK, more or less, and that a woman had been murdered. He gave her directions. She said someone would be right out.

He rolled over onto his back and drifted in and out of consciousness for what seemed like hours until the dying whine of sirens in the parking lot announced the coming of the law. He wondered how the cops would get through the locked gate without a key? He tried to stand up, but it wasn't happening. Then the sound of heavy footsteps alongside Trish's boat, and beams of light flashed through the windows, followed by pounding on the salon door.

"Police. Open up."

How did they get through the gate?

"In here," he tried to yell, but as soon as he opened his mouth pain shoot through his jaw, and the sound came out like a pathetic whine.

The door slowly opened and the beam from a flashlight whirled around the room. Then a uniform was kneeling down beside him, with another shadowy figure standing behind it. The blinding light from the flashlight shined in his face. He covered his eyes with his arm.

"Sir, are you all right? Dan, find the light."

Suddenly the salon was lit up and crowded with uniforms; two cops and two others ... paramedics. The best he could muster was to meekly point toward the passageway to Trish's cabin and mumble, "In there."

The two cops headed for the doorway followed by the male paramedic. The other one came over and replaced the cop at his side. He looked up into the most bright blue eyes he had ever seen. The paramedic was a woman with light brown hair pulled tight into a bun revealing her young face.

"Sir, sir. Do you know who you are?".

She wasn't bad looking for a uniform, but her face was far too serious for such a pretty young woman.

"Me?"

"Yes, do you know your name?"

"Hmmm, last time I looked in a mirror I wasn't me. But I was Isaac Smith."

"Do you know where you are?"

"Sure, I'm on Trish's boat."

"And who is Trish?"

"Trish, nice lady. She's dead I think."

"Mister Smith, how many fingers am I holding up?"

He stared at her for a moment until her hand came into focus. "Three?"

"Are you in a lot of pain?"

"Sister, you ask a lotta questions. Look at me. What do you think?"

"I'll give you something for that in just a second."

She strapped a blood pressure cup on his arm, and while it was inflating she got a syringe from her bag of tricks and stuck it in his arm. An immediate feeling of euphoria spread throughout his body. He thanked her and managed to smile. She smiled back. At that moment she was the most beautiful woman in the world . . . an angel.

"You're going to be all right, sir."

The last words he heard were, "Don't disturb anything. We have a homicide victim in there. The investigators are on their way..."

Smitty dozed off, or passed out, he wasn't sure which.

When he opened his eyes the pretty uniform was still kneeling beside him, holding something cold against the side of his face. Behind her was a nondescript man in a white shirt and tie with closely cropped gray hair.

"This man needs to go to the hospital," the pretty face said.

"He's a suspect in a homicide," the man said. "We're taking him to the station for questioning."

"He may have a concussion," pretty face insisted.

"Sorry honey, this is a police matter and he's going in for questioning. Now help me get him up."

Pretty face looked at Smitty with that same serious look. "Can you get up Mister Smith?"

"You can call me Smitty."

"Can you get up...Smitty?"

"I think so."

He made an effort to sit up, but his head started spinning again. The man bent down, grabbed him by the arm and yanked him to his feet like a ragdoll. New pains shot though his body. The pretty face paramedic tried to hold the cold compress on the side of his head. She had a helpless, apologetic look on her face.

"Cuff this man and take him to the station," the man said to the two uniformed cops.

"This man needs to go to the hospital," my protector yelled. "I'm going to report this,"

The cops hesitated.

"Do what I said," the plain clothes guy barked.

The cops gentle put the cuffs on him.

"Sorry pal, but orders is orders," one of them said, as they helped him out of the salon into the cool night air.

"Say, how did you guys get through the gate?" Smitty mumbled.

*

The blaring lights of the interrogation room made everything look the same sterile white. The plain clothes guy had been joined by a partner. They identified themselves as detectives Hass and Martinson, but Smitty called them Doctor Jekyll and Mister Hyde. The injection the pretty face paramedic gave him was wearing thin and his head had settled into a dull ache while the side of his face was throbbing. The cop playing the good Doctor Jekyll had given him a cold wash cloth that had long since become a warm rag. It seemed like he'd been there for hours. He glanced at the clock on the wall. Two-thirty. They kept asking what they wanted to hear and he kept telling them what happened. Mister Hyde—Smitty recognized the cop from the boat—made all kinds of accusations. Smitty kept telling them about the estranged husband who was probably getting away with his girlfriend on a yacht while they were holding an innocent man. They didn't buy it.

"I suppose next you'll tell us the butler did it," Hyde said sarcastically.

"Fuck you," Smitty responded, which seemed to piss him off more, and for a second Smitty thought he was going to haul off and hit him. Jekyll blocked his way. It was all part of the act, except he saw a streak of meanness in Hyde, the same look he had seen when he ordered him taken in, instead of to the hospital like the nice lady paramedic had wanted.

Smitty just wanted to close his eyes and sleep, but now they both came at him as if the more they shouted the same questions, the sooner he'd tell them what they wanted to hear. It wasn't going to happen.

Finally another officer entered the room and whispered something into Hyde's ear. Then they both left the room, leaving him there sweating and aching. After about ten minutes Jekyll came in with a uniformed officer.

"We're going to hold you for awhile. You can have one call. I suggest it's to a lawyer because if the prints on the gun match yours, buddy, you're in for a shitload of trouble."

The uniform unlocked the cuffs and asked if he wanted to use the phone. He tried to think of who to he could call at three in the morning. All the attorneys he knew where labor lawyers, not criminal. So he dialed Ted's house. After all, Ted was the Oakland Tribune's crime reporter. Maybe he had some pull.

The phone rang ten times. No answer. Shit. He hung up and started to call Dede, but Hyde came up to him and yanked the receiver from his hands. "One call is one call. You had yours, pal."

He was put in his new home; a five by eight cage with a cot and a toilet. He stared at the tips of his fingers. The traces of ink were still there from being fingerprinted. Guilty or innocent, his prints would now be on file with the Alameda police forever.

It must have been a quiet night. He had the place to himself. It was nearly three, but the way the place was lit up who could tell if it was a.m. or p.m., like the casinos in Vegas; no day or night in the Alameda city jail. Every time he closed his eyes he saw Trish's face staring up at the top of the cabin. It seemed every woman he got involved with lately got his ass into a wringer. Must be karma, he told himself

His mind shifted to Mei-ling. Oakland was burning up and she had led him on a wild goose chase for some amorphous fucking panda bears. He remembered thinking how trivial it was compared to the catastrophe that had unfolded in the Oakland hills that had very nearly counted them in its gruesome fatality statistics.

It was then that he recalled the letter that he had stuffed into his pocket; the letter that seemed so important, but had faded from his mind with the events of the night. The cops had overlooked it when they patted him down. He took out the wrinkled envelope and opened it. The handwriting was meticulous and exact; every i dotted, every t crossed.

My Darling Isaac,

It appears fate has once again drawn us together. How else can one explain my meeting Johnny Wong in the middle of this city of 10 million people? Call it fate.

I am grateful that I have this opportunity to tell you the events that forced me to leave you and return to China, because I had already decided that I was truly in love with you and that I would stay in America to be with you. You see, all my time in your country had changed me more than I thought. Nothing short of death would prevent me from staying with you, but it was not to be. I was forced to choose; your life in exchange for my return. That was my agreement with Rick who had been ordered to kill you and remove the only civilian with knowledge of the entire unfortunate affair. After losing my Uncle, I could not allow the only other man I had ever loved to be killed over the corruption and greed of a few Chinese officials.

I believed that I could make a life here in China and maybe forget you in time, and at first I was welcomed back to my old position at the University. I was content with my decision. But I was wrong. Life here in China has not been what I expected. Ever since Tiananmen, everyone is suspect. Every move I make here is being watched, and I suspect that the government will go back on our agreement. I want you to be very careful.

As for myself, I cannot stay in China. There is no life here for me now. I must find a way to return to America, and to you my sweet Isaac.

Yours forever,
Mei-ling

She couldn't have known about Rick and his late night visit, but until that moment Smitty hadn't realized that her love for him was that strong. Would she return? And if she did manage to come back, what would happen then? Judging from his present circumstances he could be in San Quentin doing twenty to life for man slaughter, or worse, life for murder.. He was in a jam, and at the moment there didn't look like an exit.

His eyes grew heavy. He leaned back on the cot, rested his head on the wall and soon dozed off.

* * *

Chapter 16

Guangdong

Mei-ling stood in front of the bathroom mirror, brushing her long shiny black hair. It brought back memories from after she and Isaac had been captured by the smugglers in their hide out in the Oakland Hills. Of all days, it was the day fire swept through the Oakland and Berkeley hills destroying hundreds of homes and killing and injuring dozens of people. It was at that moment, with the flames rushing at them as they sat tied back to back in a small shed that she had realized she had fallen in love with this strange white man who had come into her life. As the fire began licking at the dry wood of the building and the room filled with the acrid smoke of the roaring blaze as it ate up everything in its path, he had declared his undying devotion and love for her, and reassured her with soothing tones that they would somehow escape. But they would have surely died, if not for the last minute rescue by Rick from the Chinese Embassy.

It all seemed so long ago, lying naked in her bed in the house she had shared with her Uncle Peter, her hair flowing against Isaac's naked chest. The memory made her smile. Then she picked up the scissors from the bathroom sink and began to cut. She wasn't a sentimental person by nature, but as she saw the long locks drop into the basin tears came to her eyes.

Ministry of State Security Special Agent First Class Xian Dong arrived before dawn and stationed himself outside Mei-Ling's apartment. Following around a female college professor wasn't his idea of an important assignment, especially after his last duty in Taoyuan County, in south-central Hunan province, where he had broken up a Uyghur terrorist organization after going undercover. His local commander made him the youngest Special Agent in the Service as a result and awarded him the Order of The Cloud and Banner medal, the nation's highest honor for service to the nation. It must not have sat well with his superiors in Beijing. He figured this new assignment was their way of humbling him.

He hadn't taken the assignment seriously until recently, after spying her meeting with a visiting American named Johnny Wong. It was then he became suspicious she was up to something. He suspected she was passing Wong anti-government propaganda to take back to America. When he questioned Wong the man denied knowing her, even though his passport said he was from Oakland, California where Mei-Ling Wu had lived for many years. But when he went to his superiors requesting they bring Wong in for further questioning they wanted nothing to do with it. They wanted no trouble with Americans, and besides that, didn't he know there were many thousands of Chinese living in Oakland, California.

That made him more determined than ever to expose the woman and prove his superiors wrong. He had even sat in on several of her classes at the University to see if she was teaching subversive propaganda to her students. But she was a smart one, and every time the subject of America came up she ignored it.

He had usually waited until later in the day to start his surveillance, but over the past week he had become suspicious she was about to make a move.

The night sky was turning a dark gray as dawn approached. Mei Ling stood on her small balcony looking out over the University where hundreds of lights sparkled through the gloom. She took a Lucky Strike and lit it. She had been surprised to find Isaac's brand of cigarette in a small shop next to a nearby Museum; a sign of China's opening up to the outside world or, more likely, knockoffs. They were more expensive than the Chinese brands, but they brought back memories of her time with Isaac, even if they didn't taste the same.

She had laid out her clothes the night before: a plain pair of cotton khaki pants, a simple white blouse and a light weight black sweater. She even had a Mao hat to cover her recently cut bobbed hair in her attempt to look as much as possible like one of the thousands of country girls in search of work in the city

She dressed and finished her tea. Then she grabbed her small back pack containing her forged passport, the money and a change of underwear. She hadn't bothered packing any cloths; she could buy new ones in Hong Kong, or, if she didn't make it, well, she wouldn't need any; they provide them in prison.

The elevator was crowded with people on their way to work. Some stared at her in her outfit, wondering how the country bumkin got into the building, but no one said anything, and it occurred to her that she had made no friends in the building since she had moved in. She stayed with the crowd to the front door of the lobby where everyone seemed to want to exit at the same time. It was a perfect cover she thought.

The wide boulevard in front of the apartment building was already bustling with people and bicycles. She tried to melt in as she made her way across to the bus stop on the opposite side where she pushed her way onto the bus going to the Guangzhou East Train Station which would take her directly to Shenzhen and the Hong Kong ferry. She couldn't help but scan the faces of the people around her. Was one of them watching her; waiting to catch her trying to make her escape. She told herself over and over not to worry; how could anyone recognize her dressed as she was—just another one of the thousands of anonymous young women heading to the Free Economic Zone in search of work, any job that would take them away from the daily drudgery of farm life where there was no future.

It had been a profound shock to Mei-Ling when she had returned to China to find out that the Revolution had done so little for the millions of people who still lived on subsistence farming in the Southern Provinces. It seemed like every day a new story appeared in the newspaper about an abandoned unwanted female baby or a group of people caught trying to get out of China. She blamed it on the Cultural Revolution. Now she looked out the window as the train passed mile after mile of construction where she remembered countryside, and she wasn't sure she approved of this new China. But, then again, who was she to approve or disapprove.

She stepped off the train at the Luohu Railroad station in Shenzhen, and made her way to the street. It would have seemed logical to just follow many of the other passengers to the Immigration Center where people with passes could cross directly into Hong Kong, but even with her new passport she knew security would be tight there, and crossing by ferry would be much safer. The old General had known this, and thus the ferry ticket. She hoped he had made arrangements with the local authorities to let her board unmolested, but she had no way of knowing for sure. She headed for the exit doors that led out into the street where buses waited.

She had disguised herself as best she could and hoped she hadn't been spotted leaving Guangzhou. But try as she did, she still had a feeling she would fool no one. Even though she was fit she was in her late thirties now and hadn't the slightest idea what went on in the mind of a young woman who had grown up in poverty, or how they walked and acted. She had very little contact with these women, confining herself to the University and the neighborhood around the large campus

She searched in her pocket and pulled out the ticket the General had given her. The ferry was leaving from the Port of Shekou.

She went to a station agent, unaware of the young man whose prying eyes hid beneath a pair of counterfeit Ray-Ban sunglasses, and asked where she could get a bus to the Shekou Ferry Terminal. The agent directed her to a kiosk where a number of modern buses were lined up. The man behind the sunglasses followed behind her at a inconspicuous distance.

She couldn't believe her eyes as she looked out over a sea of construction cranes and high rise buildings that sprung out of the ground like a forest of giant concrete and glass trees. The last time she had been there was when she was in the militia, assigned to a coastal patrol boat cruising the South China Sea against U.S. intrusions into China's territorial waters during the Vietnamese War of Liberation. Shenzhen had just been a small fishing village then. She had read about the rapid development when the city was named a Special Economic Zone in 1979—an experiment in Capitalism—and welcomed foreign investment. Its proximity to Hong Kong made it a natural. Now tens of thousands of young people poured in from all over South China to find work at one of the hundreds of factories that greedy foreign business people opened up in search of cheap labor. She wasn't sure these changes were the best thing for the Chinese people.

*

The bus went directly to Shequo in the Nanshan District, and stopped in front of the ferry terminal. The next ferry to Hong Kong wouldn't leave for another half hour—thirty minutes until she would be home free and on her way back to the arms of her lover.

She wandered over to the ferry dock and looked out over the water. Memories of when she was a young woman in the People's Maritime Militia floated back into her mind. The coastal patrol boat she had been assigned to had docked near to the present day ferry terminal. Things had been much quieter then. Fishing was the main industry and there was no such thing as night life in Shenzhen. Now the streets of Nanshan were teaming with motorbikes, cars and delivery vans swerving in and out of the slower bicycles and pedestrians. Rows of modern apartment buildings and neon lit store fronts were overshadowed by high-rises and the ever present construction cranes.

Her thoughts drifted back to those distant days, when a young Russian military advisor had taken an interest in her. Today, one would have thought he had taken advantage of the pretty, young Chinese idealist. But, at the time, he was her teacher and guide into feelings that went beyond the revolutionary zeal she had been taught since childhood. He taught her how to drink vodka and how to smoke. He had taught her many things, and aroused feelings in her that she wasn't to again experience until many years later in America. She couldn't help but recognize the irony in it all; her first lover being a Soviet naval advisor; her second an American. It wasn't as if there hadn't been other men, but they were just passing affairs. Only Isaac had aroused those feelings she had experienced so many years before while cruising in the South China Sea coast against intrusions from the American Imperialists who were murdering thousands of Vietnamese comrades in their war of liberation.

Just then she was jarred back into the present when she became aware of a presence next to her. She looked around at the young man behind the Ray-Ban sunglasses. He was dressed casually with an open front white shirt. He had a friendly smile, but she immediately became wary.

"Going to Hong Kong?" the man asked.

Mei-Ling looked him straight into the sunglasses, wondering if there were eyes behind them. "No. I am in Shenzhen looking for work."

"There are no factories in Nanshan District."

"Yes, I know." She answered, her mind racing. "I just came to see the ocean. I have never seen it before."

"You appear to be a little old to be dressed like a country girl looking for work, if you don't mind me saying so."

"Well, I do mind. It is none of your business who I am or where I am going. Now, if you will excuse me." She started to walk off when she felt a grip on her arm. It was strong and authoritative.

"I'm afraid you will be going nowhere, Ms. Wu." His voice was calm but stern.

"Who the hell are you, and how do you know my name?" she said, trying to pull her arm free.

"I am Ministry of State Security Special Agent First Class Xian Dong. I have been watching you since you came to Guangzhou, and now I believe you are attempting to leave China without permission. I'm afraid you will have to come with me."

Mei-Ling's heart was pounding. "You have no right," she insisted, but the man just tightened his hold on her.

Agent Xian motioned toward the street and a black Soviet-made Lada sedan sped up to where they were standing. By now a crowd of curious people had gathered to see what was going on.

"This man is trying to kidnap me!" Mei-Ling cried out in desperation.

But Xian pulled out his wallet and flipped it open and verbally identified himself. The mere mention of the Ministry of State Security quickly broke up the crowd and they drifted off to attend to their previous business. Any concern they may have had for the woman was displaced by their fear of the MSS.

Xian hurried Mei-Ling to the waiting car and forced her into the back seat. As the car sped through the streets, Xian pulled Mei-Ling's back pack unceremoniously from her. He dumped the contents into his lap. A self-satisfied look crossed is face. He took his sunglasses off and inspected the contents.

"Hong Kong passport—forged no doubt. More money than a school teacher makes in a year, even a university teacher. And, what do we have here. Sexy panties."

Mei-Ling grabbed her panties from him.

"You have no right. My uncle is a Hero of the Nation. The authorities will hear about this. You cannot treat a comrade like this."

"Maybe not, Ms. Wu. But I believe you are a spy and a traitor. You deserve no respect."

Mei-Ling sat back in her seat. She felt resigned. There was no way to explain the passport and the money. She would never reveal how she got them. It seemed hopeless.

The Lada pulled up to a building. Unlike the modern buildings that were springing up all over Shenzhen, this one was a gray block structure near the Luohu train station; the kind of building popular after the Revolution when Soviet engineers flooded the new Peoples Republic of China.

Xian pulled Mei-Ling from the car. She looked up at the gray structure It was the kind of place people disappeared into and never came out. This was the end. She would never see her beloved Isaac again.

* * *

Chapter 17

Alameda

The voice jarred him awake. "Smith, get up. You're being released." It was the nice cop, the one he called Doctor Jekyll, standing at the open cell door.

"What?"

"You're being released into the custody of the fucking FBI," he said irritably. "The agent and that crime reporter from the Tribune are waiting for you."

"Huh? Ted?"

"Just get your fucking jacket and get your ass out here."

His head was still foggy. He stuffed the open letter into the pocket of his jacket and glanced at the clock on the wall: Four-thirty.

Jekyll marched him through the station house to the front counter where Agent Feinberg and Ted were waiting.

"I don't know what strings you pulled," he said. "This man is a murder suspect."

"You charged him?" Feinberg said.

Jekyll stared at him.

"Well then, don't worry about it. He'll be in the custody of the FBI now. You have my card."

The uniform at the desk told Smitty to sign for his effects. His wallet, car keys, Timex, Zippo and half pack of Luckys were dumped out from a large envelope. He slipped them into his coat pocket and signed the paper in front of him. Feinberg took out some handcuffs and locked his hands together in the front of him.

"Come along Smith, the Bureau's been hunting for you for weeks."

Ted said nothing. He just stared at him like he'd never seen him before, until they got outside. The cold early morning air snapped him to life and he wasn't happy. "For Christ sake, Smitty, what the hell have you gotten yourself into this time?"

"It's a long story," he said. As they walked down the cement stairs Smitty noticed a man standing in the shadows of the building. He could make out a baseball cap and a gray sports jacket. They exchanged looks as they passed. He thought he had seen him somewhere, but couldn't remember where.

"You look like you've been hit by a freight train," Feinberg said, leading him by his arm like a common criminal.

"It feels that way."

Feinberg put him into the back seat of the car, holding his head down as if he would smash into car's roof without his assistance. They climbed into the front; Harlin in the passenger side and Feinberg driving.

"So, Ted, where the hell were you when I tried to call?" Smitty said.

Harlin turned around. "I was out trying to pull strings to get you released. It's a damn good thing Gabe showed up looking for you."

"But no one answered the phone. Where's your old lady?"

"Anh? She's in Vietnam, making arrangements to bring her mother and aunt over to live with us."

Feinberg laughed. "I could have warned you about that. You marry an Asian gal, you marry the whole family."

"And Jewish families are different?" Ted said.

"And how the fuck did you know I was here?" Smitty interrupted.

"Smitty, I'm a police reporter, it's my job."

Feinberg laughed again.

"Well, actually," Ted said, "My contact in the Alameda PD called with a tip about a possible homicide, and said they had a suspect in custody ... you."

"And could you take these fucking cuffs off please?"

"Oh, sorry about that," Feinberg said. "Had to make it look good."

He dug into his pocket while making a turn up Park Boulevard, and came out with a key ring and passed it to Ted.

"It's the small one."

Smitty stuck his shackled hands out so Ted could insert the key. The cuffs snapped open.

"You can stay with me," Ted said. "I've got plenty of room for the time being."

"Sorry," Feinberg said. "Izzy here is in the custody of the FBI. I'll drop you off."

"I'd like to stop at Alameda Hospital first. Check on the details of the woman's death. Have to file a story tomorrow, and I need details. It's just around the corner."

"Is that completely necessary?" Smitty said from the back seat, as he nursed his wounds. He wished the paramedic lady was there to stick a needle in him and stop the pain.

"Yup," Ted said.

"Probably should have a doctor look at you," Feinberg added.

"I'm okay," Smitty said."

They stopped in front of the old hospital. It looked like it had been unchanged since it was built in the forties. Ted got out.

"I'll be back in a minute."

The FBI agent and Smitty sat in silence . "You didn't shoot the woman, did you?" Feinberg finally said, breaking the silence.

"Fuck no," Smitty said. "Trish was the sweetest woman I ever knew. But I think I know who did."

"Oh, who?"

"Her ex-husband. She had called me and told me he was back in town and she was afraid he'd hurt her."

"Hostile divorce I take it."

"Something like that," Smitty said.

"You tell the cops?"

"They didn't believe me."

"Well, you can tell me about it later."

Smitty sat back and pulled the collar of his coat up around his neck. He tried to close his eyes, but every time he did Trish's face appeared. He pulled Mei-ling's letter from his pocket and stared at the dark page. Was it possible she would come back. And if she did get out of China, what then?

Ted hopped back in the car. "Well Smitty, seems you're off the hook for the time being."

"What happened?" Feinberg asked.

"They transferred her to Highland's Trauma Center in Oakland. Seems the woman wasn't dead after all."

"Not dead? She's going to be all right then?" Smitty asked, his mind popping back to the present.

"She's in a coma. No telling if she'll make it, but for now it's not murder. Kinda takes the punch out of the story, through."

"You're a fucking mercenary, Ted." Feinberg said, as he stepped on the gas. "I'll drop you off at your house."

"Where are you two going to be?"

"I got a room at the Berkeley Marina Marriott. You can get us there."

Ted got out of the car and watched as it sped off into the early morning fog. He went to the front door of his house. It was an old Victorian. Unlike a lot of the older houses in Alameda that had been remodeled or split up into units, his was just as it was when it was originally built in the late 19th century two blocks south of Park Street.

He climbed the wooden steps to the front door and went to insert his skeleton key in the antique lock only to discover the door was already unlocked—must have left it open in his rush out of the house when Gabe pulled up to get him. It seemed like days ago, but in reality had only been about four and a half hours. He went into the foyer and stopped when he noticed the kitchen light shining into the dining room. The front door was understandable, but he was sure he had doused all the lights before leaving. He proceeded slowly to the kitchen. His heart skipped a beat when he saw a stranger sitting at his kitchen table with a cup of coffee sitting in front of him.

"Wow!" involuntarily came out of his mouth. "Who the hell are you and what the fuck are you doing in my house?"

"Cool it, pal. If I was a thief you'd be dead already." The man said.

"Why are you sitting in my kitchen drinking my coffee at four-thirty in the morning?"

"Name's Lee ... Marshall Lee, with the National Security Service," the man said, flipping out his ID.

Ted eased his way to the table and inspected the open wallet. "Breaking and entering is a crime, National Security Service or not," Ted said.

"Well," the stranger said. "I didn't exactly break in. That ancient door lock was no deterrent. I'm surprised a crime reporter in Oakland wouldn't take more precautions against people breaking into their house."

"That's why I live in Alameda and not Oakland," Ted said. "Besides, the house is an historical landmark and I couldn't modify it if I wanted. So what do you want from me?"

"Sit down, Pal. I've come a long way to talk to you. Have a cup of coffee. It's really good."

Suddenly Ted was just tired. He'd been up for twenty-four hours. The grayness of dawn was starting to peek through the window. He had a story to write. There'd be no sleep. "Coffee. Yeah. Coffee."

"Sit down, pal. I'll get it."

"No. My house, my coffee. I'll get it myself."

He went to the counter and poured a cup from the pot, and dumped sugar into it, then looked at the man at his kitchen table. "So, what do you want from me?"

"I'm investigating the circumstances around the events of last fall. You're a friend of Isaac Smith, and I'd like to know what he has told you. It's that simple," Lee said.

The reporter sat down at the table across from Lee, where his wife usually sat.

"You're aware that I am a reporter and don't have to reveal anything to you. Besides," Ted added, sipping at his coffee, "I thought the NSA and the Chinese Consulate where behind the whole thing. You should be talking to your own people you want to know about that. Smitty...Isaac hasn't told me anything."

"I suggest you tell me what you do know, Mister Harlin."

"And why would I do that?"

"Because his life may depend on it. That good enough."

"So, what's the NSA's interest in this? Like I said, I'm a reporter, and anything you tell me I will use in a article I'm working on about the murder of Peter Wu." he said.

Lee smiled. "Yes, you've told me that already. There may be a story here; bigger than you can imagine. Now tell me what you know, and maybe we can work together."

"And why should I trust you?" Harlin said, wanting to wipe the Cheshire Cat grin off the man's face.

"Well, because right now I may be the only hope you have of ever getting a story ... the real story."

"I'm confused," the reporter said. "Why would you want to leak a story to me?"

"Let's just say I have my reasons. Now, are you going to talk or not?"

"Well," Harlin said. "There isn't a whole lot to tell. All I know is that since the bartender, Peter Wu, was killed, nothing has happened. No suspects, no arrests. I know that Peter Wu was a self exiled officer of the Chinese Military. I know my friend Isaac Smith felt a personal responsibility to protect his niece, Mei-Ling Wu, and subsequently fell for her. I know that on the night of the Oakland Hills fire an attaché of the Chinese Consulate in San Francisco tried to murder Smitty. The only other thing is that something happened in Sonoma County that Smitty refuses to reveal to me, and that my sources in the FBI also won't reveal to me. And finally, I know there's something big going on, or had gone on in that time period that apparently some important people in Washington don't want exposed because my editor refused to run any of my stories on the situation." He fell silent and sipped at his coffee. "That's all I know."

Lee looked at him for a while and finally asked, "What do you think this is all about?"

Harlin looked up. "Think? I'm a journalist, not a fiction writer. I don't think, I investigate."

Lee laughed and clapped his hands in mock applause. "Spoken like a true reporter."

"Now, if you have anything to add, I'll be glad to hear you and ensure your anonymity," Ted said.

Lee stood up, drained his coffee cup and headed for the door, stopping to add. "I don't suppose you'd like to tell me where our Mister Smith is?"

"No." Harlin said.

"I'll be in touch."

* * *

Chapter 18

Shenzhen, China

The cold from the metal chair seeped through Mei-ling's light cotton pants and sent a chill through her. The windowless room was cold despite the heat of the day. The walls were a dull institutional gray, adorned by only a small picture of Mao Tse-tung, the same portrait found in every government building in Red China. The cold matched her emotions. She had failed to escape and would probably never get back to Oakland.

She was pulled away from her thoughts by the opening door. It was her captor, only he had shed his civilian clothes and was in uniform.

"You have no right to hold me here," she said in the sternest authoritative voice she could muster. "I am a citizen of Hong Kong."

The man smiled and sat across from her with a metal table separating them.

"A citizen of Hong Kong does not dress like a peasant. You are Mei-ling Wu and you were attempting to leave China illegally."

"You have my passport. I am a citizen of Hong Kong which is still a part of the British Empire."

The man laughed and threw her passport on the table. "A forgery no doubt. I am Special Agent First Class Xian Dong and I have been tailing you since you came to Guangzhou. You are Mei-ling Wu, niece of the honorable Comrade Ching-Shu Wu. And you are accused of spying and passing counter revolutionary propaganda to the American Johnny Wong."

"What, Johnny?" Mei-ling laughed nervously. "Johnny is just an acquaintance from my years in Oakland, California. It was just chance that we met."

"There are over 10 million people in Guangzhou and you expect me to believe you met by accident?"

Not knowing if Johnny had gone back in Oakland, or was in some prison cell in China sent a chill of fear through her.

"That's correct. I obviously can't deny I was trying to leave China, but Johnny had no part in it."

"You know you will be sent to a re-education camp."

"If it is my destiny," she said with resignation. "But Johnny Wong had no part in it."

"They should have detained you as you re-entered the Peoples Republic of China. As for your friend, Johnny Wong, he was allowed to leave China. Now, if you will excuse me, I will discuss this with my superiors and then you will be questioned further."

He scooped up her fake passport and abruptly left the room, leaving her to her thoughts.

Apparently even the MSS didn't know of her bargain with the San Francisco Consulate or the service she had provided her country. Or perhaps this was the government's way of getting her put away where she couldn't talk to anyone about the stolen pandas, and Isaac's role in uncovering the location of the smugglers. Thanks to her, and the sacrifice of her uncle Peter, China had been spared the humiliation of international embarrassment. But it was doing her no good.

The door to the Supervisor's office was open, but Xian Dong knocked anyway.

The voice from inside told him to enter.

His superior was sitting at his desk. Another man stood behind him. The agent didn't recognize him. He was wearing an expensive tailored black suit. Xian came to attention. "Sir, the prisoner Mei-ling Wu is ready for questioning."

Xian didn't like the looks of the other man whose attire reflected wealth and corruption. .

"Tell him, Colonel," the man said."

Xian's superior hesitated for a moment. Xian could see he was angry.

"Colonel!" the man repeated.

"Special Agent Xian Dong, you are to release the prisoner immediately."

Xian was confused. "But, I caught her clearly trying to illegally leave. Here, I have her forged passport."

"Don't question me Agent Xian. You have the wrong person. The woman you have in the basement is a citizen of Hong Kong. You have made a plunder and risk an international incident."

"Sir, no disrespect, but the prisoner is Mei-ling Wu. I have been..."

"You dare contradict me, Agent. I am your superior officer and I said she is to be released."

Xian looked at the man in the suit. He could feel his cold eyes boring into him. What was supposed to be another feather in his cap was turning to shit. If he continued arguing he stood a good chance of being demoted, or worse. Was this woman worth it? There was something go-ing on that was obviously above his rank, but he decided it wasn't worth the risk arguing. He snapped to attention. "Yes sir."

"And return her passport and money, Agent."

Xian walked out. The Supervisor looked up at the man behind him. "Alright?"

The man nodded and smiled.

Xian escorted Mei-ling to the entrance of the building. He didn't say why she was being released and she didn't ask. They got to the front of the building. He was holding her back pack.

"I want you to know that I know who you are," he said. "As far as I am concerned you are a traitor, and I will not forget you. I advise you never to return to the People's Republic."

She snatched her back pack from his hands and inspected it. The money and the passport were there.

"Do I have to count my money?" she said, looking him square in the face.

He turned and stomped back into the building. It was the last she ever saw of Special Agent Xian Dong.

Mei-ling turned to the street. Everything had happened so fast, like in a blur. Only moments before she was staring at spending the rest of her life in a re-education camp, or worse, prison. Now she was free. She didn't know how or why, but she didn't question it.

A dark car pulled up alongside her. The back window rolled down. A man in a neat dark suit called to her. "Mei-ling... Mei-ling Wu? "

She was suspicious. Was she out of the wok and into the fire. "Who want's to know?"

"A friend. The General sent me."

"What General?"

"General Angúo Wang. He asked me to make sure you got on the ferry safely. It seems you had a little trouble."

She faced the man now. "But, how did you get me away from the MSS?"

"Get in. We can talk."

He had a nice smile. She believed him. He held the car door open for her and she slid onto the plush leather seat.

"My name is Li Jang Ping," he said with a nod of his well groomed head.

"So," she said, still skeptical, "how did you get me out of there?"

The man smiled. "I pulled rank you might say."

Who could possibly force the MSS, the all encompassing Ministry of State Security to do anything?'

"Well," the man laughed. "Let's just say that I make it my business to know things about people, things they'd rather other people didn't know. The Supervisor here, well, he has done things he'd rather his superiors didn't find out about."

"I still don't understand. Who are you? Not military. That's plain to see."

"I will explain it to you, but first let's get you into some different clothing. No disrespect, Ms. Wu, but a lady from Hong Kong wouldn't be caught dead in those."

She looked at herself. "I thought I would need a disguise. As it turned out, it helped give me away."

"I can certainly see why," he laughed.

It was a good natured laugh and she found herself liking the man despite her misgivings. She expected him to take her to a store, but instead they pulled up to a large cement building. They got out of the car after the chauffeur rushed to open the back door. The building seemed to be vibrating with a high pitched hum.

"Come," Li beckoned.

He led her into the barn like building where hundreds of women were sitting at row upon row of sewing machines.

"What is this place?" Mei-ling asked.

"It is my factory. No sense letting foreigners be the only ones to cash in on our cheap labor. Now come, we will select you an outfit." He called over a good looking Caucasian woman dressed in a tailored smock with a pencil behind her ear. "This is Madam Beatrice, my designer. She will fix you up. I'll meet you back in the car." He turned to the woman. *"C'est ma bonne Mei-lingue d'ami. Prenez le bon soin d'elle."* He turned back to Mei-ling. "Here, I'll hold onto your backpack while you change."

She hesitated.

"Come on. You're just going to have to trust me."

She stalled for a moment, and then reluctantly handed him the backpack.

Madam Betrice escorted a transformed Mei-ling to the front door of the factory. A white silk blouse covered in a light black suit jacket with matching slacks draping perfectly over stylish black pumps had replaced the peasant getup. She had noticed the labels in the clothes. Sacs Fifth Avenue. Knock offs? They had even styled her hair, making her wish she had not cut it the night before, but pleasantly pleased with the outcome.

"Bonne chance," Madam Betrice said, and disappeared back into the humming building.

The driver opened the back door. Li looked out at her.

"Not bad Comrade Wu. Quite an improvement," He slid across the seat and she got in. "One last thing," he said and handed her a Gucci bag, or at least it looked like the real thing. She opened it. Her money and passport where inside.

The car pulled away from the factory.

It wasn't long before she realized they were going the wrong way. "Why aren't we going back to the Ferry terminal?" she asked.

He looked at her with that winning smile of his. "I promised the General I'd be sure you got to Hong Kong safely. Well, it seems you haven't had much luck on your own, so I am taking you to Hong Kong myself. The General is quite fond of you you know."

"Uncle Angee was my Uncle Peter's best friend."

"Uncle Angee?" Li replied with some amusement.

"Yes. Every time the General came to visit—he wasn't a General back then—he would bring me a small toy of some sort. I started calling him my Uncle Angee when I was very small. But that doesn't explain who you are and what your relationship with the General is."

Li looked out the window for a moment. Then he turned back to her. "It's a long story and I don't think you want to hear it."

Mei-ling looked him straight in the eyes. "Let me be the judge of that."

"Well, if you must. Here it is in a nut shell. Back in the war against the American Aggression against North Korea the General, your uncle, and my father all served there. They had become friends during the struggle against the Nationalists after the Japanese were finally defeated. They also had family ties in Guangdong..."

"What family ties. You mean the General and my uncle were related?"

"Distant cousins I believe. As you know, many families lost touch in those days. No one really knew who survived the years of war and revolution. Millions perished. But that is unimportant to what I am going to tell you. The three of them were all serving in Korea as I said. Well, my father happened to be Quartermaster for the northern region of Korea.

Tons of food and equipment passed through his hands every day, much of it coming from the Soviet Union. Your Uncle was in charge of border security and the General—he was a major at the time —was in charge of transportation."

"So, they were all in important positions to support the war effort. That doesn't explain..."

"Just listen," Li said. "Yes, they were all conscientious in their duties and loyal officers of the People's Liberation Army, until the great scandal."

Mei-ling listened closely. Her uncle never wanted to talk about his service in Korea. "What scandal?" she asked.

"It was discovered that a group of North Korean officers had been diverting food from their troops and selling it on the black market. Many Korean soldiers died of starvation as a result. Well, China was supplying most of the food, and my father was outraged. People in Guangdong were going hungry in order to support the war effort and when he talked to his two comrades, they were all in agreement that something had to be done...," his voice tapered off as if she knew the rest of it, or wouldn't really want to hear it. It was clear he didn't want to tell her.

"Well, get on with it" she said. "I need to hear it all, if only to satisfy my academic curiosity."

He hadn't counted on that. But, of course, she was a professor in Chinese history. "Well, all right. But I don't think you're going to be happy with what I tell you."

"Let me be the judge of that. Tell me."

"The three officers—my father, the General, and your uncle—developed a plan to divert food supplies and some machinery and oil, back into China. My father had tapped into a supply network that would divert much of the food to the peasants in Southern Guandong Province. The General supplied the truck and rail connections and your uncle Peter provided the security. And that's about it."

"Wait just a minute," Mei-ling said. "You're telling me that my Uncle Peter was involved in stealing supplies from our troops in China. I don't believe it."

"I told you you wouldn't want to know."

"I don't believe you. Just who the hell are you?"

"Well, you wanted to know how I knew the General." He let the information sink in for a moment and then said, "they didn't steal a lot as to be noticed. But enough. They all came back from Korea with nice bank accounts in Hong Kong. Your uncle and the General remained in the army. My father, well let's just say, he learned a lot in Korea and put it to work for himself and his family.

Mei-ling turned away from him and stared out the window as the city passed by. But she didn't notice.

"It may help for you to know that your uncle was hesitant to go along," Li said.

She wasn't moved. She continued to stare out the window.

"My father told me that the only reason he agreed was so he could put the money aside for you."

She looked back at Li. "I never heard of the money."

"My father said he used the money to smuggle you out of China when the Cultural Revolution started, and secured a scholarship from the University of Hong Kong for you to go to America and study. He had to use the rest of it to get himself out of China. How did you think he did it? Your uncle was a true hero of China."

"And what is your relationship with the General?"

"Well, besides family, we do business together. I do things for him that he can't do in his position. How do you think you got your passport is such a short time?"

"What else do you do?"

"I make certain investments for him. China is changing rapidly. Smart people are taking advantage of the changes. In exchange he overlooks certain—let us say—transactions that could be considered irregular."

"You are part of a Triad?"

"Not exactly. My family does some favors for the Triad in Guangdong. It's like I said, everyone helps each other. Times are changing. But here, we're coming to the border crossing. With any luck you'll be safe and sound in Hong Kong, and from there you can go anywhere you like."

They passed through the border without a hitch. It was plain to see Li was well known. The guards on both sides just glanced at their passports and waved them on.

* * *

Chapter 19

Oakland/Berkeley

The reporter sat at his kitchen table sipping his coffee. He heard the front door shut. His hand was shaking as he tried to lift his coffee cup to his mouth. He knew he couldn't sleep, especially after the uninvited visit from the NSA. He wasn't quite sure what the man calling himself Marshall Lee wanted, but he wasn't about to tell him where Smitty was.

The gray morning was starting to light up the room. He had a story to write. He took his coffee and went to his study. He switched on the IBM Selectric. The hum from the motor filled the silent room. It was ready to go, but he hesitated. The urgency he had felt just minutes before was gone. He shut off the typewriter and pushed himself away from the desk. It was too late to get into the morning edition, so the story could wait. Besides, he'd have to check with Highland and see whether Patrisha Rivers—that was her name—had survived. It could change the whole story, not just for the paper, but for his buddy Smitty.

He stared out the window at the large Oak Tree on the side of his house. What was the NSA guy looking for exactly. Ted picked up his phone and called his contact in the State Department in Washington.

"Marshall Lee?" the voice on the other end of the telephone said. "Where'd you hear about him?"

"Never mind that," the reporter said. "Do you know who he is?"

"Yeah, I know. But I'm not sure I can tell you."

"Don't worry, I won't reveal where I found out. Besides, I'm not sure it means anything. I just need to know who he is."

"Lee," the voice said. "Dangerous man. I'd steer clear of him if I was you old buddy."

"Talk to me. Who is he?"

"Well, I only know what I hear. Don't know the man myself, and don't know as I'd want to. He works for CSS. Rumor is he's a specialist. A killer. That's the rumor. Can't verify it, and you'd better not print it."

"You know me better than that."

He hung up the phone. Something didn't jive about Lee. What did he mean by *'there could be a story here.'* Why had he said that? Was he planning on exposing the NSA operation or was he just using that as bait to get information about Smitty's whereabouts? Whichever, it was clear that Smitty's life was in jeopardy, as if he didn't already have enough on his plate with the possible murder rap hanging over him. He looked up the Berkeley Marriott Hotel in the Yellow Pages and dialed the number.

Feinberg had just dropped off to sleep when the phone in the hotel room rang, jarring him back into the world. He glanced at the bed next to him. Smitty was sound asleep. He answered the phone to stop it from ringing.

"Gabe," the voice on the other end said. "Is that you?"

"Yeah, it's me. Ted, what's going on? Didn't I just drop you off?"

Ted went on to tell him about his visitor from the NSA. "My contact in DC says he's a hit man, but..."

"But what? He must be hunting for our boy here. Seems our information was correct. Only I wonder how the Chinese figure into this."

"You think the NSA is doing their dirty work for them?" Ted asked.

"Could be. Or maybe the Chinese don't have anything to do with it. And why in hell did he come to you with a warning? This thing doesn't make sense."

"Well, maybe it does. You'd better keep a close eye on our buddy. And watch your back, Gabe"

"Don't worry about me," the FBI man said. "I'll talk to you later. I'm going to make a few inquiries into this Marshall Lee guy myself."

"Good, let me know what you find out."

"Oh, and you better find our boy a good lawyer. He's going to need one."

Feinberg clicked off and then dialed for an outside line. He rang his boss's direct line in New York. The phone rang only once.

"Duggart."

"It's me, Gabe."

"Agent Feinberg?"

"Yes sir."

He relayed the information he had gotten from Ted and brought him up to date on Smitty and the new situation.

"Shot some broad. What the fuck's wrong with that boy?"

"Says he's innocent, but the cops aren't buying it."

"Well, this shit is getting complicated. It won't take long for them to find out you had no authority to pull him out of jail. I can't cover this. You'd better figure something out."

"I know."

"Oh, and Feinberg ... call your wife for chrissake. She's been calling the office four times a day. Threatened to come in and raise hell. We tried to tell her you were on assignment, but she ain't buying it."

"Shit, I don't have enough problems."

"Just call her, Feinberg. Get that woman off my back. I'll look into this Lee guy."

Gabe could feel the phone slam down from across three thousand miles. His wife could do that to you. He waited for the dial tone and called her.

"Where the hell are you?" she screamed over the phone.

"I told you I would be on special assignment," he said, hoping to placate her.

"I don't care. You should be here. Your kids need a father, and dammit Gabriel, I need servicing real bad!"

He could see there was no calming her anger, and although he'd never admit it, he rued the day he fell for her round rear end and pretty Semitic face. He had thought she was a liberated woman and so he hadn't used precautions, figuring she was on the pill. He was wrong.

"Honey, I'll be home when I finish up this case. That's all I can tell you."

"You'd better make it soon. My mother says I should get a divorce."

"Don't listen to your mother. She never did like me."

"Well, I'm starting to think she's right."

Once again the vibrations from the slammed phone echoed in his ear from across the country. "Shit." He hung up the phone.

He looked over to the opposite bed. Izzy—Smitty—was snoring peacefully. Gabe decided to get up and go have some breakfast. He had some thinking to do.

*

The hotel restaurant was empty . . . too early for most tourists. The waitress served him coffee and took his order; lightly scrambled eggs and bagel. He was beginning to think Izzy would be safer in jail. If the woman came out of the coma, he could give him up to the Albany police to hold. At least the murder charge would be dropped. A good lawyer could handle the rest.

The waitress slipped the steaming plate in front of him. "Here you are sweetheart." She had a cheery voice for so early in the morning. It bugged him. His wife used to smile like that. He knew he'd have to get back to New York and see her and his kids. He glanced up at the waitress. She was smiling at him. He wondered what she would be like in bed and immediately felt guilty. If nothing else, he'd always been loyal to his wife. But first there was one piece of unfinished business he wanted to clear up. It was purely personal and unofficial, but his boss had given him permission. He would have to take Izzy with him. That could complicate it, but it was unavoidable.

* * *

Chapter 20

Oakland

A gray tidal wave of fog was blowing in from the west, slowly engulfing everything in its path. Lee watched it coming from the window of the Cadi. The rental was parked along the shore of Lake Merritt across the street from the apartment he was looking for. He had tried to see Adede Ponce several times during the day, but she was never home. He slid out from the black leather seat and carefully crossed Lakeshore Drive. He climbed the steps—fifty seven he had counted on a previous visit—leading up to the apartment overlooking the lake where the woman lived with her young daughter, Chanel. He found himself breathing hard when he got to the top. He had been smoking two packs of Marlboros a day since he was given the order to eliminate the innocent union guy, Isaac Smith.

The gate leading onto a long patio was unlocked. He marveled at how people were so careless with security. Didn't Oakland have one of the highest crime rates in the nation? Anyone could just come in with access to the four units in the building.

The apartment he was looking for was just across a small patio from the gate. He went into the small alcove to the front door and rang the buzzer. He heard footsteps and felt someone's gaze through the peep hole. Then the door opened a crack, stopped by the chain lock inside. He could see part of a face and felt someone's eyes peering at him.

"Yes, can I help you?" a voice came from within.

"My name is Marshall Lee. I'm looking for Isaac Smith. I believe he goes by the name of Smitty."

"Yes, and if I did know someone named Smitty, what would you want from him?"

Lee smiled. "You know Ms. Ponce, it would be easier if you opened the door and let me in so we could talk."

He could feel her eyes inspecting and analyzing him. Then the door closed and he heard the chain slip off the inside.

For a moment he caught his breath. The woman standing there was strikingly beautiful; tall, bronze skinned, with large intelligent indigo colored eyes. The running suit she was wearing couldn't hide the seductive figure beneath.

"Well," she said, "You may as well come in and sit down."

As was his custom, and training, he gave the place the once over: one large room with kitchen and dining area in front, living room behind and a hallway leading to presumably bedrooms and bathroom. Two large picture windows looked out over the roof top with a panoramic view of Lake Merritt and the skyline.

"Nice place. Wasn't it Smith's?"

"Still is, Mr ... Lee was it?"

"Yes, Marshall Lee."

"Well Mister Marshall Lee, you may as well have a seat," she said,0 steering him toward the kitchen table that sat next to the window.

"Please, just call me Lee. Everyone does," he said, taking a chair.

"Can I get you some coffee, Mister Lee? I was just about to make some for myself."

"Thanks, that would be nice."

She went to the kitchen and started preparing the coffee.

"I believe you have a daughter. Chanel, if I recall correctly," Lee said.

She looked at him sternly for a moment and then returned to her choire. "You seem to know a lot about me, Mister Lee. I don't know who you are other than you must originally come from the south."

She turned on the coffee grinder. It was impossible to answer her even if he intended to which he didn't. He watched as she dumped the ground coffee into the filter and pushed the start button on the coffee maker. Then she turned back to him.

"So, who are you and what's your business with Smitty. You FBI?"

He laughed. "No, not FBI. I'm just a guy with some business with Mister Smith. Important business."

He could smell the rich aroma of the coffee as it dripped into the pot. He was impressed by this woman Adede Ponce. Her manner of speaking and the sound of her clear voice reminded him of when he was assigned to observe a speech by the Black militant Angela Davis. The fact that she was able to identify his southern roots by his speech revealed a keen sense of observation.

She poured two cups. "How do you take your coffee, Mister Lee?"

"Black with sugar."

This time she laughed. "Oh, you like black women, Mister Lee."

He smiled. "Why do you ask?"

"That's what Smitty always said to me, he liked his women like he liked his coffee ... black and sweet."

"Perhaps," he said.

"But apparently his tastes have changed," she said, still smiling as she brought the coffee to the table. As she bent over to put down his cup he caught a glimpse of her firm breasts exposed by the open zipper on her sweat shirt. She sat down across from him and pulled the zipper up around her neck.

"Actually, Mister Lee, Smitty just liked women. Didn't matter what color. But he was profoundly in love with this Chinese girl, Mei-ling."

"What about you?" Lee asked innocently. "Wasn't he in love with you?"

She laughed again. "Since you seem to know everything about me, what do you think?"

"What do I think? I think you were an ego booster for a middle aged man. I certainly know if a beautiful woman like you gave me half a chance I'd grab hold of her."

"You would, would you," she said. "Smitty has been very good to me and my daughter. We've became family if you can understand that. Me and Smitty, well, we are more like kissing cousins if you know what I mean. I will always be there for him if he needs me."

Lee sipped his coffee. "You make a good cup of coffee, Miss Ponce."

"Thank you. Smitty introduced me to good coffee. I was raised on Folgers, or whatever was on sale at the market. Sometimes my Grandmother made chicory like they drink back in Arkansas."

"I understand you are studying law enforcement in school," he said, making small talk. "You want to be a cop?"

"Don't know yet. I want to do something where I can help my community"

"That's very admirable, Ms. Ponce. Maybe you can do something that will help Isaac ... Smitty."

"Why, is he in trouble?"

"I think you know the answer to that, Ms. Ponce. But to answer you, yes, he's in a lot of trouble. Someone is trying to kill him and I am looking for him to warn him."

"And you think I can tell you where he is?"

Lee nodded.

"Well, I hate to disappoint you, Mister Lee, or whoever you are, but I have no idea where Smitty is. Like I told you, he was in love with this Mei-ling. And she seemed like a sweet woman from the one time I met her, and I believe she was in love with him. But it seems she went back to China for some reason and it broke Smitty's heart. I think he wanted me to fix him, but I told him he'd have to work it out for himself. So, he left."

"Wasn't that a bit harsh of you. After all you say he's done for you and your daughter. By the way, where is your daughter?"

"She's at a friend's house for a sleep over. As for being harsh, Mister Lee, well, I don't know you, but it doesn't matter. I'll be honest. He wanted me to hold him to my breast and take him to my bed. But that would have been a temporary fix and we both knew it. So several weeks ago he up and left, like I said. He didn't tell me where he went. I got one call from him during that time and haven't heard from him since. He was worried someone was after him, and he was afraid for me and Chanel, and that's all I know. Now Mister Lee, I would appreciate it if you left."

She stood up and took her cup to the sink.

"I meant what I said,"

She turned toward him. "What would that be, Mr Lee?"

"About if you were my woman," he said.

She walked back to the table and stood over him. "Don't flatter yourself, Mister Lee. You remind me of the tricks I used to turn when I was a hooker; just another sad lonely white man."

His first inclination was to reach out and slap her face. But there was something intimidating about her. He suddenly felt very small.

"I think you are finished with your coffee," she said, picking up his cup.

He stood up and allowed himself to be escorted to the front door. As a parting gesture he handed her his card. "Give this to your friend when you see him. Tell him to contact me. I'm staying at the Fairmont in the city."

And he was out the door. Adede looked at the Card:

Marshall Lee - Special Agent
National Security Agency/Central Security Service
United States Government
Defending our nation/Securing our future

She took the small .32 revolver she had tucked under her sweatshirt and placed it on the table. Her hands began to tremble and her heart seemed to drop to the pit of her stomach. Lee was the man who was going to kill Smitty.

He was outraged that the woman had seen right through him. Was he that transparent? He drove the Cadillac back across the Bay Bridge to the hotel, and went directly to the bar and ordered a double scotch, gulped it down and ordered another.

After the second scotch he began to calm down. She was right, the woman who lived with Isaac Smith ... Smitty. He had never been able to form a relationship with a woman, not that there weren't thousands of eligible young ladies in Washington.

The bartender poured him another double. He sipped this one. Many of his fellow agents were married, leading double lives, unable to confide in their spouses about their work. He didn't think he was capable of doing that. Instead he had always found comfort in the arms of one of the many prostitutes that fed off the rich and powerful in the nation's capital where man felt above the mores and rules of the society that they ruled. He supposed she had gotten it right from where she sat. To the world he must seem like a lonely old white man. He didn't see himself that way, but he could see how others would.

"Give me that bottle of 12 year old Glenlivet you got there on the rack so I can take it to my room," he told the bartender.

"I'm sorry sir; we're not allowed to do that. There's a service bar in your room."

"Just give me the bottle and charge it.. It would be better for all concerned if you do as I say."

The bartender looked at him. Whatever it was he saw in the man sitting at the bar it convinced him he'd better do as he was told. He pulled the unopened bottle from the rack behind the bar and set it down.

Lee grabbed it up and left.

As the elevator carried him up to the fourteenth floor he thought of the beautiful Black woman, the woman who loved Isaac Smith, and he hated the man for it even though he had never met him.

* * *

Chapter 21

Hong Kong

Mei-ling stared out the window of the black Mercedes limo. She had been surprised by the modest border check point at Sha Tau Kok Road— the two lane bridge separating The People's Republic of China from the British colony of Hong Kong. But for all its modesty it was swarming with Red Army soldiers on one side and British soldiers on the other. She had never been to Hong Kong, not from the land side. On the northern edge of Shenzhen, Sha Tau Kok Road was the only land border crossing. Relations with Great Britain had never been good. The Chinese had never forgiven the imperialist white nation for bringing opium to China because they were unable to compete with Chinese business superiority. In the end they had resorted to military invasion and open warfare. It seemed the West had always excelled in war and killing, and China fell victim. The British took Hong Kong and Singapore as their bases of operation, and ran their business operations from them. Singapore gained its independence in 1963 and remained in the Commonwealth, but Hong Kong was too valuable for the Brits to give up. They had a hundred year contract they had forced down the throat of a weak emperor and they intended to stay there until the last minute.

"It's quit inconvenient this crossing," Li said, breaking the silence. "But in less than 6 years Hong Kong will revert back to us, and I suspect many more crossings will open up as will our country. Soon we will regain our superiority to the West. There will be a lot of money to be made."

Mei-ling looked at the man sitting across from her; the man who had snatched her from the jaws of the Ministry of State Security. She couldn't blame him for the things her uncle had done in the past. He had told her at her insistence, and she had no one to blame but herself. But those were different times, shortly after the Revolution in 1949, and then the war against the Imperialist West in Korea. Her uncle had been fighting all his life, first against the forces of Chiang Kai-shek, then against the Japanese, then Chang again and then the U.S.

"You shouldn't be too hard on your uncle, or the General for that matter," Li said, as if reading her thoughts. "They are great patriots and decent men."

She stared back out the window. She was amazed at the difference now that they had entered Hong Kong. Not only were they driving on the left side of the well paved highway, and all the signs were in English and Chinese, but there was a general feeling of neatness and order here. The towns and countryside were clean, and the air smelled fresher for some reason.

"My father and I mourned the death of your uncle. We were saddened by the unceremonious way he met his violent death."

She turned toward him. "What do you know of it?"

"What everyone knows, that he was mistakenly shot by Chinese gangsters. He deserved a more honorably death."

They knew nothing of her uncle's secret mission in America—that he was working with the Chinese government to hunt down the panda smugglers, or her role in the mission after her uncle was murdered in cold blood. No one seemed to know, not the immigration officer that questioned her when she returned from Oakland, not the MSS agent who had been tailing her since she arrived in Guangzhou, not the General. No one.

"Thank you," she said under her breath, and her eyes returned to the window as the countryside sped past.

From Sha Tau Kok Road they joined up on Highway 9 that wound its way toward Kowloon. They drove through the town of Tai Po onto the section of Highway 9 called the New Territories Road that skirted the Tolo Harbor where hundreds of small junks and larger fishing boats sat in the quiet water.

The road then turned inland toward Kowloon and Hong Kong Island.

Li had been quiet for most of the trip, as if recognizing her anguish as she mulled over her uncle's past. "Where would you like to be dropped off?" he asked.

"Do you know the City University?"

"In Kowloon Tong?"

"Yes, I think that's right. I've never been there, but I have some friends I met in America who teach there."

Li leaned forward and gave his chauffeur instructions.

They had merged off Highway 9 onto Highway 8, also know as Lung Cheung Road, leading into the heart of Kowloon. Mei-ling could see Kowloon Peak rising above the city of skyscrapers.

"Any place special? I know a nice hotel near the University." Li said..

"That won't be necessary Mister Li."

"Please, call me Jang, and I must insist."

He leaned forward and gave the chauffeur further instructions.

"Perhaps I could have the honor of your companionship this evening. I could show you Kowloon at night. It's very nice."

The car pulled off Lung Cheung Road onto a city street. Before Mei-ling could answer the car swerved violently and came to a screeching halt.

"What the fuck!" Li shouted in Cantonese.

Before they could look up and see what happened someone yanked open the back door on Li's side. He looked up at a man with a ski mask covering his face, and a Glock in his hand. A glance at his chauffeur revealed a similar situation.

"Who the fuck are you?" Li said with as much bravado as he could muster considering the circumstance.

"Don't worry, Li. I'm not interested in you. I want the woman."

Mei-ling recognized the familiar voice from her past. Li turned to her. She saw the concern in his face. He would have done something if it was possible, but there was no way. "It's okay, Jang. I'll be alright."

"Get out and let the woman out your side," the man said.

Li did as instructed. He watched Mei-ling slide across the seat and get out. She was a good looking woman and he regretted not getting to know her better.

The man took her by the arm. She smiled. "Rick, never thought I'd see you again," she said in English. "Or is it Agent Wang nowadays?"

"Get in my car," he said irritably. He pulled her along to the waiting black Mercedes-Benz 300 that had cut them off.

The driver hit the gas as soon as the back door slammed closed, leaving Li and his chauffeur standing on the street. The whole abduction on the busy Kowloon street took no more than three minutes.

Mei-ling settled back in her seat. The man she had called Rick was actually Wang Xiabo, an attaché at the Chinese Consulate in San Francisco when she knew him. He was one of the few people in China who knew about her Uncle Peter and her own involvement in destroying the panda smuggling operation the year before. It was Rick that made the arrangement trading Smitty's life for her return to China.

"Damn Rick, how the hell did you get here and how did you know where I was?" she said in English.

The man pulled the ski mask off his head, holstered his Glock automatic in the shoulder holster under his short leather jacket, ran a comb through his thick hair and finally put a pair of Ray-Ban sun glasses on, all in a smooth coordinated motion as if he practiced it in the mirror every day.

"I got a call from my contact in the Shenzhen MSS office. He told me he had you at the headquarters, but his superior ordered you released," he said in perfect English that he had mastered in his many years in America. Unlike Mei-ling and her uncle, who had come to Oakland as political refugees from the Cultural Revolution, Rick had been sent by the government to learn the ways of the Americans. After a number of years that took him through high school in San Francisco and several years of college in Berkeley, he returned to China for training in the Ministry of State Security, and then returned to San Francisco as an attaché to the Consulate. He was assigned as liaison with the American National Security Agency in the secret arrangement allowing China to operate in the U.S and investigate a smuggling operation.

The last time Mei-ling had seen him, he was hanging out of an attack helicopter that was destroying a ranch high in the hills overlooking the Valley of the Moon in Glen Ellen, California. About twenty mercenaries were systemically killing off the smugglers and setting fire to everything. It was burned in her memory; it was the fulfillment of her obligation to her country that she had taken over after her Uncle Peter was murdered.

"So?"

"It's a long story," Rick said, settling back into the plush leather seat.

"Better told over dinner. Right now we have to get out of Hong Kong. It's no longer safe here."

"For who, you or me?"

Rick looked at her and smiled.

Mei-ling stared out the tinted window as the car made its way through the Kowloon traffic and passed into the Western Harbour Tunnel to Hong Kong Island. After what seemed like hours they came to the Shun Tak Center, a business district of skyscrapers that ended at the waterfront. The driver pulled up in front of a sprawling two story building—the Hong Kong/Macau Ferry Building.

They got out of the car. Rick said something to the driver and the car sped away.

Mei-ling leaned on the railing looking out over at the coast of Lantau Island as the ferry plowed into the Pearl River Estuary. Rick came up to her with a beer in one hand and a plastic cup in the other.

"Vodka martini," he said, handing her the cup.

She took a sip. The warm wind stirred her new hairdoo.

"So tell me, Mei, you didn't seem too concerned when I snatched you from Li. Weren't you scared?"

She looked up from the martini. "When I recognized your voice I was more curious than anything else."

"But you were free and clear, on your way back to America."

"Yes, that's true, but somehow I knew that you would get me back to Oakland."

"Oh, why is that?"

"Perhaps you think I can lead you to Isaac. You are trying to silence him aren't you?" Mei-ling said, trying not to show her concern.

Rick laughed. "Smitty? Damn Mei, we aren't interested in him anymore. What can he say that anyone would believe; that someone was smuggling pandas out of China. They'd laugh at him."

"Then you don't want to kill Isaac?"

"No. He is of no interest to us."

She looked back out over the railing of the ferry and took another drink from the plastic cup. Could she believe him? She knew that Isaac's life was in danger. She could sense it. And, if the Chinese government wasn't trying to kill Isaac, than who was? Was it possible that his own government wanted him dead?

"If you're not interested in Isaac, then what do you want from me? Surely returning me to China is not that important to you."

"No. Besides, reuniting you two would gratify my sense of romance." He drained his bottle of Tsingtao. "I will tell you everything over a nice dinner in Macau. Your service to your country is not done."

"Promotion? Yes, well that's what I thought too after successfully completing my mission."

"Thanks to me and Smitty," Mei-ling added.

"Yes. But when I got back to the consulate they handed me a plane ticket back to China," Rick said.

He was sitting across from Mei-ling at a casino restaurant overlooking Macau. She was sipping a vodka martini. He preferred gin in his. When they had walked into the restaurant the maitre d' said all the window seats were reserved, but when Rick flashed an ID they were immediately seated.

Macau was still under Portuguese administration. Relations with China were good ever since Portugal decided to rid itself of its colonies following their own revolution in 1986, and they promised to return the city to the Chinese in 1999. Macau's bureaucrats were extremely cooperative with the Chinese knowing that they would soon be the bosses.

"When I got back to Beijing I was questioned for hours," Rick continued. "Then they sent me packing to a desolate outpost somewhere on the Mongolian border. That's where I sat for the next two months."

Mei-ling sipped her drink. "They have a strange way of rewarding success," she said.

"Well, finally they called me back and did promote me, and gave me a new assignment. And that's where you come in Mei. But let's wait 'til after dinner. What would you like?"

She glanced at the menu. "I want a thick steak, medium rare, with a baked potato and sour cream. I haven't had a good piece of beef since I've been back."

"Sounds good to me," Rick said. He called over a waiter and ordered for them both.

Mei-ling cleaned her plate, and ordered another Martini.

"So, what is the mysterious mission I have to do?"

Rick was chewing his last piece of steak. He hurried to swallow and washed it down with what was left of a glass of red wine.

"Excellent," he said. "You know, they import their meat from Japan. Finest Kobe beef in the world." He pulled a pack of Marlboros from his coat pocket and offered her one. Then he pulled out a lighter. It was a slim silver thing with a picture of Mao on it. When he pressed the ignition button it played a Revolutionary tune. "Cute, huh? I could get you one if you like."

He lit Mei-ling's cigarette and then his own, blowing a cloud of blue smoke into the air.

"It's show and tell time, Rick," she said, drawing the cigarette smoke deep into her lungs. "Why the hell did you kidnap me like something out of a Hong Kong gangster movie? And just what is it you want from me?"

The waiter came with Mei-ling's Martini. Rick ordered a brandy.

"Just like old times, eh Mei."

"What old times," she said. "Last I recall you tried to kill us, and would have if it hadn't been for that FBI guy, what's his name?"

He looked up from his brandy into her accusatory eyes. "Yes, that was unfortunate. I wasn't going to shoot you, but you were interfering with orders. Truth is, Mei, I didn't want to shoot Smitty. I liked him and argued against it. But they wanted to kill him before he—how they say— spilled the beans. They were that paranoid that word would get out about those goddamned pandas. Well, orders are orders."

They sat in silence for a minute; Rick stared into his brandy, avoiding her eyes. Then he began to chuckle, more to himself than to her.

"You know, I went to see him shortly after you returned to China. I didn't have permission from the Consulate or the State Department to cross the bridge so I waited until late. Smitty thought I'd come to kill him while I only wanted to explain to him why you left."

"You told him?" Mei said. "You told him I left him to save his life?"

"Yes, but like I said, he thought I'd come to kill him. So he takes off out the back of the apartment and heads for the lake in his stocking feet. I went after him. He started running and bam, he runs smack into a flock of sleeping geese. They start to fly and he smashes right into one, knocking him flat onto the wet grass."

Mei couldn't help but smile as Rick started laughing at his own story.

"I get him back to his apartment. He still thinks I'm going to kill him. So I make him change into some dry clothes and pour him a drink to reassure him, and I explain why you had to leave him, and that he shouldn't think you betrayed him. That you loved him."

"You did that?"

"Like I said, it's my romantic side."

Mei sipped her Martini. "Well, you didn't kidnap me in Hong Kong and bring me to Macau just to tell me that. So what do you want from me?"

Rick swirled his brandy around in his glass and then gulped it down.

"I'm offering you a chance to go back to Oakland free and clear with your grateful nation's blessing. You can marry Smitty and become a citizen of the Imperialist Empire."

She laughed. "What makes you think I want to become a citizen of the United States?"

Rick looked surprised. "Don't you?"

"Not particularly. Yes, I want to go back and be with Isaac, but citizen? I'm Chinese."

"Well, whatever. We will secure you in any country you wish. You and Smitty."

"And what do I have to do for this honor," Mei-ling said, drinking down the rest of her martini. "Who do I have to kill?"

"Well, hopefully no one," Rick said. "But we do need you for an important mission."

"So stop—how they say it in America—beating around the tree."

"I believe it's a bush," Rick said

"Excuse me?"

"Bush. It's beating around the bush."

"Oh, I never could get these American colloquialisms right. Whatever, tell me what you have to tell me. And order me another martini."

Rick grabbed a passing waiter and ordered her drink and another brandy for himself with an espresso.

"You remember that night at the ranch, the one in the Valley of the Moon?"

"How can I forget it. Isaac and I would have been cremated by your Americans if not for those FBI guys. It was the second time the FBI saved us."

"Yeah. Well, I would have pulled you out, but I saw those guys and figured you'd be okay Besides, I had my hands full with that crazy bunch of mercenaries the Americans rounded up for us. Anyway, those idiots went crazy; like they were attacking a village in Vietnam. They incinerated everything before we had a chance to check on the pandas. About a week after the attack our government received information that one of the pandas had been taken out of the camp before the attack."

"You mean there's still one out there?"

"Yes. I figure that's why they called me back from the Mongolian border. They gave me a promotion to placate my hurt feelings, and gave me the assignment to destroy the goddamn thing."

The waiter delivered their drinks.

Rick looked at the brandy and the espresso as if deciding which he wanted to start with. Then he looked up at Mei-ling. "I don't know about you but I am sick of these Pandas."

He took a sip of the brandy and chased it with a sip from the steaming espresso. "Needs sugar." He dumped four sugar packets into the dark liquid.

"So, you know where this last bear is?" Mei-ling asked.

"He looked up from the espresso. "No. Maybe somewhere in Central California."

"Where?"

"That's what I need you to find out. The Americans don't know and they claim our arrangement was over, and besides, it was theoretically confined to San Francisco and Oakland Chinatowns. But you ... you still

have an active green card. You can move around. I thought maybe you could recruit Smitty to help you."

Mei-ling took the olive from her martini and slowly pulled the tooth pick through her lips. She rolled the olive around in her mouth for a moment as she rolled Rick's proposition around in her mind.

"So, if I do this, just what do you propose for compensation?"

"Like I said, we will relocate you and Smitty if you like, anywhere you want to go. We will also provide a large sum of money to get you settled."

"How much are we talking about?"

"Rick was taken aback. She was fucking bargaining with him. "The mere fact that you are fulfilling your pledge to the People of China should be enough," he said hopefully.

"If you will recall, Rick, if it wasn't for me you would never have found the pandas in the first place. I consider that obligation fulfilled," she said. "I believe I was treated pretty poorly by our government. Is that the kind of rewards a patriot can expect? My uncle was murdered and I was forced to return to a country that didn't want me. Is that gratitude?"

"Damn Mei-ling. You have changed."

"How much?"

Rick looked into his brandy, as if the answer was there, then back up at her hardened face. "One hundred thousand U.S. dollars," he ventured.

"Mei-ling laughed. "You have any idea what I could get from the international media for this?"

"Two hundred and fifty thousand...?"

"A million, deposited in the bank of my choice. Now."

"Damn."

"That's my price. You want that last panda dead, you're going to have to pay this time." She smiled and looked out the window at the lights of Macau's Casino District. The city was undergoing a remake since the 1990 Grand Prix had brought it to international attention, and the lights from the large casinos turned the night sky into day and construction cranes spotted the landscape like ancient dragons watching over the city.

"It will take me some time to get this approved," Rick said. "A million dollars is a lot of money."

Mei-ling turned toward him and smiled. "Take your time. I'm beginning to like it here in Macau."

* * *

Summer 1992

Chapter 22

Berkeley Marina

The warm days of Spring were gone and the signs of summer were showing their full colors as the gray cold fog poured in through the Golden Gate like an announcement of the season. When people everywhere else were digging through drawers for cutoffs, sleeveless shirts and skimpy summer dresses, the people of the San Francisco Bay Area were dragging out coats and wool hats.

Isaac peered out the hotel window trying to think if the events of the day before were just a bad dream. But as his mind cleared it became all too evident that it was true—that Trish was dead and he was suspected of killing her. He went to the bathroom, peed and then looked in the mirror. The left side of his face was swollen and bruised as the a memory of being beaten flowed painfully back to him. He recalled slithering like a wounded salamander across the floor of Trish's salon toward the telephone with her dead in the captain's cabin. Then his brain returned to the present by the sound of the front door opening and closing.

"Feinberg, that you?"

Agent Gabe Feinberg came in holding a styrofoam cup. "Coffee?"

"Yeah. What time is it?"

"Almost eleven."

Isaac sat down on the bed. "Shit, what a fucked up night."

"Damnit Izzy, this situation is complicated enough without you getting involved in a murder rap. What were you thinking?"

Smitty couldn't blame him for being upset. He had been asking himself the same question since Trish's panicked call the day before. "No choice in the matter," he said. "Wrong place at the wrong time."

"Well, you better hope she comes out of her coma and confirms your story."

Smitty slowly opened the plastic lid on the styrofoam cup. "Sugar?"

"Three," Feinberg said and sat down on the chair by the window.

"And in the meantime, boss, what's on the agenda?"

"In the meantime I'm going to take a nap. You're free to wonder around if you like. Just don't get any stupid ideas, or you'll have me after you as well as whoever else is hunting for you. When I wake up we're heading for Glen Ellen."

"Glen Ellen," Isaac said, almost spilling his coffee on himself. "What the fuck you want to go there for?"

"I want to go up to the Stover place and check it out, that's why."

"There's nothing there," Smitty said, recovering from his shock. "Hell, you were there—they burned the fucking joint to the ground."

"Well, we went up there—me and Berman. You remember him."

"Sure the wine merchant."

"My partner. We went up there several days after we pulled you and the Wu woman out looking for evidence."

"Yeah?"

"And someone opened fire on us. They hit my partner so I want to go back up there to see what's what."

"Berman was shot? He okay?"

"Yeah, wasn't serious. But I still want to get a second look at the place."

"And then what?"

"Then. . .well, then I decide what to do with you. Now get out of here and get something to eat. Give me a couple of hours."

Smitty started for the door, but then stopped. "I got to ask you. Why did you spring me from jail last night?"

Feinberg looked at him and sat down on the unmade bed. "Someone is gunning for you, Izzy, and my boss sent me to protect you."

"Would it be out of line to ask why?"

"Yes. Oh, and Izzy, don't leave the hotel."

With that Feinberg stretched out on the unmade bed and was snoring in a few seconds.

Smitty made his way to the lobby of the Hotel. It was built like a fancy motel, with a large restaurant and bar, and banquet rooms. All the rooms opened onto balconies overlooking the marina. He went to the bank of pay phones and dialed the Lakeshore apartment. Dede would hear about his arrest and he felt a need to explain to her.

The phone rang a number of times and then the answering machine clicked on. Dede had changed the message he had left on it to her own:

"This is the Ponce residence. If you have a message for Adeda...Or Chanel"—the little girl's voice squeaked in—"please leave us a message."

"This is Smitty. Dede. If you hear anything about me—about me being arrested—don't jump to any conclusions or come looking for me. I will be in touch and explain everything."

He hung up, a little discouraged for not having spoken to her. Aside from Mei-ling, Dede knew him better than anyone, and when it came right down to it, she probably knew him better than anyone, including Mei-ling.

He walked across the lobby toward the restaurant, resisting the urge to go into the hotel lounge and order a double JD.

He sat down at the counter facing the kitchen. It reminded him of the Merritt Restaurant where he had breakfast almost every day when he lived on Lakeshore. Only the hotel's version was more like a Denny's and far less crowded..

"Can I help you?" a young Black waitress asked. "Coffee?"

He looked up at her smiling face. His first instinct was to talk to her about the union. They had been boycotting the place for over six months and making a feeble attempt at organizing the workers. But, under the circumstance, he decided it wasn't a good idea.

" Please," he said. "And I'll have bacon and eggs, over easy."

"Toast?"

"Rye. Dark."

If he hadn't been consumed by his own thoughts he may have noticed the man who was sitting a number of seats on his left. He was sipping at a cup of coffee and glanced over at Smitty. Then he slipped a five dollar bill on the counter, grabbed a gray sports coat and A's baseball cap and slipped away from the counter.

"Nice morning," he commented as he passed Smitty and was out the door just as Smitty looked up. He called the waitress over.

"You know who that was?" he asked.

"Never seen him here before. Might be a guest of the hotel. You know him?"

The man just felt familiar. He swore he'd seen him somewhere. He got a momentary chill. "No," he said. "How them eggs coming?"

"Coming right up, sir."

He picked up a copy of USA Today that was sitting on the seat next to him. Boris Yeltsin had overthrown the elected Parliament of the Soviet Union thus putting the last nail in the coffin of the glorious Russian Revolution. Isaac could see the CIA behind the scenes. China had broken the nuclear moratorium, preparing to fill in the void left by the collapse of Soviet Communism. The world was getting screwier and more dangerous every day.

After he finished his breakfast he walked out into the lobby. He stood at the glass door leading out onto a small patio and the marina beyond and had a sudden compelling urge to be among the boats. Over the past ten years he had lived on a boat on and off. He missed the lapping of the water on the hull and the clanking of the halyards on the masts. He had felt at peace on his boats—ironically, the last two having been violently destroyed. He still had a gate key to the Berkeley Marina from when he had taken Mei-ling there to hide out from the Chinese gangsters who were hot on her tail. It was on his boat that he first made real love to her —where he fell in love with her.

He ventured out the hotel gate onto the walkway that skirted the marina. The sun was beginning to crack through the gray as he passed by a young man holding a skate board. They exchanged good mornings. A woman in a pink sweat pants suit was trying to control a huge pit-bull that strained at its leash. He glanced over at the adjacent parking lot that was filled with cars and wondered where the people were that belonged to them. It was a week day and not many people were out sailing. Perhaps they belonged to live-a-boards. His thoughts drifted back to when he lived aboard his own boat and the few quiet nights he had spent with Mei-ling. It seemed so long ago.

He made his way to the dock gate and searched for his key. It was still there, on his key ring where he had left it all this time. He didn't see the eyes that were fixed on him as he inserted the key into the lock. He heard the sound of the skate board rambling down the paved path, and then everything that followed seemed to happen in slow motion.

Just as he opened the gate and slipped inside he caught sight of a flash in the corner of his eye. The kid on the skate board suddenly was hurling toward him and smashed into the gate. Smitty ducked just as the iron mesh on the gate seemed to explode. He glanced up and saw a large hole just inches from his head. The skate board kid lay sprawled in front of the gate. The pit bull was now howling and barking like a trapped wild animal as the woman fought to control it.

Feinberg couldn't sleep. He had felt uneasy about letting Smitty off on his own, and had only dozed for about thirty minutes. When he went out onto the balcony of the hotel room he spotted Smitty headed for the docks. It took him a moment to realize something was terribly wrong. Then he saw the kid on a skate board go down in front of Smitty.

He jumped over the balcony onto the lawn. There were more gun shots ringing from the parking lot. The FBI agent had recognized the first couple of shots; they were the muffled sound of a long range sniper rifle with a silencer—you learn those things in his job —but the shots that he heard as he rushed toward the docks where Smitty was trapped were from a 9 mm. He glanced over at the parking lot where the shots were coming from and instinctively pulled out his own Glock automatic. A nondescript gray sedan peeled rubber out of the driveway and headed toward the street. He spotted another man holding a smoking hand gun get back into a late model Cadillac and drive off slowly, apparently in no hurry to pursue the first man.

The skate boarder was covered in blood and probably dead. The woman was screaming hysterically. She let the loose leash and the pit bull that came rushing at him. He shot it dead in its tracks, and then went up to the woman who had become even more terrified and he slapped her in the face. "That's enough!" She collapsed into his arms and began sobbing. He heard sirens in the distance.

A small crowd of gawkers were starting to gather.

"Someone call an ambulance," Smitty was yelling from where he was still trapped behind the dock gate.

Feinberg turned the sobbing woman over to another woman who had come up to them. He started walking toward the gate as the gathered crowd backed away and he realized he still had his gun in his hand. He stuck it back into his shoulder holster and went to the gate, kneeled down to the skate boarder and checked for vital signs. He was bleeding from a gash in his his head and his shirt was covered in blood, but he was alive. The bullet seemed to have hit him in the shoulder, but the force of it had sent him head first into the gate. He eased him away from the gate allowing Smitty to get out.

Two police cars came roaring into the parking lot. Feinberg pulled out his ID. He had left the skate boarder in the care of a woman who claimed to be an RN, and with Smitty close behind, he approached the cops. One of them stepped out while his partner crouched by the open passenger side of the car with her gun at the ready.

"What in hell's going on here?" the cop said. He was an over weight middle aged man with a shock of white hair and a voice that sounded like years of cigarettes and whiskey.

"This man is under federal protection," Feinberg said nodding his head toward Smitty as the police man checked his ID. "Someone took a shot at him. There's a kid over there that got in the way. Better call an ambulance."

"This says you're with the New York Bureau," the cop said.

"Yes, I'm transporting this man back there. You'd better put out a APB on a man in a 1990 gray ford sedan, only I doubt you'll find him."

The cop looked over the ID once again, as if he missed something. "Where you staying, Agent"—he looked at the ID again— "Agent Feinberg?"

Feinberg nodded his head back toward the hotel. "We're checking out today."

The cop handed Feinberg back the ID. He glared at Smitty for a moment. "Make sure you do. I don't need this shit in my town." He called back to the woman cop. "Get the paramedics here quick."

"They're on their way," she responded.

Feinberg grabbed Smitty by the shoulder. "Come on Izzy. We're outta here."

As they walked back to the hotel Smitty asked why he hadn't mentioned the second guy in the Cadillac to the cops.

"No sense in confusing them," Feinberg said. "Both those guys will be long gone in no time."

"We still going out to Glen Ellen?"

"It's that or I take you back to the Alameda police."

"Glen Ellen then."

* * *

Chapter 23

Washington, DC

Marshal Lee made a b-line straight to the bank of pay phones after landing in the Dulles Airport and dialed the direct line to his old comrade Mac McCraven at the State Department.

"Mac, I need to talk to you. Meet me at the Sackler in two hours."

"Lee, old buddy. You sound a little angry. What's this all about?"

"I think you know, pal. Meet me."

He slammed the phone down for emphasis.

Lee took a taxi directly to the Capital Mall. It took more than an hour to get there from Dulles. He still had an hour to kill, but was surprised to see McCraven sitting on a bench in front of the museum. Lee took out a cigarette and lit it before walking up to his old CIA comrade.

"Mac."

"Lee, you're early."

"Yeah, so are you."

"Wanted to get out of the office. Now, what's on your mind?"

Lee stared at him for a moment and then dropped his cigarette to the ground and stepped on it.

"You know damn well what's on my mind. You send another one of your mercenaries to interfere in my assignment I'll send him home to you in a pine box."

"Just hold it up right there, amigo. You're upset." McCraven had never seen Lee mad. They had both always acted with professional cool. "You're taking this thing too seriously."

"I told you I was taking care of this assignment personally. You and your friends at State keep hands off or you all will be..."

"Be what? Sorry?" Mc Craven said. "You'd better cool down, pal. You can get into a lot of hot water you keep this shit up. Now, just go back out to the West Coast and finish this thing."

"Don't worry, old buddy. I'll do what I have to do. I always have."

He didn't wait for a response. He knew he was flirting with catastrophe, but he didn't care. He turned and walked away.

MacCraven waited for Lee to disappear down the crowded mall and then pulled out a cell phone from his brief case.

"This is McCraven. Who the hell set up the Smith hit?" This time it was his turn to be angry. "Goddamned incompetents. Yes, he blew it. And what's worse is Lee caught him in the act. I want Smith dead. I don't care if he's being protected by the FBI. I want this thing done and if we have to take out the FBI agent, well, we'll blame it on the Chinese. I'll talk with Lee. Man is worth ten of the amateurs you're running. If necessary I'll go out there and take care of it myself."

* * *

Chapter 24

Berkeley Marina

Feinberg sent Smitty to their room with strict instructions not to go anywhere. Then he went to the pay phones and called his boss in New York.

Duggart: Agent Feinberg. All's well I presume.

Gabe: No exactly.

Duggart: Something happen to Smith?

Gabe: No, no. He's okay, only...

Duggart: Only what, Gabriel? Don't fuck with me.

Gabe: Well, seems he got himself mixed up in some legal prob

lems.

Duggart: What kind of legal problems?

Gabe: Well, he was arrested for murder. But I got him released.

Duggart: Murder?

Feinberg: Well, no... that is, they haven't charged him and there's a possibility the victim might live. Also...

`Duggart: What else, agent. Goddamnit.

Gabe: Well, someone took a pot shot at him a few minutes ago... but he's okay.

Duggart: I told you to take care of him. I thought you were capable of handling that agent.

Gabe: Well boss, I was thinking I would like to bring him back to New York so we can protect him...

Duggart: Here? there's no way, agent. I told you, this operation is off the books. This shit is coming from high up. In fact we shouldn't be discussing this over the phone. It's higly probable the office lines have ben tapped You do what you have to do, and don't contact me again unless it's absolutely necessary.

Duggart slammed the phone down. If the NSA had wind of what he was doing they surely had tapped his phone. He wouldn't put it past the bastards. He never approved of the secretive agency. No one really knew what they did, and there didn't seem to be any oversight. They were an animal of the State Department, and as such were an instrument of political schemes. They looked down their noses at the FBI and the CIA. As far as he was concerned they were a shadow agency that trampled on the constitution.

He fingered a folder that was on his desk. He had gotten the forensics report the day before. According to the report the animal hair Agents Feinberg and Berman had found at the Glen Ellen ranch came from a bear; not just any bear, but a panda bear. He was sure it was some fuck up, so he sent it back for further examination. The head of the forensics lab called him. They too had found it hard to believe so they had sent it to an animal forensics lab in Hong Kong. There was no doubt; the hair came from a young Giant Panda.

It all started making sense to him. Panda bears; smuggled into the U.S. Priceless. Apparently the NSA had worked with the Chinese government to destroy them. And the State Department was, no doubt, calling the shots. What was in it for America he couldn't figure, but there it was. And if what Feinberg and Berman had said about the military style attack on the Glen Ellen ranch house was true, than anyone with knowledge of it was in mortal danger, from the NSA and the Chinese. And Isaac Smith was at the top of the list.

Feinberg stared at the phone as the dial tone buzzed in his ear. He couldn't believe what he had just heard his boss say. He was on his own, and he alone was responsible for the life of Isaac Smith. There would be no one to call; no backup; a hired assassin or a gang of hired assassins laying in wait. And he knew he would take a bullet before letting them kill his charge. It's what they paid him for. He should call his wife, but on second thought decided against it. She wouldn't believe him anyway. Instead, he called Ted Harlin who was in his office at the Tribune. Feinberg told him about the botched attempt on Izzy's life. "He'd be dead except for some guy who opened fire on the would-be assassin ... no I don't know who it was ... how's the woman doing? .... good, let's hope she comes out of it and can clear our buddy. Meanwhile, I'm going to get Izzy out of town."

Harlin didn't press him on where he was taking Smitty. He just told him that if he needed anything to call.

Well, at least she wasn't dead, Feinberg thought. That, at least, was good news. The rest of it seemed rather murky. He went to get up when the pay phone rang. He looked at it for a moment, deciding whether or not to pick up.

"Hello, can I help you?"

"Yeah, you shmuck."

It was his partner, Richard Berman. "Rich, how the hell did you get this number?"

"We traced it. The old man hung up pretty quick, but we got it. Why the fuck don't you turn on your cell phone?"

"Huh?"

"You were issued a cell phone before you left. It's an unregistered line. Secure. The old man wants me to keep tabs on you."

"Cell phone? That's what was in the packet they gave me? I thought it was another useless manual. It's far too small to be a mobile phone."

"Well, it's not. Latest technology. So turn the thing on and erase all the messages I left and then call me. You do know how to use a cell phone?"

"I'll figure it out," Feinberg said, and hung up. The last thing he needed was to be lectured to by Rich Berman.

He went to his room. Smitty was in the shower. He opened his bag and found the package with a box that said IBM Simon on it. He opened it to find a ... what the fuck ... a small telephone? and a booklet which explained all the applications; calendar, fax, a note pad with an electronic pen ... what the fuck did he need all that shit for? — a worthless manual after all. So the first thing he did was plug it in to charge it, and then he called Berman. He was surprised to hear his old partner's voice answer. "Shit, it really works."

"What did you expect you shmuck. Of course it works. Hasn't been released yet, we're the only ones got them."

"So what do you know that I should know, aside from the fact that I'm on my own here."

"Only that the hair we found at Stover's was that of a Panda bear. You believe that?"

"You're kidding. A Panda?"

"You got it partner. I got shot over a *fershtnkner* Panda bear. So, where are you going to go?"

"You sure this thing is secure?"

"Guaranteed by IBM."

"I'm going to get Smitty out of town—probably head up to Glen Ellen and check out Stover's place again."

"Stover's. Why? We went over it pretty well."

"Yeah. And someone shot you because there must have been something we missed."

"Well, okay. But you should know that we have received an escaped fugitive warrant for your buddy. It just came over the wire."

"Shit."

"Yeah, shit. You better get him to turn himself in before some trigger happy cop finds him. Anyway, keep in touch. I'll do everything I can to help you on this end."

"Rich."

Huh?"

"A panda? All this over some fucking bears?"

"Go figure."

"Thanks."

"Oh, and Gabe..."

"What?"

"Take care of yourself pal, and call your wife would you."

Feinberg disconnected the call. "A Panda. Shit."

Smitty stepped out of the bathroom with a towel wrapped around him.

"You have some extra underwear. I pissed in mine."

* * *

Chapter 25

San Francisco

Lee went to the window of his Fairmont Hotel room and looked out onto Union Square. A light rain was falling and people were rushing around as if it were a downpour. They were mostly tourists decked out in summer clothes. Someone had failed to tell them that San Francisco was cold and wet in the summer.

He took off his coat and laid it on the bed. Then he took out his 9mm Beretta Px4 and put it on the table to be cleaned, and poured himself a generous shot of Scotch. He was still angry. He hoped Mac had gotten the message, but the meeting left a bad taste in his mouth. He had made the trip back to Washington to make a point, and to force the State Department to call off their dogs, but now he realized he had made two mistakes; first by letting his old comrade know of his misgivings about the mission in the first place; and second by storming back into Washington like a irate cuckold husband. He took a long drink from the glass of Scotch and silently cursed his stupidity for trusting McCraven.

He was jarred from his thoughts by knocking on the door. He had left word at the desk that he was not to be disturbed. He tried to ignore it, but whoever it was was persistent. He picked up the Beretta from the table and went to the door.

"I said I didn't want to be disturbed. Can't you read? That's why they make those signs."

"Open up, Agent Lee."

"Who the fuck are you?"

"Just open the door, goddamnit."

Lee left the chain on the door and turned the knob, opening it just enough to see outside. His eyes were greeted by an open wallet with ID and a badge. Frank Duggart, Bureau Chief, Federal Bureau of Investigation, New York.

"Frank Duggart. The Frank Duggart?"

"Open the fucking door, Lee."

He slipped the chain off and opened up. The man walked in. "Close and chain the door."

Lee did as told. "Frank Duggart."

"You know me?"

"Who in government service hasn't heard of Frank Duggart, the man who told Hoover to go fuck himself and lived to tell about it. Drink?"

"I'll pass."

Lee went and retrieved his glass. "Twelve year old Scotch."

"Gave it up a long time ago. Listen Lee, I didn't come all the way out here to shoot the bull. I know who you are and what you do for the NSA, and I don't approve."

"You come all the way from New York to tell me that?"

Duggart sat down on the side of the bed. He was feeling his age. It had been years since he had done any fieldwork, and the quick trip across the country and time change were catching up with him.

"First off, why don't you put down the weapon."

Lee looked at the pistol in his hand for a moment, and then put it back on the table.

"That's better. I came to warn you."

"Warn me of what?"

"Well, there's some folks at State and NSA who are questioning your loyalty."

"And how do you know this?"

"I have my sources. We know all about the operation with the Chinese, the armed assault on the Glen Ellen ranch, the pandas, and the contract on Isaac Smith. This is a blatant violation of the Constitution and the authority of any government agency..."

"Whoa there partner," Lee interrupted. "What armed assault? Pandas? What the fuck are you talking about?"

Duggart looked at the NSA man, as if searching his face for some sign of duplicity. "You don't know, do you?"

"The only thing I know is what I read in the FBI files. Pandas?"

"That's what this whole goddamn mess is about. The Chinese were trying to cover up the fact that three young pandas, their National Treasure, were smuggled out of the country right under their Communist noses. They couldn't stand the international embarrassment I suppose."

"How do you know all this?"

"Because Isaac Smith is in the custody of the Bureau. Well not exactly the official FBI, but under my jurisdiction. My agent witnessed the whole thing."

"Don't tell me; Agent Feinberg."

"Yes, him and his partner. Anyway, this Mei-ling woman had traced the smugglers to a ranch in the hills above the small Sonoma County town of Glen Ellen last year. Apparently, she had contacted the Chinese Consulate in San Francisco, but she dragged Smith up to the ranch in case the smugglers tried to move the bears. I don't know what her plan was, but they ended up getting caught. Luckily my agents had been watching them and were able to pull them out just when a Black Hawk helicopter touched down. Commandos—I suspect private contractors hired by your people—killed the smugglers in a firefight and torched the place, bears and all."

The two men sat in silence for a minute, just staring at one another. Then Lee gulped down the scotch and stood up to refill his glass. The pieces were all falling into place.

"I think I'll take that drink," Duggart said. He took the glass Lee offered and took a sip. The warmth felt good sliding down his throat like an old friend. "Good Scotch. So, the way I see it, there's some people in State with some of your buddies at NSA who are involved in some deep shit, and it stinks to high heaven as far as I'm concerned. That's why they want Isaac Smith silenced. And, from what I hear, you're not comfortable with the operation, and have been asking some embarrassing questions."

"How do you know that?"

"Can't be in the Bureau for as many years as I have without cultivating friends. My source said you confirmed their suspicions when you chased off their hired hit man at the Berkeley Marina." He took another sip from the scotch and let his words hang in the air.

"So, they've put out a contract on me."

"That's why I'm here. To warn you."

Lee wandered over to the window facing Union Square and stared out as if expecting to see something that hadn't been there before. Then he gulped down his drink and mumbled just loud enough for Duggart to hear. "Cocksuckers."

The FBI man stared at Lee's back for a long moment. There was nothing more to say. He glanced at his watch.

"Well, I've said what I came here to say. I need to get back to New

York. It's far too cold here for me."

He left the glass of scotch on the end table and made his way to the door, glanced back at the NSA hit man who sat on the side of the bed staring into his own glass, and then let himself out.

* * *

Chapter 26

Glen Ellen, Norther California

The girl behind the check-in counter stared at the two men. "I know you guys. But not together," she said.

Feinberg was signing the guest register. Smitty stood behind him.

"You think?" Feinberg grunted.

"I pride myself for remembering faces, but you two don't fit. Oh, I remember. You," she nodded toward Smitty. "You were with that good looking Asian chick. Right?"

Smitty nodded noncommittally.

"And you ... oh yeah, you're that FBI guy. You had a partner. You were asking about this guy. I see you found him."

Feinberg finished registering and looked into the girl's eyes. "This is official FBI business. This man is in my custody and I expect you to cooperate by not talking to anyone about our being here."

"Oh yes. Of course, sir." She handed Feinberg a key. "Room twenty-four, top of the stairs. Welcome to the Jack London Inn."

Smitty was glad it wasn't the same room he had shared with Mei-ling on there last night together when she made passionate, urgent love to him. Too many memories.

Feinberg got Smity up early. They went downstairs to the restaurant, had a quick breakfast and hit the road. The bright Spring sun came out and heated up the car's interior. Feinberg shed his jacket.

It was all too familiar to Smitty. Through the small town, past the Country Store, on up to the junction with Highway 12, north to Trinity Drive, then up the winding road into the hills that made up the eastern ridge of the Valley of the Moon. They almost passed Wall Road. It had been early morning the last time he had been there, a dark starless night until a full moon rose over the hills casting an eerie blue light over the entire valley.

They had been a raiding party of two—a fool's errand. It was the second time out, and he feared they would fare no better than the first when they were nearly cremated in the Oakland Hills fire after being caught by the smugglers. But Mei-ling was determined, and he couldn't let her go alone

Feinberg slowed as they approached the rusty sign leading up Wall Road until they saw the For Sale sign slashed across the wooden plank announcing Stover's Winery.

Smitty laughed. "Winery."

"What's so funny?"

"Old man Stover changed the name of the ranch to winery. He told everyone that since everyone else in the valley with a couple of acres were growing grapes and calling themselves wineries, he'd do the same. But there's not a grape vine anywhere."

"Last time I was here there wasn't anything here."

He made a right off of Wall and slowly drove up the rutted gravel road until they got to the gate. It was open. Feinberg stopped the car and got out. He walked to the front of the car, and looked down the gravel road leading to where the ranch house once stood. Something was not right, but he couldn't put his finger on what exactly. Then he got back into the car.

"What's up," Smitty asked.

"Been some traffic through these gates recently."

"Yeah. Well, the place is up for sale. Someone probably been looking at it."

"Of course, that probably explains it."

He put the car into gear and proceeded slowly down the road to where he and Berman had inspected what was left of Stover's Winery. The lot had been cleaned up; the charred hulks of vehicles towed away, the ground raked clean. Feinberg stopped the car next to a blackened tree stump in the center of the lot where he remembered the ranch house was.

"Stay in the car," he instructed Smitty. He got out and looked around. It was quiet—too quiet; no birds, no bees humming ... nothing. He scanned the trees and brush that covered the hillside behind the property, a hodgepodge of scrub pine, eucalyptus and oak, with a carpet of chaparral, yellow blooming acacia and black berry bushes white with blossoms; perfect cover for anyone wanting to hide. Then he noticed what appeared to be a break in the scrub and trees before it continued on up the hill. He must have overlooked it the last time he was there—probably a fire road not shown on maps. His eyes caught a glint of reflected light from the trees. A car.

"Say, what's going on," Smitty called.

He had opened the car door and was starting to get out, just as Feinberg saw the flash.

"Duck!" he yelled as he hit the ground behind the tree stump with his 9mm drawn. The glass on the open car door shattered into a million pieces.

 He glanced back at the car. No Smitty.

"Izzy, you okay?."

"I think so," Smitty shouted back.

"Keep down, and when I start firing get the fuck out of here."

"What about you, Gabe?"

"Just do what I tell you goddamnit."

Another flash and the bullet pierced the windshield.

Feinberg opened up on the location of the flash. "Get the fuck out of here!" he yelled.

Smitty kept low in the car and slid into the driver's seat. The engine was still on. He managed to get the transmission into drive and stomped on the pedal. He didn't dare sit up. He made a fishtail U-turn just as another bullet struck the trunk. He could hear Feinberg's gun blasting away, so he sat up enough to see where he was going, and headed up the road through the cloud of dust.

Feinberg rolled over on his back, ejecting the spent clip from his automatic, pulled a new clip off his shoulder holster and reloaded his gun while watching Smitty speed out the gate. He rolled back onto his belly and pointed to where he remembered the flash of the sniper rifle. Another shot smashed into the tree stump, beginning a standoff that lasted about ten minutes. He fired a couple of shots. The sniper returned fire. Finally there was no answer to his blind shots at the trees. The sniper was gone. He heard a car start up and saw the dust rise from the break in the tree line. Whoever it was, he wasn't after Feinberg and he had to be pretty annoyed by now; twice missing his mark; twice being chased off.

He stood up and wiped the dust from his pants and shirt when he noticed his hand shaking. Then he realized he was marooned. The cell phone drove off with his jacket with Smitty. "Shit!" He put his automatic into its holster and started to walk.

The sun beat down hot as he made his way down Wall Road. It hadn't occurred to him how far they had driven. Walking gave a sense of distance, and everything seemed further with no points of reference like on New York's streets. The heat from the asphalt soaked through the rubber soles of his sports shoes. His thoughts drifted as he walked, resting on his wife and their last conversation. Would she file for divorce? God knows she had every reason to. But they had two kids, and he loved them, and when it got down to it, he loved his wife. He had neglected her and the kids. And he hated the suburbs where her father had bought them a house. He probably should give up the apartment in the city and go home to his family at night like everyone else.

His throat was parched. He sat down on the side of road. Didn't anyone ever travel on Wall Road? It was like being stranded on a desert island. He thought about walking up one of the dirt driveways leading to who knew where, or who or what was at the end. He dismissed the thought.

Hopefully Izzy hadn't returned to the Jack London Inn. It was sure the assassin knew that was where they were staying and he was just desperate enough to make a rash move. He got up and started walking again with a sense of urgency. He had no faith that his charge would be smart enough to figure it out.

Finally he saw the junction with Trinity Drive just as a pickup truck rounded the corner. He waved his arms desperately hoping whoever was driving would be foolish enough to pick up a stranger on a lonely road wearing a shoulder holster..

The truck stopped and a familiar face looked out at him; old man Toliver from the Glen Ellen Country store.

"There you are Agent Feinberg. Thought I'd have to go all the way to Stovers, and hopefully not find you dead," Toliver smiled. "Brought my medical kit just in case."

"How'd you know I was stranded up there without a car?"

"That fella—said his name was Smitty—stopped by the store and told me to come retrieve you. Said some guy was trying to kill you. Get in."

"Where'd he go?"

Toliver ground the gear into reverse and backed out of Wall Road onto Trinity, ground it back into first and headed back to civilization. "Didn't say. Just handed me your jacket here and said you needed rescuing."

They drove down the hill toward the valley floor and Glen Ellen.

"I remember that Smith guy. He stopped by the store last year and I gave him directions to Stover's. Lots of folks were looking for Stover's including yourself and your partner, Agent Berman was it; the fellow I patched up? Anyway, Smith had this pretty Asian lady waiting in the car. Yeah, I remember him. How is Agent Berman doing?"

"He's fine. You did good work."

"How's come he's not with you?" Toliver persisted.

"Said the West Coast is too dangerous. He prefers New York."

* * *

Chapter 27

Oakland China Town

After stopping off at the country store Smitty headed straight for Oakland without looking back. Hunted by a paid assassin, not to mention the cops., he wasn't sure where he could go. For all he knew he was a murder suspect, and in Oakland cop parlance that meant shoot on site. He felt bad about leaving Gabe, but he had no choice. The FBI agent was either dead or making his way back to Glen Ellen. In either case, Toliver would find him.

It was early afternoon. Spring may have sprung everywhere else in Northern California, but the Bay Area was shrouded in a cold grayness. Where could he hide out? The cops would most likely be watching the Lakeshore apartment, and he didn't want to drag Dede and Chanel into it anyway. Who knew what was happening with Ted. His wife could be back from Vietnam with her mother, and besides, the cops would surely be watching him.

He found himself getting off I-80 at the Chinatown exit. Something was drawing him to Mei-ling's house. It could have been sold sold far ss hr knew, but if it was vacant it would make a good place to cool out. He found himself slowly moving through the usual Chinatown stop and go, maneuvering around double parked cars and deliver trucks, to the small two story wooden framed house on Jefferson. No For Sale sign, but that didn't mean anything. It had been nearly six month. If it had been sold, the new owners would have moved in by now. But he wanted to see for himself. He still had the key Mei-ling had given him. Luckily a car was pulling out from the curb across the street from the house. He quickly pulled into it before someone else claimed the rare parking spot.

He got out of the car and looked around. He was a marked man. The cops were looking for him. He was scared, but in a bizarre way, exhilarated at the same time. He climbed the steps to the front door. He waited for a minute and then knocked. After several long minutes he heard footsteps. Damn, someone must have moved in and he'd be shit out of luck. The door slowly opened. Then... a familiar pair of eyes peered out.

"Who's there?"

He knew that voice, the voice he had been hearing in his waking hours and his dreams.

"Mei-ling?"

"Isaac. Is that you?"

The door swung open and the next thing he knew Mei-ling was in his arms.

* * *

Chapter 28

San Francisco

The afternoon sun peeked out from under the overcast as it set in the west, casting a shadow across the front of the Fairmont Hotel. Lee sat on a bench watching the continuous cast of characters entering and exiting San Francisco's premier hotel. His first thought was to check out after Frank Duggart's warning. There was no reason not to believe the man. But instead of checking out and running like any sane man would, he decided to flush out his would-be assassins. He spotted them immediately—two men entering the hotel lobby. To the untrained eye, they would seem like two businessmen; but Lee had been in the business for a long time and could sniff out a company man or an assassin from a crowd. He checked his Rolex. It would take them about twenty minutes to check on his room number, break-in, search the place, and plant their bugs to overhear anything that went on in the room.

"Hey mister. Give me a dollar."

Lee's attention turned to the raggedy looking young man with long hair and beard who had dropped down onto the bench next to him.

"Huh?"

"You heard me motherfucker. I said give me a fucking dollar."

Lee smiled. "You got to be kidding, pal. That's the worst strong arm I ever seen."

"Huh?"

"That may work on old ladies and tourists, but you really should be more careful about who you pull that shit on."

Lee opened his coat revealing his shoulder holster holding the Beretta automatic

"Oh shit man, I'm sorry. Please, don't arrest me."

Lee saw the fear in the kid's eyes. "I'm not a cop, pal. Now here's five bucks and get the fuck out of my face," Lee said, handing the man the money.

An astonished look of relief showed through the man's scraggle whiskers. He grabbed the fiver and ran.

"Fucking San Francisco," Lee said, and then shifted his eyes back across the street. He spotted the men trying to get around a group of Japanese tourists. Mission accomplished, they hurried up Powell Street and crossed Post where a White Panel truck was parked with orange traffic cones around it. Lee saw the men rap on the door of the truck as they passed and then disappear down Powell. He got up from the bench and walked across the street, dodging a cable car and pushing his way past the Japanese tourists.

He made his way through the elegant classical lobby and went up to the check-in counter where an older man in a meticulously neat black suit and bright yellow bow-tie asked if he could be of assistance.

"Room 1415," Lee said.

The man checked the computer. "Marshall Lee?"

"Yes."

"What can I do for you sir?"

"Did two men just ask for me?"

"Hmmmm. I don't recall, but maybe Miss Young would know," he said, calling over a neat young woman dressed in a too tight blazer with Fairmont Hotel embroidered on the pocket.

"Oh sure. I gave them your room number. Why not?"

"Privacy might be one reason," Lee said.

The woman flushed and rushed off to tend to another group of Japanese tourists.

"The Fairmont make it a habit of giving out people's room numbers?"

The older man frowned. "That would never have happened in the old days. These new kids working here, they don't think. I'm sorry if it's caused an inconvenience. I'll get the manager if you wish to lodge a complaint."

"That's alright. What's done is done. I'll be checking out in the morning. Can you call the Oakland Hyatt for me and make a reservation for tomorrow?"

"Right away, Mr Lee."

"Call me to confirm."

He took the elevator up to his room. No sign of a search, not that there was much to find. A very professional job. These weren't hired contractors, or if they were, they were very good. Probably NSA, handpicked by his buddy McCraven no doubt. Not a job for the open market. He probably knew them. He made a quick check of the phone; bugged as he suspected. He made a call to the Oakland Tribune and connected to Ted Harlin's answering machine.

"This is Marshall Lee. We met the other day in your kitchen you might recall. Important that we meet tomorrow. I'll be staying at the

Oakland Hyatt in downtown. Contact me there."

He poured himself a glass of scotch, lit a cigarette and sat down at the chair overlooking Union Square, trying to make sense of his new role hunted rather than hunter...a rogue agent.. All those years of service to his country and now he was slated for elimination. The funny thing was he hadn't made up his mind about the Smith assignment yet, despite his strong doubts. Whoever was behind this operation, besides his old comrade, McCraven, were so paranoid they were taking no chances. His time was up. It made sense. Hadn't he participated in such actions himself? Sure, he could have gone along with the program and killed Smith, but something about it stuck in his craw. Maybe it was his sense of romance; the unlikely love story; Smith and Mei-ling. Besides, he would probably be eliminated, even if he carried out the assignment. These guys would want to cover their tracks, especially after what Duggart described as a commando attack on American soil on behalf of a foreign country. But what really pissed him off was McCraven. He suspected his old pal was orchestrating the whole thing.

The phone rang. It was the man at the desk. His reservation was made. Just the message he wanted his assassins to hear.

He finished his Scotch and snubbed the cigarette out. Then he put his shoulder holster and coat back on and headed out the door. It was time to put the rest of his plan in motion.

He spotted the aggressive young panhandler holding up a lamp post.. The young man saw Lee approaching him and looked around in a panic.

"Hold on there pal. I got a proposition for you."

The man stayed put somewhat reluctantly. "What do you want with me? You want our five bucks back?"

"No. Just hear me out and there's a hundred bucks in it for you"

The man's bloodshot eyes lite up, and a sly smile peered out from underneath his unkempt whiskers. "A hundred dollars?"

"Yes. You interested?"

"Always. Who do I have to kill?"

Lee laughed. "No one. You just have to come with me. We'll have to clean you up."

The man tailed after Lee back across the street into the Fairmont. The doorman tried to stop the young panhandler, but Lee assured him that he was with him.

Inside Lee headed straight for the hotel barber shop. He told the young man to take a seat in the chair and instructed the barber to shave off his whiskers and give him a haircut. The young man said nothing.

Next they went to the men's clothing store. Lee picked him out a sports coat, slacks and a fedora hat, all similar to what he was wearing.

"That's better, my friend. You almost look handsome."

He then took the young man up to his room.

"You want me to take a shower and get ready."

"Yes. Take a shower, put on your new clothes and I'll take you out for dinner."

"Is that all you want?"

"For now," Lee said.

The Tonga Room in the Fairmont was art deco tropical harping back to the 50';; the kind a place you'd see in a Rita Hayward black and white flick. Lee and the young man, now presentable with his clean face and new clothes, went to the Hurricane Bar. Lee ordered a scotch rocks. He looked at his young companion who had identified himself as Jimmy.

"Drink?"

"Anything I want?"

"Sure, Knock yourself out."

"Long Island Ice Tea?"

"You know what that is?"

"Not really, but some guys were talking about it. Said it's got a kick."

"You heard the man," Lee said to the bartender.

They didn't talk until the bartender set their drinks in front of them, complete with paper umbrellas which Lee immediately discarded.

"So, you been on the streets a long time?" Lee said, not really caring.

"About a year. I got kicked out of Berkeley over some Frat shit and was ashamed to tell my folks. I didn't have any money and have been hustling since then."

"Well, my advice is to use the hundred bucks I'm going to give you and go home." But he knew the kid would probably use the money to buy his drug of choice and end up back on the street. It didn't matter.

"What do you want from me?" he said, sipping the tall drink with the umbrella in it. "I'll do whatever you want."

Lee looked at the young man. "No pal. You got the wrong idea."

"But I thought you wanted to...."

"No kid, you're not my type. I'll explain to you what I want you to do. Now enjoy your—what did you call it— Long Island Ice Tea, and listen closely."

The young man did as he was told.

"You're going to spend the night here, but not with me. In the morning I want you to dress in the clothes we bought. Then you're going to go down to the garage and give them the room number. You will tell them you're picking up the car. It's a Cadallic Sedan de Ville. I'll make arrangements so you don't get hassled. You know how to drive don't you?"

The young man nodded affirmative.

Lee took out his cigarettes and offered one. The young man, Jimmy, begged off.

Lee lit up and blew out a stream of blue smoke. Then you're going to drive to the Oakland Hyatt Hotel. You know it?"

Jimmy nodded again, pushing the little umbrella aside and sucking on the straw in his drink.

"Good. You'll drive up to the front and give the valet your keys and go into the hotel..."

Lee sipped his drank and sat silently for a minute.

"And?"

"And nothing. You hang around the lobby for a while and then you're on your way. You never met me. Clear?"

"That's all?"

"That's it. But if you fuck up I will find you and I will kill you. Now finish your drink and we'll have dinner. They have a great seafood buffet."

. . .

Chapter 29

Oakland

The sun flowed into Mei-ling's bedroom illuminating the two weary naked bodies on the bed. They had been up most of the night telling their stories between bouts of passionate love making. Both had left out important details of the separation over the past months since Mei-ling had returned to China; neither wanting to say anything that would interfere with the moment.

Smitty looked up from a plate of scrambled eggs and spam he was eating, calmly listening as Mei-ling told him about how she ended up back in Oakland. All the tension and fear that had built up inside of him over the past several days poured out in a tirade. "What the fuck are you telling me; that having escaped China, Rick, of all people, snatches you up off the streets of Hong Kong; literally kidnaps you, and then whisks you away to Macau. And, after all we went through you make a deal with him, dragging you, and me, back into the middle of this *meshuggeneh* Panda shit..."

"Isaac, keep your voice down. And stop swearing my love."

"Don't 'my love' me." And against his better judgment he blurted out what was happening with himself. "Not only have I got professional assassins hunting me and a warrant out for my arrest, now you want to drag us back into this shit? Mei, you don't owe them anything. You did your part, and for all we know the Pandas were destroyed. Now they're telling you one ... one fucking bear got away and they want you to find it."

She reached across the table and put her hand on his. "Isaac, is this true. Why is anyone trying to kill you? Rick reassured me the Chinese Government had no more interest in you. And how come the police are looking for you?"

"Never mind that. If a bear was taken from the ranch before we got there, that was months ago. How do we know it hasn't been sold and is living in some Saudi prince's private zoo!"

"My love," she said soothingly. "I made a deal with them. If we can find this last panda they will give us a million dollars and move us to anywhere in the world we want to go. Isaac, it's just like what you always wanted for us. We could buy any boat you want and sail anywhere we want."

"And you believed them. Mei, I can't believe you're so naïve."

It was her turn to get mad. She pulled a pack of Dunhill cigarettes she had bought in Macau, and lit one up.

"Damn it, Isaac. I was thinking of us. I have no reason to believe Rick was lying. The money is on deposit in a Caribbean bank. If you don't want to help me, well, I'll look myself and when I find it I'll send for you."

"Shit," Smitty said. "I didn't mean to fucking upset you. Of course I'll help you. You didn't think I'd let you out of my sight again. I just think it's hopeless. But at least it will get me out of the Bay Area and away from all my problems. And we'll be together."

She smiled and handed Smitty her cigarette to smoke. "These are really good, sweetheart. And don't swear so much."

He took a drag and handed her back the Dunhill. "I like my Luckys better," he smiled.

* * *

Chapter 30

Alameda

It was late morning when Ted pulled up to his house. He left work early after his wife had called. She had recently returned from Vietnam with not only her mother, but her aging aunt as well. He heard what he thought was a tone of panic in her voice. While she didn't say what was wrong, he had images of Immigration threatening to send his in-laws back to Saigon, which would have been all right with him, but would upset his wife awfully.

He saw the Black SUV parked in front and figured he was right, but when he walked in, he was met by a scene he hadn't seen since he was covering the war in Nam; a man, dressed in all black clothing with a balaclava hiding his face and holding an AK47 on the three Vietnamese women. He could see the terror in the older women's faces. His wife had a bruise on her cheek, but a look of defiance.

"What the fuck's going on here?" he said.

Then he felt the cold steel sticking in his ribs.

"Just take it easy and nobody needs to get hurt," a voice behind him said. "Now pull up a chair and sit down, Mister Harlin."

"Fuck this. Just who the hell are you?" he shouted, forgetting the gun in his ribs and turning toward the voice behind him.

He was meet with the steel butt of the gun, knocking him back into the chair and rattling his teeth so hard that he tore a piece of his inner cheek. He could taste the blood begin to fill his mouth and hear his wife screaming far off. His eyes finally came back into focus. The man standing in front of him also wore a balaclava, and was wearing black, but his weapon of choice was a MK23 automatic which Ted had already been introduced to.

"Teddy, you all right?" his wife's voice floated in through the fog.

"It's ok, sweetheart," He heard the words dribble from his throbbing mouth after spitting out a glob of blood.

"Fine. Now that we know everyone's fine, I have a question for you Mister Harlin. You cooperate with me and we'll leave you and your little family of rice eaters alone."

"I'm all ears," Ted said.

"You received a call from a man identifying himself as Marshal Lee yesterday. He asked you to meet him at the Downtown Hyatt. Is this correct?"

Ted looked at the man with a blank expression. "Huh?" was all he could force out of his sore mouth.

"You heard me. Marshell Lee. He's with the National Security Service. He contacted you yesterday."

Ted remembered that the man who had broken into his house and was looking for Smitty said his name was Lee, but he hadn't heard from him since. "I'm sorry, buddy. I don't know what you're talking about."

"Don't lie to me, Harlin. We overheard his telephone message to your office. We know you were in your office this morning. Don't you listen to your fucking messages?"

Ted wiped the blood that now trickled out the side of his mouth.

"Yes I do. And no, I didn't get a message from this Lee person."

Ted thought he heard the front door open, but it was probably just the wind and wishful thinking.

"Goddamnit," the man shouted. "You start talking or we're going to kill your little harem of rice eaters here."

Ted craned his neck and caught a glimpse of the man behind him grab his wife by the hair and hold a knife to her throat. He could see the terror in his wife's eyes.

"No. Don't hurt her," Harlin said in panic. "I'll tell you whatever you want. Just don't . . ."

Suddenly a new voice shouted from the doorway.

"FBI. Hold it right there!"

Ted looked back. Gabe Feinberg was standing in the doorway with his ID out and gun in hand.

"Drop your weapons now!" Feinberg ordered.

The man with the knife looked up. The other man stood frozen, and then slowly raised his hand with the gun in the air and turned around facing Feinberg.

"There's two of us. You think you can stop us both without hitting one of these civilians, FBI man?"

"Look buddy. I've had a bad week. I'll shoot the whole bunch of you if that's what it takes. I don't give a fuck."

There was a moment of silence, and then suddenly the man holding Ted's wife grabbed his AK47 and blindly opened fire. Ted felt the bullets rush by his head as he dropped to the floor. Gabe dove to his right as the stream of bullets smashed into a china cabinet behind him. Then there was a blood curdling scream, and the old woman, cringing next to Ted's mother-in-law, grabbed the gunman from behind. The rest of the bullets smashed into the wall and shattered the door frame sending wooden chips flying. It was as if all the fear and anger she remembered from the

Vietnam War came rushing back into the old woman and she was going to take her revenge. A long kitchen knife appeared in her hand and she jammed it into the man's throat. Gabe opened fire from his position on the floor and hit the other man in the chest just as he got a burst of shots off in the direction of the old woman.

The room went deathly silent as gun smoke drifted up and the smell of gun powder permeated the air. Then the mother-in-law screamed and started to wail. Ted stood up and went to his wife who folded up in his arms weeping. Her mother-in-law was holding her sister in her arms; rocking back and forth as blood trickled from a hole in the old woman's head and her eyes were wide open as if she was seeing her ancestors coming for her.

Ted poured two mugs of coffee and brought them over to the kitchen table where Gabe was sitting. Ted's wife had taken her mother upstairs to calm her down.

It had been a couple of hours since the cops had arrived, the questions answered, and the bodies carried out. Thanks to Gabe being an FBI agent, and Ted a respected crime reporter, the cops settled for *we'll come down to the station to file statements.*

"Say, aren't you the two guys that sprung Isaac Smith?" one of the cops asked.

"Yeah. Why?" Gabe said, hoping the man wouldn't ask where Smitty was.

"Well, tell your boy he's off the hook."

"Why? What's happened?"

"The woman came out of the coma last night. Seems she's going to be okay, and she cleared Smith of the crime. So, when you see him, give him the news and tell him she's been asking for him. Oh, and have him stop by the station when he has time. We got some questions to ask him and he needs to sign some forms."

Gabe and Ted looked at each other in disbelief.

"I'll do that," Gabe said. "He'll be relieved to hear the news."

Gabe dumped two heaping teaspoonfuls of sugar into the steaming coffee with the Oakland A's insignia decorating the mug. He lifted it to his mouth and noticed his hands were still shaking.

Ted had poured himself a glass of vodka and was nursing it. "So, just what the fuck is this all about, and who the hell is Marshall Lee?" he said, almost accusatory, as if it was Gabe's fault the two men had terrorized his family. "My wife's auntie for gods sake."

"Marshall Lee..." Feinberg said, more to himself than Ted.

"Yes. Who is he, this guy that almost got my family murdered? Shit, my marriage was shaky as it was. This ought to put the lid on it."

"Marshall Lee. Well, He's the guy people in the intelligence agencies use to scare their kids. Like, you'd better behave or I'll get Marshall Lee after you. He works for the NSA; well actually the National Security Service. Marshall Lee is the man in charge of all covert assassinations throughout the world. If these guys were looking for him, it appears he's either gone rogue, or someone else is seriously trying to kill him. For what is anyone's guess, but I'll bet it has to do with our pal Izzy." He took another sip of the coffee.

"Smitty? Where is Smitty. I thought he was with you. He'll want to know about the woman. Shit. There's a hell of a story here if I can put it together."

* * *

Chapter 31

Lincoln Monument/Washington, DC

McCraven took his routine afternoon walk from the State Department to the Lincoln Memorial. He considered it his daily constitutional; the only exercise he got. He liked sitting in front of the memorial and contemplating Lincoln's response to the threat to the union during the Civil War, and it somehow made him feel exonerated for his own deviations from the Constitution in the name of national security. What a great invention; Homeland Security. It gave him license to do anything he wanted. But none of this was secret within the intelligence community. After the JFK assassination, it was clear that the restraints were off. There were no boundaries if it threatened the military domination of the United States. When Congress placed restraints on the CIA after it was discovered they had been dealing with the Iranians, the NSA, under the State Department, picked up the ball. There would never again be a president of the United States who would challenge their power.

These were the things McCraven pondered while looking up at the statue of the Great Emancipator.

He hadn't gotten much sleep over the past week after approving the elimination of his old pal, not because he was his old pal, but because Lee was no fool. He was, in fact, one of the most dangerous and intelligent agents McCraven ever knew. He was asking too many questions; had too many doubts. Marshall Lee was a true patriot. He believed in the Constitution, and believed he was protecting that piece of paper against all enemies. But it was clear he couldn't justify the elimination of Isaac Smith, and if he found out why Smith had to be killed, he would possibly blow the whistle on the whole operation. When he knew the truth he would not only object, but fight back. There was no alternative; Lee had to go.

It was a warm day in the Capital and he found his eyes growing heavy and finally closing.

The next thing his knew he was awakened by the feel of cold steel poking into his ribs. His eyes opened.

"So Lee. You've come for me at last. I was expecting you."

"I doubt that," Lee said.

"I knew you'd spot our team right off."

He felt the gun dig deeper into his rib cage.

"You know, I've done a lot of questionable things for my country, but conducting military operations on U.S. soil for a foreign power ... Jesus Mac, what were you thinking?"

"I thought I told you all about it."

"Yes, you told me we were allowing the Chinese to conduct investigations within the confines of San Francisco and Oakland Chinatowns in return for cutting one of our assets lose. Well, okay, tit for tat. But seems to me you went too far with this thing. I'll tell you, I was willing to go along for a while, despite my misgivings; but you people seem to think my usefulness is at an end. You, you sonofabitch, my old pal, put a kill order out on me. After all we've been through; Vietnam, Eastern Europe, Congo, Chile. How many times did I pull your ass out of the fire. And now...for Chrissake, Mac, fucking Panda bears."

McCraven just dropped his head onto his chest and shrugged his shoulders as he felt the gun slide up to right under his chin.

"Who else is involved in this caper of yours?"

McCraven turned his head, pressing against the barrel of the gun, and looked at Lee. "You don't seriously think I'm going to tell you that..."

"No, I suppose not..." Lee whispered as he squeezed the trigger.

The muffled shot was the last thing McCraven heard. Lee was an expert, sending the low caliber bullet through McCraven's throat to the back of his skull, knocking out all motor responses, and then spinning along the top of the skull to become imbedded in the frontal lobes, confining any bleeding to inside the brain.

McCraven slouched into the bench. Lee sat him up; stuck his hat over his face, wrapped his dead hand around the gun, and then walked away.

* * *

Chapter 32

Oakland China Town

Smitty was sitting at the kitchen table sipping a cup of morning coffee when he heard someone knocking on the door. He had been sequestered for four days. Mei-ling wouldn't allow him to leave until she could arrange to get them away. She had gone out to buy some groceries, and now someone was knocking at the door. Must be Mei-ling. Maybe she forgot to take her keys, but better not to take chances.

He got up, grabbed Mei-ling's Takarov that a Russian officer had given her many years ago, and went to the front door and opened it a crack. He saw a man in a light colored London Fog rain coat and wide brimmed hat holding a copy of the Oakland Tribune.

"Don't sweat it pal, if I was an assassin you'd be dead by now. Now open the door. I have good news for you if you haven't already heard."

Smitty opened the door with one hand, holding the gun with the other. The man crossed the threshold and closed the door behind him.

"Put the weapon away, Smith. Like I said, if I was going to kill you, you'd be dead."

"Well, you know who I am. Who the fuck are you," Smitty said, still pointing the pistol at the man's mid section.

"Names Lee ... Marshall Lee. Say, that's a TT-30," he said eyeing the pistol in Smitty's shaky hand. "Haven't seen one of those since my CIA days."

"Never mind. What do you want?"

"Seems you and I have something in common, Mister Smith ... or do you prefer Smitty?"

"Smitty's fine," he said, lowering the gun.

"Good. Now, is that fresh coffee I smell,?" the man said and walked past Smitty toward the kitchen.

"Whoa buddy. Just what the fuck are you doing?"

"Getting a cup of coffee. I haven't had any this morning."

Smitty followed behind the man as he breezed past him heading for the kitchen, then stood dumbfounded as the man helped himself to a mug, filled it from the half empty pot and sat down at the table. Smitty sat down across from him. The man put the newspaper on the table and pushed it to him.

"Page two, Local section," he said.

Smitty took the paper and opened it up. A small item on page two:

"It's by your buddy, Ted Harlin I believe."

Smitty read it:

Assault Victim Comes out of Coma.

A woman identifid as Patrisha Rivers, 39, who was shot on her boat in the Alameda Marina ten days ago and had been in a coma ever since, regained consciousness.

Police had been looking for suspect Isaac Smith since the shooting. But now Rivers has cleared Smith of any wrong doing, and asked to see him, claiming they had been good friends and that he would never harm her.

Smith had been apprehended at the scene of the attack, but it appeared he had also been badly beaten up. The police, however, considered him a prime suspect.

Police sources say Smith was released into the custody of the FBI, but later put out an arrest warrant after local FBI officials said they had no knowledge of the
case...

Smitty stared at the open paper. The article went on, but he had read
enough. "Thank god," he said under his breath. He tried to conjure up a
vision of Trish; sitting behind her desk in her tight white shorts with her
long tanned silky legs spread slightly apart; her blue eyes smiling at him
as he stood in the galley cooking. But all he could see was her laying face
up on her bed, her long blond hair fanned out around her, and the trickle
of blood that oozed from her scalp and flowed down in red rivulets forming a red puddle on the pillow. There had never been any talk of love
or permanency between them. They were just two lonely people finding
comfort in one another the only way they knew how.

Suddenly the slamming of the front door sent his thoughts flying out
the open kitchen window into the small space between the houses, and
his eyes looked up to where Mei-ling stood in the door gazing at the two
men sitting at her kitchen table.

"What's going on, Isaac? Who's this man?"

Lee stood up and smiled. "Well, if it isn't the infamous Mei-ling Wu,"
he said. "Let me take those groceries for you."

"I can manage on my own," she said, and turned her back to them to
set the bag on the counter. She had no way of knowing that he had been
thinking about Trish, but Smitty oddly felt like a husband caught cheating by his wife. She was wearing a short green summer dress that clung
to her round hips. Smitty notice the man across from him watching her
as she took several things from the bag and went into the small service
porch where she kept the refrigerator.

"I can see why you got yourself involved in this mess," Lee said.

Smitty just stared at the man.

"So just who the hell is this Isaac?" Mei-ling snapped as she stepped back into the kitchen with the small automatic pistol she kept in her purse. She never swore. '

"Says his name's Lee. He's the man trying to kill me."

"Was assigned to kill you. If I wanted you dead, Smitty, you'd be dead by now. Or I'd have let the punk in the marina parking lot finish you off."

That was you?" Smitty remembered the shots being fired and the two cars driving out of the parking lot while he was hunched behind the gate to docks C-D, and the young skate boarder laying on the other side bleeding from the bullet meant for him.

"And I suppose you were at Stover's when someone opened fire on us."

"Missed that one," Lee said. "Thought that FBI guy, what's his name, Feinberg was protecting you. Where is he anyway?"

Smitty hadn't thought about Gabe since he got back. He was totally consumed by Mei-ling's return. For all he knew the FBI man had been killed back at Stover's.

Lee stood up. "Here, let me at least pour you a cup of coffee, ma'am. And please be careful with that gun," he said to Mei-ling.

"I can get my own coffee, thank you. And don't worry; I know how to use this." She poured her coffee with one hand while holding the gun on him, and took the cup to the table. "So, enough of this chit-chat; that's correct, Isaac? chit-chat."

He nodded.

"Just who the hell are you Mister Lee, or whatever your name is, and what the hell are you doing in my house?" she said, leveling her gun at the man.

"Just hold on there little lady, and hear me out. After that, well you can shoot me, or we can part company, but I think I can get you the information that you need."

Smitty sat there watching Mei-ling. She was fearless and he loved her.

"Well, maybe you should get out right now!" Mei-ling said.

"Or what, you'll shoot me?" Lee smiled.

"Hold up a goddamned second," Smitty cut in. "I've had enough shooting over the past few days to last me for a while. Mei, sweetheart, let's hear what the man has to say. What can hurt?"

She looked at him with the same determined expression as when she talked about her mission to destroy the Pandas.

"Come on Mei, put the gun down."

She leaned over to him and kissed him on the lips, all the time looking at Lee and holding the gun steady. "Alright Isaac, if you say so."

Smitty looked across the table at Lee. He was still smiling. Mei-ling settled back in her chair and rested her gun on the table.

"I don't know how many people I've killed because someone in Washington said they were a threat to national security. Sometimes there was what we euphemistically call collateral damage; innocent people who just were in the wrong place at the wrong time. I felt bad about those. I suppose somewhere they know how many it was. They like to keep records of those things."

"Yes, and then you're assigned to kill me, but they send someone else to do it and you scare him off before he..."

"And that's the point, Smitty. Don't you see? For the first time in my career I'm ordered to eliminate a citizen in the United States. So I say to myself, this dude must be a serious threat to national security. I look up the file, and it turns out to be some insignificant small time union functionary."

"Excuse me?" Smitty said defensively.

"I'm sorry, Smitty, but you're just not worth my killing. I know most of the story about what went down, and there's nothing there worth killing someone for, you or Ms. Wu. As far as I can see, you're no threat to anyone accept a small group of people in the State Department who apparently orchestrated this whole fucked up panda operation."

"So, now you're coming to us to what? To ask us for forgiveness for all your past crimes?" Mei-ling said.

"I don't need forgiveness for anything, Ms. Wu," Lee said. "What I did, I did for my country. And don't tell me you wouldn't have taken those smugglers out if you had to."

Mei-ling and Smitty exchanged glances. Smitty knew it was true, that Mei-ling wouldn't have let anything interfere with her determination to destroy the pandas.

"It's not the same." Mei-ling protested and set the gun on the table, holding her hand over it. "So, what are you here for?"

"Okay, let's cut out the—what did you call it?—chit chat. First off, Ms. Wu, I know about how you got back to the United States and the deal you made with the Chinese Government."

"Mister Lee. My deal with the Chinese Government had nothing to do with my escape. I was already safe in Hong Kong when I was kidnapped off the street and taken to Macau."

"But you did make a deal with them to find the last Panda —the one someone, I suspect the Russian, got away before the commando attack. And you haven't got a clue as to where it is. Correct?"

"How do you know this?"

"Look, I'm going to be honest with you folks," Lee said, his face hardening. "As far as I'm concerned this whole affair stinks. But I feel like I owe you people. If you want to know where that last Panda is I can help you find out. You have to come with me for a ride down the coast."

"Why would we do that?" Smitty said. "So you can kill us where our bodies can't be found?"

"I told you, I got no reason to kill you."

"But Smitty is wanted by the police. He shouldn't leave the house," Mei-ling said.

"Show her the paper, Smitty," Lee said, standing up and putting the gun he had under the table back in its holster. Tomorrow morning, 9 a.m sharp, if you want to find that bear."

Smitty and Mei-ling watched as Lee walked out of the kitchen. They waited to hear the front door close.

"Sonofabitch had his gun out all the time," Smitty said.

"What's he mean, show her the paper?"

Smitty slid the Tribune in front of her. She scanned the article and then looked up at him.

"Just what was going on between you and this woman, Isaac?"

* * *

Chapter 33

Highland Hospital, Oakland

"What do you mean he's not in the office. He's always in the office," Gabe said into the cell phone, trying to keep his voice down as he lurked in the hallway of Highland Hospital. It was after visiting hours. Several patients still lingered outside their rooms, while interns and nurses where making their final rounds.

"Well, he flew to San Francisco a couple of days ago and when he returned he was instructed to report to Washington. I don't think he's coming back, Gabe," Berman said."

"What happened?"

"Well, if you're asking me, Gabe, I'd say someone found out what we've been up to here."

"But what about Frank?"

"Retirement I suspect. We've been notified he was being replaced."

"Shit"

"Yeah."

"What about me? Has anyone said anything?"

"Only your wife, Gabe. She's worried out of her mind. She's calling everyday now. A real nudnick your wife. You should call her. Better yet, you should get on a plane tonight and come back."

"Can't do that, partner. As far as I'm concerned my boss gave me an assignment, and until I hear different, that's what I'm doing. Nothing's changed. Izzy's life is still in danger and my assignment is to protect him."

"Isaac Smith? Not your responsibility anymore, old buddy."

"I think it is. Besides, it's personal now. Someone tried to kill him, and me."

"All the more reason..." He knew he was wasting his breath. "...at least stay in touch. And Gabe, call your wife."

Feinberg snapped the phone shut. He looked down the hallway and spotted Ted Harlin getting off the elevator. They had agreed to meet and talk with Trish together.

"Sorry I'm late, Gabe. Traffic from the airport was heavy."

"Airport?"

"Yeah. They're going back to Vietnam. After what happened they wanted no part of America."

"Your wife?"

"Yeah, her too. Guess we're quits."

"Damn Ted, I'm sorry. She'll come back."

"Don't think so. She said she'd rather be a poor dentist where she could live in peace, then a rich doctor where she will live in fear all the time. It's been coming for a while. Things weren't working out between us."

Feinberg flashed his FBI badge at the cop guarding the hospital room.

They were both surprised by the woman in the bed; the nurses had snuck her in makeup and fixed her bandages so they looked more like a fashionable head band than dressing for the hole in her skull. Her blond hair was neatly gathered into a bun. Her hospital gown was slid off her tanned shoulders like a peasant blouse.

"Mr Harlin," she said, extending her hand for him to take. "So nice meeting you in person. You look surprised."

He pulled a chair close to the bed and sat down taking her hand which she squeezed and held on to.

"I'm sorry, Ms. Rivers. You look more like you're ready to go out clubbing than a woman who came out of a coma only two days ago."

"Why thank you," Mister Harlin. "Smitty had told me about you. Said you were his best friend."

"Ted," he said looking into her piercing blue eyes. "This is my friend, Agent Gabriel Feinberg of the FBI."

She nodded without relinquishing her hold on Harlin's hand. "Mister Feinberg."

"We'd like to ask you some questions about what happened," Feinberg said.

"Are you the agent who got Smitty out of jail? Ted told me about it when he called to interview me."

"Yes."

"Where is he?"

"Well, to tell the truth, I don't know. We were hoping something you told us would help us find him."

She looked at Ted and smiled sadly. "I can't tell you anything more than I told the police.'

"And that was?" Feinberg insisted

"Only that Smitty had been staying with me for a while. He needed somewhere to crash since his boat was destroyed. I sold him his last two boats, you know. He always seemed like a sweet man. He cooked for me. I never learned how; always too busy trying to make money, and eating out was getting expensive. Boat sales have been down since the recession. Anyway, I had filed for divorce because my husband had left over a year ago. When I heard he was back in town I got scared. He was a violent man and he knew about the divorce action. Smitty was out, but when he called I asked him to come back."

As she talked she looked at Feinberg, but had pulled Harlin's hand close to her breast, as if for comfort.

"Anyway, before Smitty got there, a man came onto the boat and into the salon where I was at my desk."

"Was it you husband?" Feinberg asked.

"My ex. No, this man was a stranger. He wanted to know where Smitty was. Well, I shouted at him to get off my boat. That's when he grabbed me. I think I hit him with the telephone, but he hit me back. I ran into my bedroom and was going for my gun, but he was right on top of me before I could take aim. He wrestled the gun away from me and hit me hard in the face and I fell onto the bed ... that's all I remember."

Tears had welled up in her eyes and she buried her face into Harlin's chest.

"Maybe we should leave her in peace," Feinberg said."

"You go on, Gabe, I'll stay with her for a while."

"Okay," he smiled. "Think I'll go back to my hotel and make some calls. Smitty's got to be somewhere."

* * *

Chapter 34

Oakland China Town

After the mysterious appearance of Marshall Lee, Smitty spent half the day trying to explain his relationship with Trish to Mei-ling. In the end she convinced herself that he probably had no way of knowing if he would ever see her again, and so he filled the void with another woman. Men were like that.

Nevertheless, she had taken so many risks escaping China, and she had rationalized to herself that she had done it for Isaac; that she had to get back to him because his life was in danger because of her. But when it got right down to it, she had to admit that she left China for herself; that after so many years in America she could not fit back into her beloved country. What she had found was not the revolutionary China she had grown up in. Mei-ling was a historian and told herself she should have known that even the revolution could not erase thousands of years of mercantile culture. Business was in the blood of the Chinese. She saw it plainly as tens of thousands of peasants poured into the cities to find work and make money. She also knew that no matter who was in charge in China, they would always be watching her.

By the time the sun was setting over the Golden Gate Bridge she and

Smitty were locked in each other's arms in her bedroom. The past few months were swept away by their passion for each other..

Smitty sat at the kitchen table sipping his morning coffee. Mei-ling was getting dressed. It was eight in the morning. They had decided to go with Lee; Mei-ling had decided; Smitty reluctantly agreed. He found it hard to trust the man who had been sent to kill him.

He heard a knock on the front door. Lee wasn't supposed to be there for another hour, so he went to the foyer with Mei-ling's Tokarov in hand. The knocking persisted. Why the hell wasn't there a peep hole in the door? The chain would have to do, so he stepped away from the door so whoever it was couldn't blast him in the face, and slowly turned the lock until it clicked and turned the doorknob. "Who is it?" he said.

"Izzy, is that you?"

Izzy? It had to be Gabe Feinberg. He was the only one in the world aside from his dead uncle to call him that.

"Gabe?"

"Yes, you fucking wandering Jew, open the fucking door."

Smitty threw the door open. He grabbed the FBI man and threw his arms around him. "Damn, I'm glad to see you alive." And then pulled him inside the foyer and slammed the door shut.

"Where the fuck have you been, Izzy. I've been racking my brains trying to figure out where you'd gotten too. And put away that cannon, would you?"

Smitty looked down at the gun in his hand like he couldn't figure out why it was there. Not knowing what else to do with it he stuck it in the front of his pants.

"Come on, Gabe, I'll buy you a cup of coffee."

He led the FBI agent into the kitchen and bid him sit down. Then he went to the counter, poured a mug of coffee and brought it to the table.

"How did you know where I was?"

"A hunch," Feinberg said.

"Hunch?"

"Yes. I thought of all the places you might go where anyone looking for you wouldn't think to look and this is all I could come up with."

"Mei-ling is here. She's gotten out of China. I didn't know it until I came here on the outside chance the house was vacant and I could hide out. But she was here."

"Cream," Feinberg said.

"Huh?"

"Cream. For the coffee."

Smitty suddenly felt foolish. The grin on his face dissolved as he realized not everyone would be as thrilled to see that Mei-ling had come back as he was. He went to the porch to get the milk from the refrigerator, just as Mei-ling came into the kitchen with a towel wrapped around her hair and a short terry cloth robe wrapped tightly around her. She stood in the doorway for a moment.

"Agent Feinberg?"

Gabe looked up.

"How did you get here?"

Smitty came in with a quart of milk. "Look Mei, its Gabe. He isn't dead."

"I can see that," Mei-ling said with a frown. She hadn't seen the FBI agent since he had handed her over to the NSA to be transported to the San Francisco airport. "So what are we suppose to do now?"

"There's a problem?" Feinberg asked.

Smitty set the milk down on the table.

"Well, we're about to go with this guy, the same one who drove off that prick that was trying to kill me at the Marina."

"Slow down, Izzy. What the fuck's ... sorry Ms. Wu ... what in God's name is going on?"

Smitty went over to Mei-ling and put his arm around her waist. He explained about Marshall Lee and the continued hunt for the missing Panda. When he had finished, they all were silent for an uncomfortable minute.

"Well," Feinberg said, breaking the silence. "I'm coming with you." He poured the milk into the coffee mug.

"What do you mean, you're coming with us. What for?" Mei-ling said, stepping away from Smitty's arm and going to the counter to pour herself a mug of coffee.

"Just what I said," Feinberg said. "I was nearly killed protecting your friend here. Those were my instructions, to protect him, and the job isn't done. So I'm coming with you."

* * *

Chapter 35

Santa Cruz Mountains, Ca

"So, Agent Feinberg, your boss tells you to come out here to protect Smitty," Lee said as he pulled onto Highway 880 South.

"That's right," Feinberg said, as he adjusted his seat belt in the Lincoln Navigator. He was sitting shotgun, with Smitty and Mei-ling in the back seat.

"So, where were you when I had to chase that creep off who almost killed your charge at the Berkeley Marina?"

"Well, if you are his self-appointed protector, where the fuck where you when that same creep opened up on us at Stover's ranch?" Feinberg shot back.

Smitty was sitting in the back smiling as the two men in the front argued over who was his best protector. Mei-ling just stared out the window unimpressed by any of it.

"I had business elsewhere," Lee snapped back. "Listen pal, I don't mind you tagging along, but you have to swear to not reveal where we are going to anyone."

"Or?"

"Or I will kill you."

Feinberg remained quiet. He knew who Marshall Lee was, and that he was quite capable of doing just that.

After that no one spoke for the forty-five minutes it took to get to San Jose. Feinberg kept glancing over at the man behind the wheel. Everything he knew about him said he was a monster; a cold blooded killer, no different than the criminals and gangsters he had investigated in his long career, only worse, because his crimes were condoned by the government, the same government that paid him to hunt down men far less brutal. It was hard to believe that this killer claimed to have had a sudden change of heart because of a insignificant target like the Jewish union man and his Chinese girlfriend.

Lee continued straight past the 101 turnoff where 880 turned into Highway 17 heading to the beach town of Santa Cruz.

Seeing where they were going, Smitty leaned forward. "We're going to the Boardwalk?"

Lee gave him a look in the mirror that let him know he'd better shut up. He leaned back into the plush leather seat and shrugged his shoulders to Mei-ling who had remained uncommonly quiet throughout the entire ride.

After climbing into the mountains for about twenty minutes Lee pulled off the highway onto Summit Road that meandered into the back hills. Smitty felt Mei-ling's hand tighten in his and her fingernails dug into his skin. They looked at each other and he saw the fear in her eyes. For all they knew the government assassin was driving them into the hills to murder them all. After all, they had no reason to believe his story other than his word.

They soon turned off of Summit onto a dirt road that lead into a thicket of manzanita, Douglas fir, California scrub oak, and brightly colored chaparral pea that dotted the landscape in a deep chartreuse.

Lee noticed the growing apprehension on his passengers faces as he turned off onto a single lane gravel road leading higher into the mountains as the vegetation started to give way to a pine forest.

"What are you worried about? You still have your weapon Agent Feinberg," and peeking into the rear view mirror, "and I assume you have your gun in your bag, Ms. Wu."

"Your friend must not like company," Feinberg said.

"You could say that."

After about ten minutes of climbing they came to a heavy security gate. What looked like an electrified fence spread out in both directions. The Navigator came to a halt and Lee got out and went to an intercom next to the gate. The others watched as he said something, and then the gate buzzed and swung open. Lee checked his weapon and snapped a round in the chamber.

* * *

Chapter 36

Highland Hospital, Oakland, Ca.

Harlin returned to the hospital the next day. He told himself he wanted to question Trish for more information, but the truth was he was strangely attracted to her. He oddly felt a sense of responsibility for her well being, perhaps because she had nearly been killed as a result of her association with Smitty.

He entered the hospital room. The policeman was no longer standing outside her door, so he just walked in. She wasn't in her bed and then he caught sight of her, standing in the bathroom with her back to him, looking into the mirror and brushing out her long blond hair. The ties of her hospital gown were undone, revealing her long shapely legs, and what his friend Gabe Feinberg would call, a cute tush. She slowly turned toward him, looking more beautiful than the day before. There wasn't the slightest sign of embarrassment as she spotted him in the mirror and she made what Ted interrupted as a seductive smile. .

"Ted, I didn't hear you come in. Could you help me tie this damn thing? I hate hospital gowns."

"Well," he stammered. "You do them justice, Ms. Rivers."

"Trish. I thought we agreed you'd call me Trish," she said, and walked up to him and turned her back. "Do me up."

His fingers fumbled with the ties. Unlike her long legs and shoulders, that were tanned, the skin on her back was alabaster like that of a Greek statue, and after years of being with an Asian woman and idolizing all things Vietnamese, this woman seemed exotic to him.

His fingers clumsily tied the back of the gown and then he helped her slip back into the hospital bed.

"My ex-husband came by today, but they stopped him at the nurses' desk. The cops had told them about the restraining order."

"Where are they ... the cops?"

"Said now that I cleared Smitty they didn't believe I was in danger. They didn't count on my ex."

"The divorce has gone through?" Ted said.

"No. Hal's contesting it, the son of a bitch. And they're going to release me tomorrow."

"Where will you go?"

She looked down. The gown slid off her shoulders as she shrugged.

"I can't go back to my boat. My ex is bound to show up, and there's no telling what he'll do," she said in a low voice.

"Of course you can't. Why don't you come and stay at my place?"

She looked up at him questioningly. "But what about your wife?"

Ted told her about his wife returning to Vietnam with her mother, and about the violence at his house, omitting the death of his wife's aunt. "I don't blame her for leaving. Truth is, our marriage had been over for a while, if you know what I mean."

"Oh, you poor thing," she said, and put her hand on his arm. "That must have been terrible for you. I wonder if one of those men was the same one who came to my boat and...."

"Well, if it was, he won't be bothering you anymore." He took her hand from his arm and held it. He was looking into her eyes now and getting lost in their deep blue.

* * *

Chapter 37

Somewhere in theSanta Cruz Mountains

Lee slowed down as the Navigator approached what appeared to be a large log cabin, with an even larger mobile home attached at the rear that sprouted a gigantic short wave radio antennae. Someone stood in front of the building, and as the dust settled, Smitty saw that he was a small man, maybe five foot five, with old fashioned wire rim glasses, a stubbly white beard and long thin gray hair tied in the back into a rather scraggly pony tail. The man held a twelve gauge pump shotgun firmly in his hands.

Lee stopped the car and told them to stay put as he got out and greeted the man. They watched him grab the government assassin in a bear hug causing him to disappear from view for a moment. The men seemed to be talking about the people in the Navigator as the host kept looking in their direction. Finally, Lee waved for them to come out of the car and join him and the other man.

Smitty noticed that their host was older than he first thought. His face had the tired look of a man who had led a long intense life, but his green eyes sparked with intelligence behind the wire rim glasses.

Mei-ling held onto Smitty's hand, still unsure of what was happening until the old man came up to her with a big grin and put out his hand in greeting.

"And this must be the mysterious Mei-ling Wu, the woman who single-handidly outwitted the Chinese Secret Police and escaped from behind the Chinese Red Curtain."

She smiled and took his hand. He had a firm grip and gave her a slight, polite bow, and she returned it. She smiled. "Not alone. I had help." She liked this old man immediately. She told herself it was cultural; honoring the elderly.

"Of course you did, my girl. We all need friends. Lee here, he's my friend ... maybe my only friend. We go back."

Lee laughed. "Longer than I like to remember."

"And Isaac Smith." He offered his hand, which Smitty accepted with a skeptical look on his face. "A fine kettle of fish you wound up in, but I can certainly see why," the old man added glancing back at Mei-ling.

Then he turned to Feinberg. "And you? Special Agent Gabriel Feinberg from New York. You know, of course, that your boss has been removed from the New York Office, and that you are AWOL. Your wife is very worried about you."

"How do you know that?" Feinberg said. "I just learned of it myself."

The man smiled. "It's what I do," he said. "But come in. You all must be tired and can use a drink."

The interior of the log cabin was a single spacious room with a brown leather couch, matching love seat and easy chair wrapped around a large glass top table sitting on a polished tree trunk base. Shelves lined the walls, with rows of books haphazardly stacked to overflow. The attached bedroom revealed a neatly made rolled up futon and the kitchen along the rear had a large stove, refrigerator and freezer with a small kitchen table. A locked rear door Smitty figured opened into the adjoining mobile home.

The man bid his guests to make themselves at home. They took seats; Lee in the easy chair, Smitty and Mei-ling on the love seat and Feinberg on the edge of the couch.

"What are we drinking," the host asked. "Lee, single malt scotch if I remember correctly."

"Do you ever forget anything?"

"Not much," the host said, opening a well stocked liquor cabinet and pulling out a fancy bottle. "Highland Park ok?"

"Jesus, where did you get that?" Lee asked.

"I've been saving it for you," the host smiled.

"And you, Ms Wu?"

"Vodka and ice will be fine, thank you."

"I can make you a martini if you like."

"How did you know I drink martinis?"

"Like I said, it's what I do."

"Vodka and ice will do fine."

"Mister Smith? Or do you prefer Smitty"

"Smitty's fine. Jack Daniels, if you have it."

"Knob Hill's the best I can do."

"Thanks. No ice"

"And Agent Feinberg?"

"Water."

"You sure. I won't report you," he laughed.

"Water will be fine," Feinberg said.

With drinks all around, the host hovered over them like a mother hen. "So, here we are, a gang of wanted desperados."

"I'm sorry, sir, but I didn't catch your name," Smitty said.

"I didn't give it," the host said. "Just how much did you tell them, Lee?" he said turning to the CSS, now ex-CSS killer.

"Nothing. I thought I'd leave that up to you to tell them as much as you want them to know. All I said was you might be able to help them find the location of the missing Panda."

"Hmmmm," the host said, scratching at the stubble on his chin.

"Well, if you want, I can explain who you are, or who you were," Feinberg said.

Everyone's eyes turned to him.

"And just who do you think I am?" the old man said with a smile, as he poured himself a glass of red wine.

"You're a lot older than the picture I saw of you, but if I'm not mistaken you are Malcolm Stanford the Third, born September 8, 1922; first born to Samuel and Martha Stanford of Richmond, Virginia. Youngest student ever admitted to the University of Virginia at age 16; graduated in 1932; excelled in linguistics and science; accepted at Yale in 1938 after several years of study abroad; studied Radio and Communication Technology; recruited into the Office of Strategic Services in 1941 where you were put in charge of setting up and running surveillance and intelligence interception and monitoring. After the war you were one of the key organizers of the Central Intelligence Agency in 1947." He turned to Mei-ling and Smitty. "He remained head of electronic surveillance and intelligence gathering, providing information to the FBI, CIA, NSA and a number of other agencies. He remained until retiring in 1984. Present whereabouts unknown; retirement checks mailed to the National Bank of Switzerland."

The old man clapped his hands. "Excellent Agent Feinberg. You've done your homework well."

"Apparently the FBI wants to know where you are because there is an active file on you."

"Malcolm Stanford the Third?" Lee laughed.

"I'd still like to know why we are here and just how you have so much information," Mei-ling blurted out after finishing off her vodka.

"Perhaps I should start off by showing you my little operation here," the old man said.

"But I still don't understand," Smitty said. He hadn't had a drink in over a week and the bourbon had gone down easily. "Why do you want to help us? And why should we trust you and this professional murderer."

"The name's Lee ... Marshall Lee. Can we cut out this assassin killer dog shit?"

"Look my friends," the host broke in. "Whatever we were previously, we're all in the same boat now. Some powerful people in this government are out to kill us, except for you Ms. Wu. They don't seem to know you've returned to the States."

"And me," Feinberg said. "I am still a sworn agent of the FBI."

"I'm afraid you are a fugitive now, Agent Feinberg. We intercepted the communication yesterday. They think you know too much and there's a contract out on you as well. They're calling you a rogue agent. So you and Lee here have a lot in common."

"That's bullshit." Feinberg started, fumbling around in his pockets. "We'll see about that," he said, pulling his cell phone from his pocket.

Lee abruptly yanked it from his hands.

"You fool. Shit, I should have searched you. I'm sorry, Malcolm. I didn't know he had a cell phone."

"Why," Feinberg protested. "What's wrong with it?"

"What's wrong, you idiot? This thing probably has a tracking device in it," he said as he dropped it on the floor and smashed it with his heel. "Let's just hope they haven't been monitoring it. I ought to break your fucking neck."

The old man stepped between them. "Now, let's just calm down. Agent Feinberg, Lee is right. That phone could lead them here. We wouldn't want that now, would we."

Gabe fell back in the couch. It hadn't occurred to him that they could do that, but he had no idea they could make a small cell phone either. The old man was right, of course, if they could do the one, they could do the other, although he had no idea how. He was just angry with himself for letting Lee snatch the phone from him.

"That's better," Stanford said. "Now, let's all have another drink, and then I'll show you my little operation and tell you what we've found out."

"Well, I don't get it," Smitty said, eagerly handing his glass to his host. "You retired after years of service to your country. Why are they after you?"

The old man poured a generous amount of Knob Hill in Smitty glass. "Same as the rest of you. I know too much."

"What could possibly be so damning?" Feinberg said.

Stanford took Mei-ling's glass and fetched the vodka.

"He's much too modest," Lee said. "You're looking at the man who knows where all the skeletons lie. They realized that he had too much power, controlling all communication intercepts, both internally and foreign. This was a man they couldn't allow to retire and live. He knew it and so he disappeared."

The old man handed Mei-ling her glass

"You're going to tell me where the Panda is?" Mei-ling asked.

"*Yŏu nàixīn de niánqīng nǚshì. Suŏyŏu zài shí fàng de shí hòu.* Patience young lady. All in due time," the host said in perfect Mandarin.

Mei-ling smiled and gave him a polite nod. "*Duìbùqǐ, xiānshēng,*"

"Now, if everyone will finish your drinks I will show you my little clandestine operation." He led them through the door that led into the mobile home. It was one large room with a bank of TV monitors and computer stations. A shiny black head topping a short cropped beard sat at one of the monitors.

"This is my partner in crime, Jamal." The man turned his head to them and nodded.

"Jamal was arrested ten years ago for hacking into the CIA's computers. But they were so impressed with his skill that instead of putting him in jail, they gave him a job. He was working in counter surveillance where his talents were being wasted in my opinion. Anyway, when I decided to retire I met with him. He confirmed his continued hatred of the system, but he considered working for them an educational opportunity. Better than the hoosegow," he laughed. "So I recruited him to join me in retirement."

"Yeah, well there's an arrest warrant out on me now for ditching them," Jamal put in as he stared into the computer monitor. "And if they catch me I doubt they'll give me back my old job." His face lit up as he laughed at his little joke.

"Ah, yes," Feinberg said. "I knew I'd seen your face before. Jamal Duclois; born in French West Africa; family immigrated to France in 1975; studied at the Sorboone. But if I recall from your photograph correctly you didn't have a beard and you had hair. Short cropped. Very collegiate."

Jamal laughed. "I'm on the run as you know. I'm surprised you recognized me."

"It's what I do," Feinberg said.

"Jamal can hack into any system in the world," Stanford said, breaking into Feinberg's wanted poster description. "We are also able to access cell phone calls, e-mail and any electronic communications from the President of the United States on down. Anyway, when Lee here contacted me and told me about his assignment, and that he was seriously troubled by it and was thinking about jumping ship, well, I was delighted. The Lees and Stanfords go way back in Virginia, and Lee's father and I were great friends. So naturally I took an interest in his son. I became his friend and confident through the years although we disagreed over many things, including his career choice." He looked at Mei-ling. "Lee's great grandfather was General Robert E. Lee, the general in charge of the Confederate Army in our Civil War," he explained like a school teacher.

"Yes, we study American history in our schools in China,"

"Good, good, you have the advantage over most American school children unfortunately."

Jamal looked up from the monitor. "My great white father here thinks anyone born outside the U.S. doesn't know anything," he smiled.

"You were about to tell us what you were doing when Mister Lee here confessed his sins to you," Feinberg said.

"Ah yes. To the point, eh Agent Feinberg. Well after talking with Lee we turned our focus on the only lead we had, that being Mac McCraven." He turned to Lee. "Apparently McCraven is now dead. Suicide they said."

"Yes," Lee said with a straight face. "Tragic."

"I knew McCraven," the old man continued. "Didn't seem the type for suicide."

"You never know."

"No, you don't. Well, we were able to intercept his cell phone calls and his land line."

"That's impossible," Feinberg said.

"No, actually it was easy. You see, all employees of the government services phones are monitored. Telephone calls are recorded on a main frame computer in the basement at Langley—that's where our CIA headquarters are located in Virginia," he explained for Mei-ling's benefit.

"Yes, I know Langley," she said, growing increasingly irritated by the old man's condescension.

'Well, only a select few people can access the information, but Jamal here—genius that he is—made sure to create a back door for himself before he left.

Duclois smiled. "At Malcolm's direction I might add."

"Come on, Malcolm, let's dispense with the technical shit and get on with it," Lee said.

"Always the impatient one. Jamal, tell the folks what you found."

"Well," Duclois said, looking up from the computer screen, "we started monitoring all of McCraven's calls, both incoming and outgoing. From his conversations we were able to pin down what appeared to be a group of conspirators; that is, what they discussed concerned a certain secret operation involving the People's Republic of China..."

"Yes, we know all about that," Lee said. "What I'm interested in, is who exactly is involved."

"Yes, well, it seems to have originated with the Assistant Secretary of State in charge of Southeast Asia, Gregory Parsons. He had come in with the new administration," Duclois explained.

"Yes, Parsons," the old man scoffed. "Ambitious fellow. Worked for State in the first Bush Administration. I remember he'd always try to get close to Chaney whenever he had a chance. Chaney, he was the Secretary of..." he said turning to Mai-ling, but her look stopped him from explaining. "I suspect that's how he got the appointment when Bush Junior came in. Still can't phantom how the American people voted that idiot into office..."

"Okay Malcolm," Lee interrupted. "What happened next, Jamal?"

"Well, from what we were able to gather, Parsons contacted the Chinese Embassy about two years ago after information reached him about one of our most important assets being exposed and arrested in Beijing. He apparently believed that if he could get the guy out it would be a big feather in his cap."

"And so he made the deal with the Reds," Lee said, recalling his conversation with McCraven. Apparently the truth was the opposite of how Mac had explained it that hot summer day in the Sakler Museum. "And he didn't get it approved first?"

"You got to know this guy," Stanford said. "He's got a lethal ego that gets people killed."

"My Uncle Peter," Mai Ling said.

"Yes, your uncle, Peter Wu" Stanford said.

"But my government would never have attempted this operation alone."

"No," Stanford said. "But it was a perfect opportunity for them. They knew that something was going to happen that would threaten their national security. They also knew that the 14K triad was behind it..."

"Hold up there a second," Smitty said, lighting a Lucky. "For us simple citizens, just who is the 14K?"

"I think I can answer that," Feinberg said. "The 14K is the largest triad in China. It was formed during WWII as an anti-communist action group under the Nationalists led by Chiang Kai-shek. After the communist takeover they moved their operations to Hong Kong and are now the largest smuggler of drugs, guns and people in the world."

"Very good, agent Feinberg," the old man said. "Couldn't have said it better."

"I've been tracking them down in the U.S. for two years, Mister Stanford. I discovered them through the Ghost Shadow gang from New York when they came to San Francisco."

"But what's a New York Chinese gang got to do with this —what did you call them—14K?" Smitty said.

"All the Chinese gangs in the U.S. are controlled by one triad or another," Feinberg explained. "The triad had started smuggling operations into the United States. That's what I know."

"Well, Parson offered the Chinese government the opportunity to operate on the West Coast," Stanford went on as if the exchange never happened. "So the deal was struck. From the Chinese perspective it was a win-win proposition; they could keep an eye on the triad's operations in the U.S. and at the same time get the traitor out of their hair without causing much disruption or scandal."

"Just wait a minute," Mei-ling interrupted. "This is all very interesting, but what does it have to do with where the last Panda is?"

"Just hang on, Ms. Wu," Stanford said. "We'll get to that. But first Lee here wants to know just who was involved in this operation beside Parsons and McCraven."

"Why do you care, Mister Lee?" Mei-ling asked.

"Simple. These are the people who have put the kill order out on all of us. That's why."

"Well, that's easy," Jamal said. He turned back to the computer screen and typed something in. A chart appeared looking like a family tree, with Parsons name at the top and branching out. Lee recognized most of the names; high ranking officials with their agencies and departments listed under their names.

"I have also listed the contracting groups they have enlisted to hunt you folks down. I can print them out for you, Mister Lee, and then we can get on to Ms. Wu's problem."

Lee glanced over at the small Chinese woman who seemed so out of place in the group of men.

"Yeah, sure, that will be fine. Thanks Jamal."

While Jamal pushed the print button, Stanford explained:

"Your Panda, Ms. Wu. We discovered it quite by accident. It really started when we got an alert on the Security outfit called X-Men. We've been tracking these guys for a couple of years. They're an exceptionally violent crew, hiring out mostly to dictators and corporations operating in Third World countries. We discovered a large sum of money being deposited into their bank in Zurich and traced the source to a CIA Secret account used for covert operations..."

"I've used the same account on occasion," Lee added.

Smitty snuffed out his cigarette on the floor. "You think I could get another drink."

"Sure," Stanford said. "Go in and help yourself."

Smitty looked at Mei-ling, but she was engrossed by the tale Sanford was telling, so he just wondered off through the door leading back into the house. He went straight to the liquor cabinet and filled his glass with the Knob Hill.   He took a gulp and let the warmth fill his stomach and lit a cigarette.

Something had been gnawing at him since Mei-ling had returned. Ever since he had first met her she had been dedicated to fulfilling her uncle's assignment. She said she was doing it for her country and for him. But since returning she had changed somehow. He wondered what he would have done if he had known what he was getting mixed up in when he made the promise to old Peter Wu; whether he might have just forgotten the whole thing. But by the time he figured it out it was too late, he was madly in love with her. Since escaping from China she seemed to have discarded her lofty ideals in exchange for money-—a million dollars, true enough—but he questioned if he was willing to die for money alone. It was against his principles. But, on the other hand, she seemed to want the money for them, so they would be free to go anywhere they wanted, and—as the old phrase goes—live happily ever after.

He gulped down the rest of the bourbon and shrugged. "Fuck it," he said out loud and went to rejoin the others.

*

Smitty stood at the doorway looking at his four companions. They seemed to all fit. They all had their own agendas, but they had one thing in common; they had turned on the governments they had served all their lives, except for Jamal. They were all once agents of their own governments. He and Jamal were along for the ride.

Mei-ling noticed him and, quite unexpectedly, flew into his arms.

"Isaac, Jamal here is a genius."

"Huh, what did I miss?"

"Tell him, Jamal."

The man sitting at the computer smiled. "Do you other fellows mind?"

"Go right ahead," Lee said.

Stanford nodded his head. "If you don't mind, I think I'll excuse myself and get a drink."

"I think I'll join you," Lee said.

The two old friends disappeared out the door.

"This is amazing, Izzy," Feinberg said. "I had no idea they could do this. Jamal here's a genius."

Pleased with his appreciative audience, Jamal told the tale, elaborating on his first telling. "Well, we had long suspected that certain people in Congress and at the White House of having connections with some of the oligarchs in Russia. These men are very powerful and have billions of dollars stashed in European banks."

"Why would they do that?" Smitty asked.

"Its obvious, Izzy," Feinberg said. "Money. Untraceable, unreported money. For the oligarchs, who are consolidating their power over Russia's industrial wealth, buying influence in the U.S. government is important. It's no secret the U.S. played an important part in the overthrow of the Soviet Union, and we are instrumental in introducing free market capitalism to Russia. Some men are making fortunes at the expense of the Russian people, all thanks to that drunkard Boris Yeltsin, America's sweetheart, who is pushing through a new constitution that will fundamentally change the socialist economy."

"Go on, Jamal," Mei-ling interrupted Feinberg's current events commentary.

"Yes, well anyway, I've been monitoring this one particular guy named Viktor Rashnikov who is cornering the coal industry in Siberia with the help of a ruthless mob led by Igor Mikhalov; The Bear of the North they call him, uncle to Sergai Mikhalov, head of Solntsevskaya bratva, the largest organized crime outfit in Moscow. Well," Jamal continued, "about a year ago, I was monitoring Igor's cell phone and what do you think? He was talking to an associate in the 14K. His boss, Rashnikov, wanted a Panda bear for his private zoo on his estate in Israel."

"Israel?" Smitty said. "This Russian prick has a place in Isreal."

"Not just a place," Jamal said. "More like an estate; a five hundred acre palace outside of Haifa overlooking the Mediterranean. Israel is very hospital to Russian Jews, and this one has money; lots of it. I don't know why, since most Russian Jews aren't religious. But what is it they say? Money can buy you into heaven."

"Jews don't believe in heaven," Feinberg said.

"Anyhow," Jamal said, ignoring the FBI man's correction, "that's what you've got tangled up in I believe. If successful, Rishnikov would own the only Panda in the world that doesn't belong to China."

"But wiat a nimute. Don't they have a Panda in the Washington Zoo?" Smitty asked.

"On loan," Feinberg answered. "It's part of Red China's foreign policy. Good will gesture."

"And htat's what got my Uncle Peter murdered," Mei-ling added.

Smitty notice a tear form in her eye, and he put his arm around her. She sniffled once and then shook him off.

"That was then. This is now, and I want to know where the last Panda is so I can finish this thing once and for all," she said.

"Well, as you know, the NSA— probably cleared by Parsons—responded to the San Francisco Chinese Consulate's request for assistance and mounted a full scale military attack using the X-Man Security company."

"Yes, we know all that," Smitty said impatiently. "We were there."

"Yes, of course. But what you don't know is that a helicopter came in earlier that day and took out one of the smugglers and one Panda in a crate."

"That Russian son-of-a-bitch I'll bet," Smitty said.

Just then Stanford and Lee rushed back into the room.

"Quick Jamal, turn on the surveillance monitors."

"Why, what's up?"

"Just do it."

Jamal swiveled his chair to a bank of three monitors and switched them on. The first monitor revealed three black Land Rovers slowly coming up the hill leading to the front gate.

Feinberg, who had been standing toward the back, poked his head into the gathering.

"What's going on?"

"It means they traced us here through your cell phone," Stanford said.

"Oh shit, I didn't know," Feinberg said.

"You prick, why didn't you tell me you had...." Lee shouted moving toward the FBI man with murder written all over his face.

"Just hold up there, Lee," Stanford said, stepping between the two men. "It's not his fault. There's no reason he should have known about it. This is new technology. Now you folks have to get out of here."

The three Land Rovers appeared in the next monitor heading for

261   The Last Panda

the front gate. Stanford glanced at it.

"Jamal, the escape route."

Duclois hit a switch and all the computers went dark except for the surveillance monitors..

"Quickly, come with me," he said, grabbing a laptop computer from the desk and a backpack.

They followed behind him as he exited the back door of the mobile home. Then Lee hesitated.

"Arn't you coming?"

The old man looked at his friend. "I'm seventy-five years old, son. I'm too old to be on the lamb. But I want you to take this."

He handed Lee a bundle of CD discs. "It's my memoirs."

"I won't leave you Malcolm."

"No, you go on. They're going to need a man with your skills. I'll be all right."

Lee frowned, and then hurried after the others just as the buzzer to the intercom at the front gate went off and the surveillance monitor revealed the Land Rovers that had stopped. Several heavily armed men jumped out of the lead vehicle wearing fatigues with baklavas over their faces.

The old man glanced at the monitor from the camera at the rear of the building and saw the Jeep Wrangler, that had been hidden in a camouflaged shed, start up the steep hill in the back. He calmly walked to the front house. The men in the Land Rovers were surely preparing to crash the front gate. He went to the far wall and removed a picture of a seaside landscape he had painted when he first arrived on the West Coast. A small safe was imbedded in the wall. He quickly punched in an electronic code and opened it to reveal an electronic timer which he set for three minutes.

"There, that should be about right," he said..

By now the Land Rovers were rolling up to the house. He went to a closet and took out an Uzi sub machine gun and went to the front window. The Uzi could pierce body armor, and the men jumping out of the Rovers surely wore them. They were professionals and they were there to kill.

He stuck some earplugs in and covered his eyes with darkened goggles in preparation for the flash grenades which would surely be smashing through the windows at any moment.

"Everyone inside! Come out now! I'll only give you one warning!" a voice blasted from a megaphone.

It was his cue. He opened up with the Uzi blasting out the front windows. As he expected, the front door slammed open by a powerful force outside. He saw the hands toss the grenades and he ducked behind the couch just as they exploded in blinding flashes. The concussion was absorbed by the couch. Before the smoke cleared he withdrew to the door leading to the attached mobile home while firing the Uzi in a scatter. He heard the muffled sounds of shouting and a blast of gunfire intrude through the earplugs. He fired back, drawing his enemies deeper into the house ... into his trap.

The sound of automatic gunfire echoed up the hill. Jamal stopped the jeep and got out, followed by his four companions. They all looked down the hill overlooking the house at the bottom of the dirt road. They couldn't see the front of the house, but they could imagine what was happening. Suddenly there were several small explosions followed by more gunfire.

"Damn," Smitty said under his breath. He felt Mei-ling's hand holding his tightly. Then moments later there was a huge explosion and they watched as the entire house seemed to disappear into a huge cloud of smoke and fire. No one spoke; they all simple stared, as if in a trance, at the expanding smoke and debris, somehow expecting to see the old man miraculously appear out of the fiery cauldron.

Lee was the first to break away, turning his back on the scene. "Come on," he said. "Let's get the hell out of here."

The others remained, staring as the cloud of black smoke slowly drifted into the sky until Mei-ling grabbed hold of Smitty's hand. "Let's go, Isaac." They slowly walked back to the Jeep and got in.

"Shit, I haven't seen anything like that since Vientnam," Feinberg mumbled.

Jamal contnued staring. "Inshallah," he said.

"You're Muslim?" Feinberg asked.

"When it's convenient. Let's get the fuck out of here. This place will be crawling with fire trucks and cops any minute now."

No one spoke as Jamal shoved the gears of the Jeep into compound gear and steered over the ridge into a bleak landscape of charred earth dotted by the black skeletons of burned out trees. They slowly descended until hitting a dirt fire road that would lead them back to the main high-way.

* * *

Chapter 38

Monterey, California

The fire road eventually intersected with Highway 17. They drove out of the mountains into Santa Cruz and connected to the Pacific Coast highway south. Smitty had suggested staying at a motel, but Lee had nixed it.

"I only stay at the best places. They owe me that after all I've done. It's on the NSA."

"They'll trace your credit card if you use it," Feinberg said. "Bad idea."

"Shit Feinberg. You're right," Lee said grudgingly.

"Not a problem," Jamal replied, opening his laptop computer. He spent about five minutes punching keys.

"There, four beach front rooms reserved and pre-paid."

When they got into the lobby to register, there was an older couple at the front desk arguing with the clerk, insisting they had reservations.

"I'm sorry," the young Asian woman behind the counter said. "You are not in the computer. I can see if we can find you another room. I believe we still have a couple of Garden rooms available.

"We've been coming here for over twenty years and never had a problem," the irate elderly man said, but he finally relented.

Jamal smiled and shrugged his shoulders. "There are three more parties that are going to be disappointed I'm afraid," he said under his breath.

"How did you do that?" Smitty asked over the crashing surf just outside the picture windows overlooking the ocean from the hotel's cocktail lounge. He and Mei-ling sat side by side across from Jamal at a small table facing the ocean.

They had all checked into the hotel, and agreed to meet after settling into their individual rooms. Jamal had cut off his beard before coming down and they noticed that he wasn't as young as they had assumed, but probably well into his thirties and handsome by any standard..

"Wonders of the computer age," Jamal smiled. "I hope I got it right, reserving one room for the two of you."

"You got it right," Smitty said.

"Those poor people," Mei-ling said.

"It's a hell of a lot better than a Motel Six," Smitty said.

"They'll get over it," Jamal said.

"They have a great restaurant here. At least they did when I stayed here a couple of years ago. Believe it or not, this is a union hotel," Smitty said.

"You mean there are hotels without unions? In France everyone belongs to a union." Jamal said.

"Yeah, well welcome to America."

"I'm sorry about what happened to Mister Stanford. You two must have been close," Mei- ling said, sipping her vodka martini.

Jamal forced a smile. "Don't worry about it; he knew they'd catch up to us sooner or later. He never told me he had the place wired to blow up though."

"Well, I see you people have started," Lee announced as he came up to the table. "Are you going to tell us where that phantom bear is?"

"Sit down and have a drink," Jamal said. "I was just getting to that."

Slow down there," Smitty said. "We've all been through a rough time. Perhaps you should sit down and have a drink and relax for a minute."

Lee pulled another chair over and squeezed into the small table. A waitress was johnny-on-the-spot.

"I'll have a scotch over," he ordered. "Single malt."

"Were's Gabe?"

"Agent Feinberg. Suppose he'll be down soon."

As if on cue, Feinberg appeared at the entrance to the lobby and cocktail lounge. He looked around and spotted Smitty waving to him.

As soon as he sat down the waitress was there with Lee's drink. "Can I get you something?"

"No thanks. I'll pass." He turned to his companions. "So, what's happening?"

"We're waiting on Mister Duclois here to reveal the whereabouts of that bear," Lee said.

All eyes turned to the Jamal. He took a sip from his beer. "Yes. Well, I'd better tell you because there isn't a whole lot of time left." He looked at Mei-ling. "Personally my advice is to forget about the whole thing and be on your way."

"I can't do that, Jamal. Isaac and I have come too far to leave this thing undone," Mei-ling said. "Agent Feinberg can tell you."

"I suppose not. Well, where were we? Seems like a year ago since we were in the computer room."

"You had been monitoring a Russian oligarch named Rasnikov," Feinberg said. "So he called in his gangster buddy. I believe his nickname is Bear of the North. Bad man."

"Ah yes," Jamal said. "Rashinkov. He wanted a Panda for his private zoo so he asked his mob partner, Igor Mikhalov, to get one. Mikhalov made arrangements with the Chinese triad X14 in Hong Kong that control the drug and immigrant smuggling out of Guangdong Province."

"Hold up a second," Feinberg said. "You know how to speak Chinese?"

"No, but the old man does ... did."

"Malcolm was affluent in Chinese, Russian, German Spanish, Japanese, Arabic and god knows how many other languages," Lee added.

"Anyway," Jamal continued. "The triad enlisted the service of your Uncle, Ms. Wu, to use his influence with Chinese officials in Guangdong to smooth out the passage of their shipments. I think you can take up the story from there."

"Yes," Mei-ling said. "When they found out Uncle Peter was leaking information they had him murdered."

"Yes, your uncle found out about a special shipment being made and was about to contact the Chinese Consulate when they gunned him down."

Smitty felt Mei-ling's hand tighten on his leg where she had been resting it.

"Anyway," Jamal continued, "two days ago I picked up a transmission from somewhere in Central California to Mikhalov. The man said something like, 'the package being ready for delivery,' only in Russian of course..."

"The Panda?" Mei-ling blurted out.

"Yes, the bear," Jamal said. "Not long after, Makhalov called Rashnikov to report that his Panda was being held at a private wild life ranch outside a place called Mojave, California. It was under the care of a veterinarian—who I presume was your Russian friend—and was ready to be flown out of the country. Arrangements were made to have a private jet fly to the ranch and pick the bear up. That was two days ago. I suspect that means the bear will be transported sometime within the next two weeks."

"We have to get started right away. Where is this place?" Mei-ling said, nearly jumping out her chair.

Smitty put his hand on her shoulder, hoping to calm her down.

"No Isaac.! We have to get started right away."

"So, where exactly is this so-called wild-life ranch?" Lee said.

"Well, that's the problem. As far as I could tell, the call came from somewhere near this Mojave ... within a fifty square mile radius."

Mei-ling collapsed back into her seat. "That will be like finding a pencil in a haystack," she said.

"I believe it's a needle in a haystack, but never mind," Jamal said. "They have to feed this thing and my research says an adult Panda eats at least 40 pounds of bamboo a day. Someone in the area must have noticed so much bamboo passing through. I guess you'll have to do some detective work. Isn't that what you guys do?"

"I suggest we get a good night's sleep and leave first thing in the morning," Feinberg said. "It's been a long day."

"I have to agree with the FBI man on this one. I have to make some arrangements before we go anyway," Lee said, drinking down the rest of his scotch and getting up.

"Goddamnit Lee. Would you start calling me Gabe? That's my name," Feinberg protested, as he too stood up.

"Well, if you'll stop referring to me as the mad dog killer."

"Agreed," Feinberg said.

"Seven o'clock sharp, in the lobby. I'll eat dinner in my room." Lee said.

"Me too," Feinberg said, as they both made their ways to separate exits.

Jamal saw the distress on Mei-ling's face. He felt like he knew her and Smitty. He placed his hand over hers. "I wouldn't be worried, Ms. Wu. From what I understand you and Smitty here tracked down those Pandas twice already. Seems to me you should have no trouble finding this one. And now you have an experienced FBI agent working with you, not to mention one of NSA's top operatives."

"You see," Smitty said. "We'll find that last Panda, and then we can put this whole thing behind us and maybe find some peace."

Mei-ling forced herself to smile and nodded to Jamal. Then she kissed Smitty on the cheek and excused herself. "I think I'll go to the room. I'm suddenly very tired."

"I'll be right up," Smitty said. He turned to Jamal. "So, what's your plans. You coming with us?"

Jamal took a sip from his beer. "You know this could be very dangerous."

"You think the NSA is still after us?"

"No, it will take weeks before they figure out we weren't in the cabin when it went up. I mean the Russians. Those people don't play."

"What do you plan on doing?"

"Well, I suppose I'll tag along with you folks. Maybe I could be useful. But if the shooting starts, don't look to me for help. Basically I'm a physical coward."

"Brother, you aren't the only one."

Feinberg saw Lee standing on the third floor balcony smoking a cigarette and staring at the ocean.

"Marshal," he said, walking over to the NSA man and standing next to him.

"You talking to me? Name's Lee."

"Yeah, but your first name is Marshal."

"Well agent Feinberg, what can I do for you?"

"I thought we agreed that you'd call me Gabe? Agent Feinberg sounds so formal under the circumstances."

"OK agent Gabe, what do you want?"

"Just a question. You can tell me to fuck off if you like."

"Shoot."

"Haven't you ever felt guilty about all the people you have killed over the years?"

Hmmmm," Lee said taking a puff from his cigarette. "Fuck off."

"Sorry Marshall. I was just curious."

Feinberg started to walk away.

"Hold up, pal," Lee said. "To answer your question, no. Most of the people I killed, or had killed, were bad men; killers with no conscience about who they killed or hurt in order to further they're goals. I have no regrets. In war, innocents sometimes get hurt. Does that answer your question?"

"Well, I guess I should have figured that out myself."

"You don't approve. Fuck you."

"Doesn't matter I suppose. I was just curious." He turned his back and walked away.

The sun was setting into the ocean as the lights from Monterey across the bay began to come on. Mei-ling and Smitty walked hand in hand down the nearly deserted beach in silence. Several large Mexican families had built fires and were cooking while children scampered along the shore, playing tag with the water as it swept onto the shore and then receded back into the pounding surf.

"Well, it's all going to be over, one way or the other," Smitty said, breaking their silence.

Mei-ling let loose of his hand and walked toward the water. She stood there silently, looking out into the gray dusk that rose out of the black water of the Pacific Ocean. Her thoughts drifted to China. It seemed like so long ago since she had escaped from that land that had become foreign to her. Then she felt Smitty's arms wrap around her waist. She placed her hands over his and pressed them against her.

"I have to do everything I can to get that last Panda, Isaac. I owe it to my Uncle. I owe it to us."

* * *

Chapter 39

Monterey, Ca

They met in the lobby at seven and grabbed paper cups of complimentary coffee. Lee herded them out and to the Jeep.

"What's the rush?" Feinberg protested, eyeing the croissants and sweet rolls on a platter next to the coffee.

"I have to meet someone in about half an hour. It's not far from here."

They drove out Highway One, the way they came in, and connected with Highway 56 inland. It wasn't long until Lee instructed Jamal to pull off the highway onto a two lane road cutting through what seemed like miles of green artichoke plants to a lone building housing a large fruit and vegetable stand.

"This is it," Lee said. "Pull in and park."

Jamal did as instructed, pulling the jeep onto the dirt parking lot and stopping in front of the stand.

They all sat quietly in the car for a few minutes.

"Well," Feinberg said. "What are we waiting here for?"

"I'm expecting someone," Lee answered.

"I'm not sitting here in this hot car. I think I'll go shop," Mei-ling said.

"Yes. I'm hungry," Jamal agreed, and they all piled out of the jeep, leaving Feinberg and Lee."

It wasn't long before two Caddis, one red convertible, the other a black sedan, pulled into the parking lot and stopped alongside the artichoke field away from the open front of the fruit stand.

"That's them," Lee said. "Wait here."

As Lee approached the two cars, Feinberg saw two men get out. Lee talked to them for a couple of minutes and then walked to the trunk of the sedan and opened it, looked inside, and then shut it. He nodded to the two men who then got into the convertible and drove off, leaving a cloud of dust in their wake.

Lee waved to Feinberg to join him.

The others had seen what had happened from the cashier's line, and walked to where Lee and Feinberg stood behind the Cadillac.

"What was that all about?" the FBI agent asked as the others gathered around.

"Some acquaintances of mine," Lee said. "I want you to ride with me. We'll meet up with you three in Lancaster."

"What's in the trunk?" Smitty asked.

"It's the reason agent Feinberg here is riding with me." He unlocked the trunk and opened it.

They all stared into the huge space; more weapons than Smity had ever seen in his life.

"Shit. We going to war?"

"I hope you don't think I'm going to participate in any gun play," Jamal said.

"No," Lee answered, and then back to Feinberg. "You've been trained in these weapons I assume," Lee said.

Feinberg kept his eyes on the arsenal in the trunk and nodded an affirmative.

"I know how to us military weapons," Mei-ling said.

Lee laughed. "I'm sorry, Ms. Wu, but these are much different than what you trained on twenty-five years ago. I know all about your stint with the People's Militia. Maybe in a pinch."

"That was an AK47 I saw. I was trained on that."

Lee didn't seem to notice her remark, or he chose to ignore her.

"You think we're going to need these?" Smitty said.

"I've had experience with Russian gangsters, as I suspect Gabe has. What do you think?" Lee said, closing the trunk lid.

"But how did you get these and the car. Who were those guys?" Feinberg said.

"Come on pal, you know what I've been doing all these years. A man has to plan ahead. I have contacts all over the world, and don't think I haven't stashed a whole lot of dough away for a rainy day. We'll meet you folks in Lancaster. There's a hotel on Highway 14 between Rosamond and Lancaster. It's called the High Desert Inn. We'll meet there and plan our strategy."

* * *

Chapter 40

Lancaster, California

The High Desert Inn was a fancy motel with rooms along two long covered walkways facing a large swimming pool with crystal clear blue water. A long row of tropical shrubbery and palm trees blocked the traffic along Highway 14. The motel had an adjoining restaurant with a bar attached; the kind of place where husbands and wives came for a one nighter with someone else's husband or wife, and families came for Saturday dinner. The bar had a small band stand with a dance floor where local groups played on the weekends.

It was a Monday evening when the black Cadi and the Jeep met up in the parking lot. There were plenty of rooms available. They took their small travel bags to their assigned rooms, and met up in the restaurant after freshening up.

The restaurant was well suited for them with large high backed red naughyde booths that could easily accommodate six.

The waitress served coffee tothe five strangers in the booth and was convinced they were a gang of bank robbers hatching a job. When she related this to the chef he scoffed: "They're just strangers passing through, you dummy."

Feinberg spread out a map of the area on the table.

"I think we should split up into two groups. One takes the northeast section. The other the northwest. Ms. Wu will come with me and...

"No, no, that will never do," Mei-ling objected. "Isaac and I won't be separated."

"But neither of you are professionals," Feinberg said.

"I agree," Lee said.

"No," Smitty interrupted. "Mei-ling and I—well Mei-ling actually— found those bears twice when no one else could."

"That's why the Chinese recruited me," Mei-ling added.

"It couldn't be because they couldn't do it themselves," Lee said.

"Or maybe the million dollars they're willing to pay you," Jamal said.

Everyone turned to Duclois who hadn't said anything since they had come down from their rooms.

"How do you know about that?" Mei-ling asked, although she wasn't surprised since the Jamal seemed to know everything about everyone. He grinned. Lee and Feinberg stared across their coffee cups at Mei-ling.

"Is that true?" Feinberg asked.

Mei-ling nodded.

"Shit," Feinberg said. "A million?"

"Personally, I'm okay with that," Lee said. "These people didn't ask to get mixed up in this thing. Smitty here did it because he fell in love with Ms. Wu, and I can't blame him for that."

Smitty unconsciously took Mei-ling's hand.

"And Ms. Wu did it out of love for her uncle. As far as I'm concerned Ms. Wu should have held out for more," Lee said.

"Well, I don't know," Feinberg said. "It seems I'm getting the short end of the stick here. By all accounts I've lost my job, and now I'm a hunted man, if what you say is true."

"No one's twisting your arm," Lee said.

"I know you've just been trying to protect me, Gabe," Smitty added. "No one will hold it against you if you want to bail out."

"Or maybe you'd rather get a cut of the money," Lee said.

Feinberg took a sip from his coffee cup. "Well, I've come this far. I guess I'll see it through."

"And what about you, Jamal?"

"Me? Oh, I'll tag along. I'm curious to see how this works out."

"Good, then it's settled," Lee said. "Gabe and I will go north, and Smitty and Ms. Wu will head west on Highway 38. We stop at every gas station, feed store and country store and ask questions."

"And by the way," Jamal said. "I question if what we're looking for is actually a wild life refuge. It's possible, but it could just be a ranch or any large land holding big enough to accommodate an airstrip."

"You didn't say who Jamal will go with." Mei-ling said.

"I'll remain here and see what I can find on the computer."

`Good then," Lee said. "It's settled. This calls for a drink. But first..." he put a small leather bag on the table and pulled out four cell phones and passed them out ... "these are clean. Each person's number is listed. Now then, let's drink to it."

He called the waitress over. This time he took a good look at her. She wasn't bad; in her thirties with a jumble of dirty blond hair piled on her head that gave her a kind of wild sensuous look. She left the top three buttons of her uniform unbuttoned, and had hemmed the bottom of her uniform to show off her long shapely legs.

She looked around at the group, staring at Mei-ling for a moment, and then turned back to Lee. "You people bank robbers or something?"

They all began laughing. The waitress' naive question broke the tension.

"What makes you say that?" Lee finally managed.

"Well, I was just wondering," the waitress smiled.

"We'll have drinks all around."

They all ordered their usual. The waitress took another long look at Mei-ling who ordered her vodka martini, and then disappeared into the bar.

"She's suspicious," Mei-ling said.

Lee laughed. "No Ms. Wu. She wants to join up. She's jealous. Didn't you see the green envy in her eyes as she stared at you?"

The others laughed.

"I don't understand." Mei-ling said.

Smitty put his arm around her shoulder and kissed her on the cheek. "Mai, look at us. Five suspicious looking strangers huddled around the table concentrating on a map. And you the only woman with four men. For a lonely waitress in the middle of nowhere this smells of excitement."

"Why would she want that?" Mei-ling said.

The waitress returned with their drinks. She had a good memory and set them down one by one in front of the person who ordered it. Then she slipped a piece of paper to Lee and whispered. "I get off at ten. Call me."

He slipped the paper into his pocket. "We'll be ordering dinner in about twenty minutes."

The rest of the evening was spent drinking and eating, with Lee and Feinberg trading humorous stories from their experiences that kept them all laughing, except Mei-ling who still had a hard time understanding American humor.

It was after ten when they finally paid the check and left for their rooms. Lee glanced in the nearly empty bar as they left and saw the waitress with a cocktail in front of her. She looked back at him and raised her glass as if in toast. He smiled.

*

It was a hot night with a gentle breeze blowing across the desert. It reminded Mei-ling of her home in Guangzhou.

"I wish I had a swimming suit," she said, as Smitty opened the door to their room overlooking the swimming pool.

"So, lets go swimming naked," Smitty said.

She hugged him and laughed.

"No. I'm serious," he said. "We wrap ourselves in towels and go down to the pool and get in. Hell, there isn't anyone down there and there aren't many cars, so we have the place pretty much to ourselves."

She hesitated and then; "Let's do it ."

Jamal wasn't sleepy. He stood by the walkway railing on the second floor in front of his room looking out into the star filled sky when he saw two figures slip into the pool below. He knew who they were and smiled.

Mei-ling swam across the pool while Smitty admired her perfect golden body and felt his desire for her surge. They hadn't made love since they had left Oakland. He swam after her and pinned her against the side of the pool. She wrapped her arms around his neck and they kissed. She pressed her body next to him, welcoming him to her. It was over in a moment of desire and they lingered.

"Ngóh oi néih. I love you, Isaac," she whispered

"This will all be over soon," he said. "Maybe then we can finally find peace and just be together. You are all I ever wanted."

She pressed her lips to his.

*

Feinberg also couldn't sleep and stood in the shadows by the door of his room smoking a cigarette when he heard someone's footsteps coming up the stairs and heading down the walkway. It was a woman silhouetted in the dim light. She stopped at Lee's room and knocked softly. The light from the opened door revealed her face; the waitress. She slipped in and the door closed. It was dark again.

Gabe Feinberg was not a sentimental man, but he suddenly felt homesick for his wife and children. "Son-of-a bitch," he said to himself and stomped out his cigarette.

* * *

Chapter 41

Mojave Desert

Lee and Feinberg headed north toward Mojave. The sun was beating down on the Cadillac, but the air conditioner kept the interior a comfortable 69 degrees.

"So, I noticed you had a visitor last night," Feinberg said.

"Agent Feinberg ... Gabe, you were spying on me."

"I was just having a smoke when she came to your room. You recruit her?"

Lee laughed. "Poor girl, she desperately wants to get out of here. I think she sees me as her ticket."

"I hope you didn't make any rash promises. A sexy woman can do that to a lonely middle-aged man."

Lee laughed again. "Gabe, old buddy, I've had women all over the world. Every one of them wanted something from me. Some even wanted to kill me and were willing to fuck me just to get close enough. No, I didn't make any promises. I did get her to agree to keep her eyes and ears open and to report to me anyone mentioning a captive bear, or a shipment of bamboo. I don't think she put the two things together, but at least we have eyes and ears at the High Desert Inn. Better than nothing."

"I suppose," Feinberg said.

"Hey, she's a naive sweet lady, and I don't meet many like that in my line of business. Besides, she has a great body."

Their plan was to first drive out Highway 14 to the Mojave Grain and Feed store and start their search there, and then systematically make their way west to Tehachapi.

Mei-ling and Smitty were not professionals. They started stopping at truck stops, feed stores, and roadside business, along Highway 138 west, always asking the same questions: Is there a wild life rescue ranch nearby, or do they know of such a place; has there been any shipments of bamboo in the area? There wasn't a lot to see along the Highway and fewer places to stop. They took a side trip to a small community called Fairmont, and stopped at the old gasoline station and market combo. Aside from some flirtatious remarks toward Mei-ling, no one knew anything. When Mei-ling persisted, an old man took her by her elbow like a school girl being punished, and walked to the edge of the station.

"Look out there young lady," he said.

She looked out at mile after mile of flat wasteland, and then looked at the old man whose face was the same color as the barren landscape.

"Does that look like a place where things grow? There's no bamboo around here, young lady."

By the time they pulled into the High Desert Inn parking lot the sun was going down over the coastal hills, casting a golden and pink glow that faded into a dark blue. The far away rumble of thunder came out of the east with flashes of lightning threatening to ignite the dry summer terrain.

They entered the lobby. A sad Country Western song came out of the bar. Lee, Feinberg and Jamal were huddled together in a booth. The drinkers were sparse at the bar. A few couples sat hidden in the other booths. Smitty figured the place only began to rock on the weekends.

"I hate country western," he remarked as they headed toward their companions.

"Well, if it isn't Nick and Nora Charles," Lee said looking up.

"Watch it," Feinberg said, "Your age is showing."

They apparently were old buddies now, Smitty thought, as they squeezed into the booth.

"Speaking about Nick and Nora Charles, we could sure use a drink."

"Who is this, Nick and Nora?" Mei-ling asked.

"They were like the alcoholic versions of Charley Chan," Lee said. "And a lot funnier."

"I know Charley Chan," Mai said. "Racist stereo type created by Hollywood."

"No, what he meant was that the Thin Man, like Charley Chan, were famous movie detectives," Smitty said.

"Still raciest stereo types," Jamal said without lifting his face from his laptop.

"What about those drinks," Smitty said. "I'm parched."

Lee called the waitress. "Krissy, honey, how about some service."

It was the waitress from the night before, but with a big smile this time.

"Another round, sweetheart."

She smiled at Mei-ling. "Vodka Martini up. Can I put some extra olives, hon?"

"One will be enough," Mei-ling said.

"And a JD clean for the gentleman."

Smitty nodded.

"And you sir? Another Santa Barbara Pinot?"

"That'll be great," Feinberg said.

"And a Bud for the other gentleman?"

Jamal looked up from his lap top. "Still nursing the one I got."

"And single malt scotch, Hon."

"You're an angel," Lee said.

They all watched as the waitress walked over to the bar, moving her curves seductively.

"Well," Smitty said. "Seems we've gotten pretty chummy with the help."

"Real chummy," Feinberg said.

"She's an asset," Lee said. "Eyes and ears on the floor."

"More than just an asset, I'd say," Smitty added.

Mei-ling, totally disinterested in the banter about the waitress said, "So, did you two find out anything?"

"We went up to Mojave and checked all the feed stores from there back. No one knew anything," Feinberg said. "What about you folks?"

"Nothing. Some people were very rude," Mei-ling said.

"A few people laughed when we asked about the bamboo," Smitty added. "We worked our way up to Tehatchapi stopping at feed stores, truck stops and rest areas."

"What about you Jamal?" Feinberg said.

He looked up from his lap top. It was obvious he hadn't been paying much attention to the conversation around him. "Me? I've been trying to hack into the CIA's satellite spy system."

"You can do that?" Lee asked.

"I said I've been trying," came Jamal's curt answer to the NSA man. "This shit ain't easy, my friend."

"You mean to tell me the CIA has spy satellites circling the earth?" Feinberg said. "I never heard of that."

"You wouldn't," Lee said. "It's top secret. They can spy on everything on the earth's surface. I believe they have two of them out there."

"Three," Jamal said. "If I can hack into the system I can direct the cameras and search our area. But so far no luck."

"They can't do that," Smitty said. "That's illegal."

Lee, Feinberg and Jamal all laughed.

"These are the guys who asssainated JFK," Lee said. "You think they care about legal?"

"Ever since the Soviets shot down the U-2 spy plane over Russia, the government has developed and launched spy satellites," Jamal said. "They use high resolution cameras to spy on any part of the planet they want."

"Shit, that's fucked up," Smitty said.

"Isaac, you swear too much," Mei-ling said.

"But Mai, don't you understand? The government can spy on anyone if they want."

"It does not surprise me that the Americans would do this," Mei-ling said. "They are international outlaws. Look at what they did to the people of Vietnam."

"She makes a good point," Jamal said. "Anyway, that's what I'm doing."

"So, we have nothing," Feinberg said.

Just then the waitress came with their drinks.

"Here you go folks," she said, and passed out the drinks, smiling at Mei-ling again like they shared a secret.

"Well, Krissy here has something to report, don't you sweetheart," Lee said. "Bring over a chair and sit with us."

"Lee, I can't do that. You trying to get me fired."

"Don't worry, I'll take care of it," Lee said.

The waitress hesitated, and looked over her shoulder at the bartender. He was chatting up a couple of middle-aged women at the bar. Then she pulled over a chair and sat down, facing the five people in the booth. All eyes were on her. She felt self conscious. She had never been the center of attention.

"Don't be nervous. Tell them what you found out," Lee said.

She looked back at the bartender again and then back across the napkin holder, salt and pepper shaker and Tabasco bottle at her audience.

"It was about an hour before my shift started, so I decided to sit at the bar and have a drink. That asshole over there," she went on, nodding her head in the direction of the bartender, "wouldn't pay any attention to me, so I called him over. He said it was against company policy to serve employees. 'I'm on my own time,' I insisted but he wouldn't serve me until a man came in and sat down beside me. 'Give the lady a drink,' he said. So the asshole had no choice."

Just then the bartender sauntered over to the table. "What the hell you doing, Krissy. You can't sit with the customers. He put his hand on her shoulder as if to drag her off the chair when Lee grabbed him by the wrist and yanked him toward the table.

"The lady's talking to us." he flipped out his ID card. "This is official government business." He let go of his grip on the man's wrist.

"I'm sorry sir," the bartender said. "Sure, she can sit here as long as she has to. Everything's cool, right Krissy?"

She didn't say anything, and the bartender made a hasty retreat back to the bar.

"Go on, sweetheart. It's okay."

"Well," she said. "To make a long story short," she glanced back at the bartender again who was nervously busying himself behind the bar, and she smiled. "To make a long story short, we carried on small talk for a while. You know how it is. He said he was from LA. Anyway, it was getting close to my shift, so I asked him what he was doing out here in the middle of nowhere. He seemed to get a kick out of the question, and said I wouldn't believe him if he told me. I said, 'Try me' Well, he said he worked for a construction company in LA and they were clearing a lot for some shopping mall project. They had to cut down a grove of—would you believe—bamboo. Well, for some reason they had him bring the stuff all the way up here to deliver to a ranch."

"Did he say where the ranch was?" Mei-ling said.

"He said he wasn't supposed to say. He seemed to get nervous and said he had to go."

"And?" Feinberg prompted.

"And nothing. He got up and left. I had to get ready for my shift." She could see the look of disappointment on Mei-ling's face. "I'm sorry. I did what I could…"

"It's okay," Lee reassured her.

"Did he tell you the name of the construction company he worked for?" Jamal asked.

"Let me see. I believe he said it was Volga River Construction and Demolition Company. Yes, I remember because that's someplace in Russia, isn't it?

Jamal got busy on his laptop. "As I suspected. Owned by Svetlana and Ryko Sokolov. Most likely a Russian mafia front."

"Russian Mafia," the waitress blurted out.

Lee sushed her.

"Jeez Louise. That's who you guys are hunting for?"

"Better not talk about it to anyone," Feinberg said.

"He's right, Krissy. Keep it to yourself."

"Don't worry about me. I'm your gal. Now, I'd better get back to work," she said, standing up.

"Sure sweetheart. You did great, and if that gorilla gives you any trouble let me know."

She gave him a smile, and then walked back to the bar.

"It seems we're right back to where we started," Feinberg said.

"Maybe not," Jamal said. "Let me out. I'm going back to my room and work on some things. Bring me up a sandwich after you eat."

* * *

Chapter 42

Mohave Desert

They met in the restaurant the next morning to plot out their day's strategy. It was decided that they would explore side roads along the same routes they took the day before. Jamal hadn't come down. They suspected he had stayed up late on his computer and overslept.

They finished their coffee and went out to the parking lot.

"What's she doing here?" Feinberg said when he saw the waitress in the front seat of the Cadi. She was now in a tight pair of Levis, flannel cowgirl shirt complete with leather fringe, and cowboy boots. The only thing out of place was the LA Dodgers baseball cap, but it seemed to suit her.

"Krissy? She grew up around here," Lee said. "I thought she could help us out."

Feinberg watched Smitty and Mei-ling take off in the Jeep. He shrugged his shoulders and opened the door to the back seat.

*

Smitty and Mei-ling had headed back down to Highway 38—West Avenue D Road—and decided they would try the dirt road they had started traveling the day before. Smitty wanted to stop at the gas station first and ask if they knew where it went.

"Don't want to go on any wild goose chases," he said.

Mei-ling looked at him with a blank expression. "They have wild geese around here," she said.

Smitty laughed, "No, it's just an express...oh, never mind."

He pulled the jeep into the gas station. The same old man came sauntering out just as a gust of wind sent a tumbleweed rolling into the single pump. The old man nudged it on its way as he came up to the front window of the car.

"You folks back again?"

"We thought you might be able to give us some information," Smitty said.

"What would that be?"

"That road about a quarter of a mile up, you wouldn't know if it leads somewhere would you?"

"Son, it's like I told that there girlfriend of yours yesterday; there ain't nothing out there but more of the same wasteland you're looking at right now. So, what in God's name do you think could be out that road?"

"Well, something," Smitty said. "They don't just build roads for the hell of it, pal, and it looks to me like it's being kept up."

The old man's face suddenly turned hard. It wasn't as if he changed expressions, but Smitty could see the hint of mirth behind the gray eyes.

"Well, saying there is something at the end of that road," the old man said. "It could be something you really don't want to find, or maybe, something that doesn't want to be found."

With that said, the old man turned back to the shelter of the small adobe building just as another gust of wind blew and a tumbleweed leisurely rolled through the gas station and back out into the barren waste, kicking up dust as it did.

"He's lying," Smitty said.

"I think you are right, Isaac. Let's go."

"There's nothing out here, except maybe some Mexican goat herders," Krissy said.

Feinberg and Lee looked out over the brown landscape spotted with mesquite, Joshua trees, juniper, fan palms, and an occasional cottonwood tree. Rocks and large boulders were strewn around like some giant had randomly tossed them there without rhyme or reason.

"She's right," Feinberg said. "It's a fucking desert."

"There has to be some ranches or something." Lee said.

"Well, there are some horse stables where people who live in town board their horses. That's what my step dad did. My mom hated horses." Krissy said.

"Well, maybe you should show us some of these horse ranches," Lee said.

"Stables," Krissy said.

"Yeah, whatever."

Just then Lee's cell phone rang. He dug into his pocket and flipped it open. "Yeah."

The voice on the other end was Jamal. "You'd better come back here. I think I've found your bear."

Mei-ling and Smitty had been driving down the dirt road for about twenty minutes when they noticed a massive brown cloud coming their way.

"What the hell is that?" Smitty said.

"Mei-ling stared at the cloud for a minute. "Isaac, turn around.""

"What."

"Turn around and drive fast," Mei Ling said. "That's a sand storm."

"How do you know?"

"I've seen them in the Goby desert when I was on an archeological trip. Turn around."

Smitty did as instructed and started back down the road, but as fast as he drove the storm caught up with them, and soon they were lost in the blinding cloud of dust. Smitty turned on the headlights, but the dirt road was totally lost. He came to a stop.

"Why are we stopping Isaac?"

"If we keep going, we're going to go off the road and we'll never find our way back," he said.

They sat there silently, tightly holding hands, as the wind, sand and dirt pounded the Jeep relentlessly. It was as if they had been swept away from the world; as if the world never existed and they alone existed in a bubble protecting them from the raging storm around them. Nothing else mattered but landing safely from the raging sea of pounding dirt...

Lee pulled into the parking lot of the High Desert Inn. He had expected to see the jeep parked there as Smith and the Chinese woman had not traveled as far as they had. But they weren't there.

Krissy leaned over and kissed him on the cheek. "I'd better not go in. I'm in enough trouble with my boss as it is. You really humiliated him last night."

"Sure sweetheart. No problem," Lee said.

Then she turned to Feinberg in the back seat and blew him a kiss. I'll see you guys in a couple of hours when my shift starts. Okay?"

"Sure thing," Feinberg said.

They went into the hotel and found Jamal at their usual booth with his lap top in front of him.

"Hey," Feinberg said in greeting.

Jamal looked up from the lap top. They slid into the booth on either side of him.

"So, what's this earth shaking discovery of yours?" Lee asked.

A waitress came to their booth. "Can I help you gentlemen?"

She was an older woman who had the hang dog look of someone who had been working on their feet for too many years.

"Bring me a scotch, single malt, ice," Lee said without looking up.

"Just coffee for me." Jamal said.

"Same here," Feinberg said.

The waitress walked off without a word.

"Racist bitch," Jamal said.

"Why do you say that?" Feinberg asked.

"I've been sitting her for almost an hour and she never once came over to ask if I would like something. Then you two show up and she comes right over. What do you think?"

"Forget it," Lee said. "What do you have for us?"

"I'd rather wait 'til Smith and Ms. Wu come back so I can explain it once if you don't mind. After all, we're doing all this for them. Right?"

Lee and Feinberg looked at each other. They had both been so absorbed in solving the mystery of the last Panda that they had forgotten why they were doing it, and in all likelihood, risking their lives.

"Did you try to call them?" Lee said.

"Yeah, but neither one of them answered."

What had seemed like an eternity was more like twenty minutes until the storm passed over them and swept its way south on into the desert, gobbling up more sand and dust and tumbleweed.

Smitty had turned off the engine fearing dust would clog up the carburetor, and the temperature inside the Jeep had risen to over 120 without the air conditioner. They were both drenched in sweat and exhausted.

"Shall we turn around and keep looking?" Smitty asked.

"All I want right now is a cold shower and a drink," Mei-ling answered. Smitty started the Jeep. It cranked for a minute and finally turned over. He shoved it into fist gear and they jerked forward. The wind had exposed a roughly paved road that had been hidden under the dirt.

The jeep pulled into the parking lot of the High Desert Inn and Smitty parked next to the Cadi. It wasn't shiny black anymore, but covered in a layer of dust. The fancy new hub caps were splattered with mud. Smitty thought how Lee really must hate having to drive it that way.

They got out of the Jeep and were hit with a blast of hot air. Smitty felt himself sweating again after having been in the air conditioned car on the ride back to the inn.

"I'm going up to shower," Mei-ling said.

"I'd better go in and tell the others we're back in case they're worried."

"All right," Mei-ling said. "I'll be down in a few minutes."

Smitty turned to walk into the lobby.

"Isaac," Mei-ling called.

He turned around. Mei-ling fell into his arms and kissed him, a long passionate kiss.

"I love you, Isaac." Then she broke away and headed for the stairs leading up to their room.

Smitty stood there for a moment watching her. Despite everything, she was the best thing that ever happened to him.

*

"So why the fuck didn't you have your cell phone on?" Lee said as Smitty walked up to the booth where they were all sitting.

"And where's Ms. Wu?" Jamal added.

Smitty sat down, and dug the cell phone out o his pocket. "Sorry fellas, I forgot to turn it on." He squeezed in next to Feinberg.

The older waitress came up with their drinks and unceremoniously set them down. Then, she dropped a pile of menus on the table. "You having something, Mister?" she asked Smitty.

"Yes. Bring me a beer and a double JD. Oh, and bring a vodka martini up."

The waitress didn't acknowledge his order. She just walked off without a word.

"Well, she's a piece of work," Smitty remarked. He had known waitresses like her in his job as a business agent; women who had worked all their lives, probably had an unhappy marriage and was left with a kid or two to raise by herself; bitter and alone.

"Mei-ling's taking a shower. She'll be down when she's finished" He then related their venture down the dirt road that wasn't dirt at all, and the dust storm. "There's something at the end of that road." Smitty said. "We were told that there was no welcome for strangers there."

"Let me look into that," Jamal said. "Meanwhile, let's wait for Mei-ling to come down."

They sat there in silence while Jamal fiddled on his lap-top. Lee sipped at his scotch; Feinberg his coffee. Smitty picked up a menu and idly opened it. It hadn't changed from the day before; the same food featured in a million restaurants all over the country: Various cuts of steak, prime rib, pork ribs, roasted chicken, served with mashed potatoes, baked or fries, salads. The beef was particularly good at the High Desert Inn, with fresh meat coming from the Harris Ranch, a giant feed lot up the road north on Highway 5. But Smitty wasn't particularly hungry, and when the waitress returned with the drinks he nodded thanks, and gulped down the bourbon. It fired up his throat and stomach, so he quenched it with the beer.

A few minutes later, Mei-ling came in. They all turned to look at her. She had changed into a pair of jeans with a oversized Cal t-shirt that fell over one shoulder. They all smiled at her as she nudged Smitty and slid into the booth next to him.

"You ordered me a drink. That was thoughtful," she said, and kissed Smitty on the cheek. "Did you tell them about our adventure?"

Jamal looked at them. "I hate to disappoint you two, but what lay at the end of that road was not the ranch we're looking for."

"No, what was it then," Smitty said.

Jamal could see the disappointment on both their faces. "Well, it was the Del Sol Naturalist Commune. A nudist colony."

Feinberg and Lee started to laugh. Smitty looked at Mei-ling, and he laughed at their own folly. But Mei-ling didn't see the humor in it.

"But if that wasn't the ranch, we have to start all over again," she said.

The others stopped laughing, and everyone sat there in silence for a minute.

"Well, maybe not," Jamal said, finally. "I may have found our ranch."

Just then Krissy came up to the table, no longer in her tight jeans and flannel cowgirl shirt, but back in her waitress uniform with the top buttons open enough to show off her cleavage.

"Have we made any progress?" she said with a smile. "Refills?"

"We'll have another round and then we'll order dinner," Lee said. "And we're about to find out if we have made progress. I'll fill you in later tonight."

Krissy smiled at him. It was different from the smile she gave the others and they all noticed. Then she went back into the bar.

"Well Jamal?" Mei-ling prodded.

"Well, I've been going through the county tax records for Kern and San Bernardino Counties and guess what I found?"

"Do tell," Lee said sarcastically.

"A five hundred acre parcel north-west of Barstow registered under the Volga River Investment Corporation. Sound familiar?"

"Wasn't that the name of that construction company that the truck driver worked for; the one your friend Krissy talked with?" Feinberg said.

"Exactly," Jamal said. "The Volga Construction and Demolition Co. And guess who's the CEO and President of the Volga River Investment Corp." He looked at them one by one. "None other than Svetlana and Ryko Sokolov. the same two owners of the construction company. I'd say it's a pretty good bet that's our ranch, and that's where your Panda is right now, just waiting to be picked up and flown to Israel. Or at least somewhere it can be smuggled into Israel."

"Son-of-a bitch," Lee said. "Our friend here's a god damn genius."

Everyone clapped and Jamal nodded his head.

"Well," Smitty said. "This calls for a drink of celebration."

"I'd say," Feinberg agreed.

"What do you say Mei?" Smitty said.

She smiled and nodded, but she shared what Lee was thinking.

"Slow down people," Lee said. "This ain't going be a cake walk. You think those people are going to let us waltz in there and shoot the fucking bear. You people dealt with Chinese gangsters. Let me assure you, these Russians are worse."

Mei-ling nodded her head in agreement. "We're going to have to be just as ruthless as they are," she said.

The men's eyes all turned to her; the small sexy Chinese lady who would let nothing stop her from finally completing her mission.

Just then Krissy came up to the table. "Are we ready to order dinner?"

* * *

Chapter 43

High Desert Inn

Lee watched the woman as she stood by the window. The light from the walkway outside filtered in, silhouetting her shapely naked body.

He felt something stir inside him, a feeling he hadn't experienced in many years. Could it be affection? At least that was the strongest emotion he could make himself feel. He had only been able to make love to prostitutes in the past; no attachments, no feelings, just temporary, noncommittal female companionship. Not that there weren't plenty of eligible woman in Washington, but he couldn't bring himself to get emotionally attached to anyone. There had been too many innocent women and children killed, from either his own hand or on his orders. He had been haunted by them, so he learned to cancel out all emotions...until now.

"I want to come with you tomorrow," the woman said without turning around."

"What?"

She turned toward him. He could see the outline of her firm breasts and flat stomach. She was at least twenty years younger than him.

"I said, I want to come with you."

"That's impossible," Lee said.

"You're going to go away and I'll never see you again."

"No baby, I'll be back for you. There's nothing to worry about."

"I still want to go tomorrow."

"I can't let you do that. It could be dangerous, and you could get hurt. I couldn't have that on my conscience. I promise I'll come back for you."

"I see," she said, and flicked on the light switch.

He watched as she started getting dressed. He saw the hardness in her face. He had seen that look before on the faces of woman who knew they were being abandoned.

"Where are you going?"

"Home. I have to work tomorrow."

She pulled on her jeans and wrapped herself in her shirt. Then she went to the bed and kissed him on the cheek.

"Thanks Lee. It's been fun."

She picked up her shoes and was out the door before he could say anything.

He went to the window and watched as her Volkswagen bus sped out from the parking lot, past the shrubbery and trees, and onto the highway. It occurred to him he had no idea where she lived. He imagined it was in a small trailer at one of the many trailer parks in the area.

He turned off the lights and went back to bed. He had always had trouble sleeping, but now he was also troubled by the young woman. He was determined to come back for her. He imagined them finding an island, somewhere in the Mediterranean or perhaps in South America. Maybe opening a bar and restaurant. He would be back for her. She had been able to pry open a little piece of his heart and he didn't want to lose it.

*

Smitty lay next to Mei-ling. They had made love when they got back to their room, and had lain naked next to each other for a while in silence.

"You know, we may be both killed before this is over. We may not make it this time," she said.

"Don't be silly," Smitty said. "Of course we'll make it. We have always managed to escape in the past, and then we will be finished with it once and for all." He sat up and reached for a cigarette. "No more China, no more NSA killers, and no more godamned pandas. We'll finally be free."

She sat up and rested her head on his shoulder.

"Give me a puff," she said.

He reached over his shoulder with the cigarette. He could feel her drag on it, and then her warm breath on his skin as she exhaled the smoke onto his back. Then she laughed, a feeble sarcastic laugh.

"What's so funny?" he said.

"You, my sweet Isaac. All those times I forced you to come along with me to hunt down those smugglers and nearly got us killed, you kept trying to talk me out of it. You remember?

"Yes."

"And now it's me who's worried, and you reassuring me it will all work out fine."

"I guess."

"Isaac. Isaac, I love you."

* * *

Chapter 44

Mojave Desert

The sun was just rising above the eastern horizon when they started gathering in the restaurant. The golden globe gave off waves of heat turning the purple morning twilight into a deep blue. The forecast was for 112 degrees that day, and in several hours the sky would turn white with the burning sun.

Smitty and Mei-ling met Feinberg at the entrance of the hotel lobby and they went in together. An older Mexican woman was dragging a noisy vacuum cleaner over the red paisley carpeting that covered the lobby floor and on into the restaurant and bar. It was too early for breakfast, but they helped themselves to the complimentary coffee and sweet rolls that were neatly arranged on a table in the lobby, and then made their way into the restaurant to their regular booth where Jamal sat with his lap top open in front of him and a Styrofoam cup next to it.

"Morning."

"Good morning yourself," Feinberg said, and slid into the booth.

"Where's Lee," Smitty inquired. "He's the one insisted we get up at the crack of dawn."

Mei-ling slid in next to Jamal, and Smitty sat next to her on the end.

"Probably still shacking up with that waitress," Feinberg said. "Maybe he's backing out?"

"No!" Mei-ling said. "He's our leader."

"She's right," Jamal said. "For Lee this is his last operation. It's the last thing he has to do before retiring. He wants to end his career on a high note, knowing he did something for the good; knowing he is helping someone he feels a debt to, and not because someone else tells him he has to do it. No my friend, Lee will be here."

"I agree," Smitty said. "He's been there for us, and for you, Gabe."

"Well, we'll see," Feinberg said. "I guess I'm just getting shpilkes ... antsy."

"Good morning. Sorry I'm late, but I've been studying some maps of the area I picked up this morning from the front desk."

They all looked up at Lee. He had seemingly appeared as if out of nowhere.

"What do you mean, this morning?" Feinberg said. "This is this morning."

"Sorry. I guess it was about four."

"Don't you sleep?" Feinberg said.

"Not much. Now go up to your rooms and gather your things. I've checked us all out. This thing will probably take more than one day, so I reserved rooms for us at a motel outside of Barstow. Probably not as plush as this place, but we're not on vacation. I'll meet you all in the parking lot in fifteen minutes."

Feinberg slipped out from the booth first, followed by Mei-ling and Smitty.

"Jamal, I'll have a word with you before we go if that's all right?" Lee said as the others walked past him with their coffee cups in their hands.

Jamal stopped the process of exiting. "Sure Lee. What's up?"

Lee sat on the end of the booth. He looked straight into the Duclois' face.

"I want you to know I had nothing to do with your father's death."

"No one's blaming you," Jamal said.

"But you know I knew him in Paris."

"Yes, I do. Malcolm told me all about it."

"Well, now I'm telling you. The French government asked us for assistance in tracking down the terrorist cells that were setting bombs off all over the city. I had learned French in Vietnam so I was assigned. I met your father. He was intelligent and likeable, but not terrorist material in my opinion, and I told the French that. It wasn't until after I had been reassigned to Eastern Europe that I found out he had been assassinated."

"No matter," Jamal said. "I was only four at the time."

"I didn't suspect him. I only reported that he was sympathetic to the Algerian cause; a lot of people were, especially among immigrants from North Africa."

"As far as my family knew, he could have been killed by the Algerians, maybe because of your association with him. It's a long time ago. Don't worry about it."

"Well, I just wanted to tell you. The French may have killed him despite my report. There was a lot of paranoia at that time."

"Well, now that you got that off your chest can I go get my things?"

"One more minute. How's the satellite connection coming?"

Jamal smiled. "I've linked up with them. One won't be crossing over Central California until tomorrow afternoon, and I think I might be able to direct it. They won't be paying much attention as long as it's over the U. S."

"Great. Let's get going then."

*

Forty minutes later they had past the town of Mojave and were traveling east on Highway 58. Lee was driving the Caddi with Feinberg next to him. Smitty, Mei-ling and Jamal followed behind in the Jeep Wrangler. Jamal sat in the back seat with his head buried in his lap-top.

"Where do you think he's taking us?" Mai Ling said to no one in particular.

Smitty looked over at her. He knew she didn't entirely trust the NSA man. He couldn't figure the man out; Lee had saved his life in the Berkeley Marina parking lot, and he hooked them up with old man Stanford and Duclois.

"What do you think, Jamal?" he said, glancing in the rear view mirror.

"Yeah, what did he ask you back at the restaurant?" Mei-ling said, twisting around in her seat so she could look at the handsome black man in the back seat.

Smitty knew she liked Jamal, but reminded himself that this was no time for jealousy. They had come too far together for that.

Jamal looked up from his lap-top and smiled back at her.

"He just wanted to know if I'd hooked up with the satellite yet."

"Well," Mei-ling prodded.

"Well, maybe. We have to wait and see."

"That's no answer," Mei-ling said.

"Well, that's the best I got."

Mei-ling turned back facing the front. She took Smitty's hand and squeezed it.

Lee signaled for them to get off the highway at Kramer Road and headed north-east into the desert. The late morning sun was now beating down on the road, sending rippling waves of heat up from the ground, distorting the desert landscape and making everything appear as if in a dream. In the distance tall dust devils rose from the desert floor and swirled and danced like crazed deverishes.

"Where are we going?" Feinberg asked.

"The Barstow Gun Club," Lee said. "You don't think we're going to walk into this thing without everyone learning how to handle these weapons I have in the truck."

"You really think it will be that bad?"

"Gabe, old pal, we're going to be entering a war zone. These guys are well armed and they have a mission. Coming back empty handed is not an option for them."

The FBI man sat back in the plush leather seat, closed his eyes, and listened to the hum of the air conditioner, and the tires of the car as they sped over the hot asphalt. He thought about his wife and kids and wondered if he would ever see them again.

As if reading his mind, Lee said, "You know, it's not too late for you to bail out, pal. I mean, when it comes right down to it, you don't really have a dog in this fight."

"You got a cigarette?" Feinberg said.

* * *

Chapter 45

Barstow, Ca

Lee flipped opened his ID and held it out for the middle-aged man behind the gun counter to see. The man hadn't shaved for a couple of days, and a gray shadow covered his pudgy face. His eyes were hidden behind aviator sunglasses. The sound of a swamp cooler rattled and gurgled as it pumped cool air into the room.

"Marshall Lee. Captain Marshall Lee?" the man said. "I'll be goddamned."

"You know me?" Lee said.

"You got a partner named Mac—Captain McCraven I think his name was, or at least that's the rank he was going by."

"We know each other?"

"Well, you probably wouldn't recognize me. Me and my crew pulled you two out of Cambodia a couple of times. I had on a helmet and shades and maybe fifty pounds lighter, but I sure remember you CIA guys. Damn that was a lot of years ago."

"You were the chopper pilot?"

"Lieutenant Frank Henderson, 52nd AHC, Special Assignment Attached to Special Ops, which consisted of pulling you dudes out of bad situations."

"No shit" Lee said, "what the fuck you doing here?"

"Me and some buddies bought this land cheap after we got out. Figured it would make a great place for a shooting range, what with Edwards nearby."

"They got shooting ranges on the base," Lee said.

Henderson pushed the baseball cap he was wearing back and rubbed the balding spot of the top of his head. "Yeah. Bad call that one. We were all high most of the time. I'm the only one left. My old lady split with my last partner, and as you could probably tell by the parking lot, we don't have a lot of members. But never mind that. Marshall Lee. CSS now, eh? That's part of the NSA," he said, looking down at Lee's ID again. "Still got your fingers in the shit."

"You could say that. I need a private range where me and my companions can check out some weapons."

"No sweat, brother. I can set you up on my private range. Reserved for VIPs. We call it The John Wayne Range. How many of you are there?"

"Five."

Henderson scratched at his half grown beard. "You don't think ... could you give me a hundred bucks for its use? I hate to ask from a war buddy, but ... well, as you can see, I can use the bread."

"No problem, Lieutenant;" Lee said, and pulled a wad of bills from his pocket and peeled off two fifties.

"Take the road down the arroyo and follow the signs."

"Thanks pal," Lee said and started heading for the door.

"You know. No one gives a fuck anymore," Henderson said.

Lee stopped and turned around, surprised by the sudden bitterness and anger in the man's voice.

"What?"

"Half my buddies are dead and the rest are fucked up on drugs, homeless, in jail. No one remembers or gives a shit."

"Yeah," Lee said.

"Do me a favor. Stop by when you're finished."

"Will do," Lee said, and went out the door into the blazing sun.

"No, Mei, I'm not going to let that bastard turn me into a killer like him," Smitty protested. "And you, Gabe, I can't believe you're going along with this shit."

"Please," Mei-ling pleaded, squeezing Smitty's hand.

"Look Smitty," Feinberg said. "If we're going to do this thing we have to be ready for anything that comes up."

That was the conversation taking place when Lee got back to the two parked cars. He had expected Jamal to protest, but he hadn't been sure of Smitty. He had counted on the Wu woman to convince him. Instead he found Smitty adamant, while Jamal sat in the back seat of the Jeep looking at his lap top.

"Hey. Everything's set. I expect Gabe has explained what we're doing here."

"I have no intention of killing anybody," Smitty said.

Lee ducked his head into the back seat of the Jeep.

"You okay with this, Jamal?"

"You're the boss man," Jamal said without looking up from the computer.

"You see, Smitty, Jamal's okay with it, and he has a lot less to gain from this thing than you do."

"I don't give a shit. I have no interest in learning how to use your weapons. I refused to fight in Vietnam and I'm not interested in shooting anyone now."

Lee kept his mouth shut. He wasn't the right person to convince the idealistic union man and he knew it. It was the FBI man who stepped up.

"Smitty, come on now. Are you trying to tell me that when you and Miss Wu were captured at Stover's Ranch and held in that barn; when me and Rich broke in to get you out of there; that if we had been the Chinese gangsters come to finish you off, that you wouldn't have killed them? You know damn well you would have. You would do anything to protect Miss Wu."

Smitty stood there for a minute, staring at Feinberg. He was right, of course, and he would have done the same thing when Mei-ling had dragged him to the ranch in the Oakland Hills two weeks earlier. He looked at Mei-ling who was still clutching his hand, her eyes pleading.

"Isaac?"

"Fuck it. Let's get on with it then. If this is going to be war, I guess that's what it's got to be."

"That's the spirit, pal," Lee said.

Smitty was a natural, if there was such a thing firing a weapon. Once he got the feel of the M-16 he let losse short accurate bursts like he had been a killer for years.

Not so, Jamal. He handled a weapon like it was a fine young woman, or a sensitive computer as fit him better. The first time he fired he lost control of the weapon and dropped it. Thankfully, no one was in the line of fire. Lee gave him an Army issue SIG Pro 9mm semiautomatic pistol. Jamal was no more comfortable with the small weapon, even after Lee showed him the right way to hold it with both hands, crouch and squeeze.

"Better you stick to your computer and keep out of the line of fire," Lee told him.

Mei-ling admitted she hadn't fired an assault weapon since she was seventeen as a member of the Volunteer Militia in Guangdong. But when Lee pulled the AK47 from his trunk and handed it to her it came back to her, like riding a bike. They were old friends, and she handled the weapon with confidence.

"Have you ever killed anyone?" Lee said.

Smitty objected to the question, but she nodded.

"Maybe. I went on patrol once with the North Vietnamese militia. We were just teenagers. All the real soldiers were in the South. We got into a fire fight with some Americans who had strayed over the line. We all fired. I don't know if I hit any of them, but they were all dead when it was over."

Everyone stopped what they were doing and looked at her in amazement. She seemed ashamed of what she had done, and Smitty put his arm protectively around her.

"Good," Lee said. "You're ahead of the game."

Feinberg hadn't used an assault weapon since training with the Israeli Army, and later in training when he joined the FBI, but he was familiar with the weapons and competent in their use as Lee knew he would be. He had read Gabe's record: Investigator for the Military Police in Saigon where he busted an officer for murdering Vietnamese hookers. That was when he met Ted Harlin, a freelance reporter at the time, and, as it turned out, a close friend of Smitty's. After Vietnam, he joined the Massad where he was part of a secret mission into Lebanon to wipe out a Hezbullah missile battery. When they crossed back into Israel they had three wounded comrades, but left behind a destroyed missile base and a burned out Shi'a village. A month later Feinberg resigned from the Mossad and returned to the States where he was recruited into the FBI. Gabe was no sweat—he was a killer with a conscience—an inconvenience that wouldn't get in the way when the bullets started flying.

It was over two hours before he was satisfied that his little band of warriors could hold their own in a fire fight, depending on the odds and the circumstances. He could only hope for the advantage of surprise. He figured the Russians wouldn't be expecting a bold attack. After all, why would a bunch of Russian gangsters think anyone would make such a fuss over a fucking bear, even a cute black and white one that looked like a kid's toy. All they knew is they had their orders.

On the other hand they could all be killed, and end up buried in an unmarked grave in the middle of the Mojave Desert. But, he figured, everyone knew what they were getting into. Everyone had their own reasons for being there. One way or the other, it would be his last mission. It was something he had to do if he was going to live with himself.

"Suppose you'll be wanting to replenish your ammo." The Lieutenant had changed into a carefully ironed, but faded, camo shirt with his name tag and rank insignia sewed neatly on where they had probably been since his duty in Vietnam. It was baggy, and the man Lee remembered piloting the chopper in Vietnam was a much younger and huskier man.

Lee had come back into the Barstow Gun Club office with Feinberg at his side.

"You're an intuitive man, Lieutenant," Lee said

"I took the liberty of packing it up for you. I hope twenty-five round clips are okay."

"How do you know what weapons we have?"

A self-satisfied smile crossed Henderson's face. "Monitors. Here, come see for yourself." Then, as if noticing for the first time, "Who's your buddy?"

"This is FBI Agent Gabriel Feinberg."

"FBI and NSA. Shit."

"Thanks for packing up the ammo. Wasn't sure you'd have it."

The same all knowing smile appeared on Henderson's face, and Feinberg questioned if the vet was quite all there.

"I keep stocked," Henderson said.

"RPGs?" Lee asked.

"You crazy? I'm standing here talking with a NSA agent and an FBI agent. Those things are illegal."

Maybe he wasn't so crazy, Feinberg realized.

"Look pal," Lee said. "I'll be straight with you. If you have any kind of ordinance we could use, we'll pay top dollar for it. No questions asked."

"What's your mission?"

"Better you don't know," Feinberg said. "Come on, Lee. Let's take the ammo and get out of here." He went to pick up the ammo cases.

"Wait," Henderson said. "Captain Lee. Can I have a word in private?"

"Go ahead, Gabe. Give me a minute."

They waited as Feinberg picked up the two military issue ammo cases and hefted them out of the office.

"Well?" Lee said. "And stop calling me captain. I haven't held a ranking since I was with the Seals."

"Whatever you want, Captain," Henderson said. "Just give me a minute."

Lee glanced at the Rolex on his wrist. "You got a minute."

"Look Captain, I want to come along with you. I don't care what your mission is. I just want to get into the action. I've been dying since I got out. I could be a big help."

Lee looked at the man's desperate face. He knew the feeling; the adrenalin; the feeling of danger and the thrill of having the power of life or death over another human being. There are some men who thrived on it; who needed it to make them feel alive. He knew. He was one of those men.

Smitty sat at the wheel of the Jeep Wrangler brooding. Mei-ling was sitting next to him, but he paid no attention to her. Something had stirred inside him when he fired the M-16; something disturbing. He had recognized it in himself back in 1989 when three Vietnamese gangsters from Oakland's China Town were ready to kill him over a misunderstanding, and it took an earthquake and a collapsed freeway to drag him from death's gate. Ever since that time he had become dissatisfied with his life as an idealistic union representative. He remembered his father—a rank and file Communist—telling him back in 1967 about the Cuban revolutionary hero, Che Guavara, and how he was murdered by the CIA in Bolivia in an abortive attempt to export revolution to that country. Some men need danger to live, his father had told him. Che was a revolutionary, but he found no peace in the success in Cuba. He could only be satisfied tempting death.

Smitty looked over at Mei-ling. He had pledged himself to her and had faced death for her. And each time he had felt the same intense sense of being alive, and it made him fall more in love with her each time. He recalled a small booklet of poetry and photographs from the Student Revolt in Paris in '68. There was a picture of a young masked man throwing a tear gas canister back at police and the simple caption; *The more I revolt, the more I make love.*

"Forget it, Lieutenant. You have no idea what you're talking about."

Lee turned to walk out the door.

"You're planning an assault on the Sokolov ranch, aren't you," Henderson said.

Lee stopped in his tracks and slowly turned around.

"What do you know about the Sokolov ranch?"

"I know that every week, like clockwork, a plane lands there and they unload what I presume are narcotics—marijuana, coke, or both."

"How the fuck do you know that?"

"Because most nights I go out on recon missions. On slow days I go out too. I know what goes on at all the spreads around here."

"What the fuck do you do that for?" Lee said.

"I have to do something around here. I'd go nuts if I just sat here every night. I have night vision glasses and the whole nine yards."

Lee believed him, but he wasn't sure whether the man had already gone over the edge.

"The only thing I can't figure out," Henderson said, "is that you guys aren't DEA. NSA, FBI, and three civilians? Looks like something personal and off the books, but I don't really give a fuck. I want in."

Lee thought about it a minute, staring at the desperate Henderson. If he could be trusted he would be an asset. He was familiar with the terrain, and if his hunch was correct, Henderson had hoarded military ordinances. If he could be trusted.

"I'll have to take it up with the others," he said. "Call me at the Joshua Tree Motel. It's outside of Barstow."

"You're not staying there? It's a dump."

Lee turned to walk out, but Henderson wasn't done.

"You owe me two hundred bucks for the ammo."

* * *

Chapter 46

Historic Route 66

Henderson was right about one thing; the Joshua Tree Motel was a dump. It looked like it hadn't seen a coat of paint since it was built, and by the single story architecture that had to be sometime in the fifties. Older model pick-up's were parked in front of several rooms, and four Mexican kids were playing soccer.

The Caddi pulled into the dirt parking lot followed by the Jeep Wrangler. They parked in front of an attached Mexican restaurant and bar with a half working neon office sign. Loud mariachi music poured out from inside.

"Next time, leave the arrangements for accommodations to Jamal, would you." Feinberg said.

Lee frowned and got out of the car. A blast of hot air met him as a couple of tumble weeds rolled past.

"I don't think you got the right place," Smitty said, stepping out of the Wrangler into the furnace. "This looks like where farm workers stay."

Lee hated to be wrong, and he hated people pointing it out.

"I'll go in and check it out," he grunted and started heading for the music.

"I wouldn't do that if I was you, Lee. You have ICE written all over you," Smitty said.

Fifteen minutes later they were all sitting in a booth at the Route 66 Hotel and restaurant where Jamal had booked them four rooms. The place looked like it had been sitting in the desert since the fifties when Route 66 was a major highway stretching from California to Illinois, but probably fell on hard times after the interstate replaced it.

A small swimming pool was stark blue against the brown surroundings and large date palms blocked off the highway of what remained of the historic route. The place had recently been remodeled as tourists started rediscovering the old Route 66 made famous in song and a popular TV show.

They had all checked in, and were regretting ordering cold drinks as the central air conditioner pumped out icy air.

Lee was trying to convince them that Henderson could be an important asset, but was being met by skepticism.

"Could you ask the waitress to bring me some coffee?" Mei-ling said, trying to wrap herself up in her light sleeveless blouse. Smitty ran his hand over her bare leg and it was covered in goose bumps. "It's freezing in here."

"He says he knows the terrain and he has some military ordinance that would be useful," Lee said. "I believe him."

"And he could just run over to the Sokolovs and sell us out," Feinberg said.

Just then a nondescript middle-aged woman dressed in standard waitress with a sweater draping her shoulders came over. "Is everything all right here?"

"Could you have them turn down the air conditioning?" Smitty said, with his arm wrapped around Mei-ling's shoulder.

The waitress leaned in conspiratorially. "I've asked them a thousand times. They insist the customers want it cool when they come in from the outside. Personally, I moved out here because I like the desert heat. I swear, I catch a cold every couple of weeks."

"You can't do anything?" Mail-ling said like a pouting child.

"I'm afraid not dear. But if you like there are some patio tables just outside around the pool. They have umbrellas to block the sun. I can serve you out there if you like."

They grabbed their ice drinks and made their way to the patio doors, into the heat of the afternoon and resettled at a round aluminum table with a red and white stripped umbrella; probably some local decorators idea of chic.

"Henderson," Lee said after they'd settled in.

"I told you what I think," Feinberg said. "Why should we trust the man?"

"He's a veteran. I knew him in Nam. He was a chopper pilot."

"So, that was a lot of years ago," Feinberg said.

"What does he want?" Smitty asked. "How much?"

"Nothing as far as I know," Lee answered. "He just said he wanted to get in on the action."

"I don't trust the man, no matter what you say," Feinberg said, taking off his jacket and revealing his shoulder holster with his .38 Special.

Duclois looked up from his lap top. "I think I will be getting a satellite image in a few hours," he said, as if he hadn't been listening at all.

"I think we should use him," Mei-ling said. "I agree with Mister Lee."

Lee smiled. If the woman agreed, Smitty would agree.

"Well, I guess he's in, but I don't understand it, and I'm uncomfortable with things I don't understand," Feinberg said, and sipped his iced tea.

"Good. I'll let him know."

"Oh, one more thing," Jamal said. "I monitored a phone call to the ranch. The plane will be arriving in two days."

"I'm really hungry," Mei-ling said.

Smitty looked at her. She had hardly eaten since they had left Oakland, and rarely smiled, and now she was beaming. She turned to him and kissed him. "Let's get that waitress," she said.

* * *

Chapter 47

Barstow

Smitty drove with Jamal into Barstow. Mei-ling had wanted to sleep in that morning. As they drove through the desert into town his thoughts drifted to the night before. They had stayed up late. From the moment they walked into their room at the motel she had thrown him down on the bed, and then slowly and sensually stripped off her shorts and blouse, followed by her bra and panties. She made love to him more aggressively and passionately than ever before, climaxing a dozen times before he came.

As they lay naked side by side, recovering and sharing a cigarette, she spoke eagerly of their life together after her obligation was finally finished once and for all. She dreamily lay out plans for them. They would buy a boat with the money she would get, and travel slowly around the world, making love night and day. And then they made love again, and so the night went, until the sun was beginning to rise.

Smitty's mind was pulled back to the present as Jamal glanced at his lap top, and instructed him where to go. They came to what looked like an older part of town that appeared to have been left behind as the city expanded. They stopped in front of a small store with a faded sign—Computer Repair, Copys, Fax—that was squeezed in between a liquor store and a vacant lot where some enterprising Mexican family had set up a taco stand.

"Wait here," Jamal said. "I'll be about half an hour."

He watched as Jamal disappeared into the small store, and then got out. The morning sun was already beating down mercilessly as summer refused to give way to the usually cooler temperatures of Fall. He hadn't eaten anything that morning and so headed over to the taco stand. The woman gave him a suspicious look. Her dark face retreated into her Indian reboso that was wrapped over her head with one dangling end swept over her shoulder.

He had a way with working people that set them at ease, and years of visiting his members who worked the kitchens of restaurants and hotels gave him a passable conversational Spanish.

For some reason he had always felt more comfortable with working people of color than with white people, perhaps because both neighborhoods he had grown up in—New York and LA—he had been the minority; a Jewish kid with commie parents living where working families of color lived because they couldn't rent or buy in white neighborhoods. The girls he dated were Mexican, Asian or black. He wondered if maybe that was why he had been so attracted to Mei-ling from the start. Parents were non-judgmental and to his buddies he was *one of us*.

He noticed the young children playing in the empty lot behind the Taco lady and smiled. He asked if she had tacos de berria. He loved the flavorful spiced goat meat and few gringos would ask for it. Her face brightened and a smile of shiny white teeth changed her whole appearance.

While she prepared the tacos, he learned that her husband had been deported back to Mexico after a raid on the strawberry field he had been working. She wouldn't work the fields because she didn't want her kids exposed to that kind of hard work or the pesticides the Farm Workers Union was warning about. She saved and borrowed from relatives to buy the taco stand.

He finished the savory little tortillas, smothered in the greasy meat with guacamole, and then popped a pickled pepper and carrot slice into his mouth.

"Come on Smitty, let's go. I'm finished here."

Smitty turned as Jamal stood at the Wrangler door, laptop in one hand and a large envelope on the other.

"You should have some of these tacos. They're really good."

"Never touch street food," Jamal answered.

Smitty downed the rest of his lukewarm Coke, thanked the woman—buena suerte, señora—and went to the car and hiked himself into the driver's seat.

"Where to?"

"Back to the motel. I want to go over this chart with Lee."

"I think he and Gabe headed back up to the gun club," Smitty said, as he guided the Wrangler toward the highway entrance. He was eager to see Mei-ling.

Lieutenant Henderson stepped out into the dusty parking lot as the Caddi drove in. There were a couple of pickups parked along the ridge of the arroyo, and a sporadic sound of small arms fire echoed up from the ranges.

Lee and Feinberg got out of the Caddi and walked over to the Gun club office where Henderson waited for them with a scowl.

"Well, Mister NSA and Mister FBI. What can we do for you?"

"I hope you didn't go to the Joshua Tree Motel to meet us. You were right; the place is basically a dump."

"Well I did go and you didn't even leave a message for me. So I thought you just wrote me off."

"No," Lee said. "Can we come in and talk with you? It's hot out here."

"Well, you could have called. We're in the book."

"I have to apologize for that," Lee said. "I just didn't. No excuses. Now, can we come in and talk?"

He started walking toward the door, with Feinberg trailing behind.

"Hold up," Henderson said, pushing back his Hawaiian shirt to reveal the .45 automatic stuck in his pants.

Feinberg started to go for the .38, but Lee stopped him.

"Come on lieutenant, there's no need for that. We all agreed that we want your help."

"Is that so..."

Lee's cell phone interrupted the conversation. He reached into his pocket and answered it, listened for a minute and then flipped the phone shut and put it back in his pocket. He turned to Feinberg. "We got to get back to the motel, Gabe. Jamal has the satellite photo." Then back to Henderson. "If you want in, fine."

He turned to go back to the Caddi.

"Hold on there," Henderson said. Lee and Feinberg turned back to the lieutenant.

"Well?" Lee said.

"I want in. But I want ... a thousand bucks. Okay?"

Lee looked at Gabe .

"Don't look at me," the FBI man said. "I don't have any money."

"A thousand ... okay, but you'd better bring something special for that kind of dough."

"You won't be disappointed, Captain."

"Meet us at the motel around six—the Route 66—I want to check things out tonight. "

"I'll be there, Captain." Henderson said, giving Lee a casual salute.

"The man's crazy. You know that," Feinberg said.

"We're all crazy," Lee said. "This whole fucking operation is crazy. That's what I like about it."

Feinberg sat back in the plush leather seat of the Caddi, wondering how he had gotten mixed up in this—what did Lee call it—craziness. The AC blasted frigid air into the interior of the car, making the outside furnace seem unreal, like watching Lawrance of Arabia in an air conditioned theater. He turned on the car radio and scanned through the stations, but all he could find was Mexican ranchero and Country Western. He switched off the radio, and pushed the button on the door to open the car window so the hot air of the desert blasted on his face.

Suddenly a large funnel of dust rose from the desert floor carrying with it tumble weeds and anything else that wasn't attached to the earth. They were headed right into its path. His window went up. Lee had pushed his control button. Then the car was engulfed in the dust devil and it seemed to take them with it into its swirling chaos ... and then it was gone.

* * *

Chapter 48

Sokolov Ranch, Mohave Desert

Lieutenant Henderson pulled his Ford Econoline Van off the dirt road and stopped.

"We're on foot from here," Henderson said.

Lee stepped out on the passenger side, looking up into the star filled night. The moon had dropped below the western horizon at seven, just as Henderson had said it would, leaving almost total darkness over the desert.

It had taken a lot of arguing to convince Mei-ling she couldn't go on the recon mission. It wasn't that Lee thought she wasn't capable, but if he let her go Smitty would insist on going.

"I don't want a gang of people going up there. I'm just going to check it out."

Henderson showed up at the motel with only two pairs of night vision goggles. That settled it for Gabe not going, although Lee knew the

FBI man was suspicious of the lieutenant, and had told Lee so, arguing that he should not go up to the ranch without backup. But with no night vision goggles the FBI man knew he'd be useless and conceded as much.

They had all studied the satellite chart that Jamal had made at the computer store in Barstow, so they all had some idea of the lay of the land. The chart revealed what was probably a ranch house with a number of outbuildings around it and a half mile long asphalt roadway that went from nowhere to nowhere—a landing strip?—all tucked neatly between two ranges of low hills.

"How can they fly in without someone picking them up on radar or something?" Mei-ling asked.

"Perfect cover for the drug planes to come in unnoticed," Feinberg said.

"There's a lot of small aircraft in the area," Henderson added. "The Barstow Flying School air strip is just a few miles away. No radar so no one would notice."

"But isn't there a big Air Base nearby? Edwards I think you called it?"

"They don't pay attention to civilian traffic unless it intrudes on their air space," Henderson said.

"That would never happen in China," Mei-ling said.

"Welcome to America," Lee said.

She was getting tired of hearing it.

Lee lowered the night vision goggles over his eyes. Suddenly the desert around him exposed itself in an eerie pea green hue. Henderson came up alongside him. He had an M-16 slung over his back.

"I don't want any shooting," Lee said.

"Just in case," Henderson said.

"No shooting," Lee repeated, and ventured out into the wasteland of dirt, rocks and sage brush. Suddenly he caught sight of a figure standing to his right. He hit the ground and pulled an automatic from his belt. Then he heard Henderson snicker, and he looked up. It was a Joshua Tree, in the shape of a man, looming out of the green light.

"Relax captain. There ain't nobody out here but, jack rabbits, rattle snakes and us."

They walked on for about half an hour before the low hills came into view. Lee made a mental note.

They scrambled up the hill and flopped on their bellies at the ridge. Lee flashed back to Vietnam and Cambodia.

They were looking over the ranch and outbuildings. Beyond the compound there was a landing strip about 6,000 feet long—big enough for a private jet to land. One of the buildings looked like it could be a hanger, and piled up next to a barn like building there was a large pile of cut bamboo.

There were lights on in the ranch house, and two flood lights lit up the compound. Lee was trying to figure out how they could attack the place without being detected, when a man came out of the building with the bamboo stacked along side. Lee figured it was the Russian veterinarian; probably the same man Smitty and Mei-ling mentioned had been with the Chinese smugglers.

"That's probably where they are keeping it," he said, not meaning to be heard.

"Keeping what?" Henderson asked. "Just what are you people after here?"

Lee watched the Russian as he walked to the ranch house and disappeared under its eaves. Then he looked at Henderson.

"I mean, I don't have to know if you don't want to tell me," Henderson said. "Hell, we never knew what our mission was when we went into

Cambodia and got you and your partner out of there."

"It's okay, Lieutenant," Lee said. "You're a volunteer. You deserve to know."

"I'm all ears," Henderson said.

Lee lifted the night vision goggles from his eyes and rested them on his forehead. "We believe they have a panda down there."

"A what?"

"A panda, as in panda bear. It's one of three that were smuggled out of China last year. The other two have been killed already. Our mission is to kill this last one before it's flown out of here."

Henderson lifted his night vision goggles and looked at him. "And I thought I was crazy."

"You can still back out of you want,"

"Oh, hell no. I wouldn't miss this for the world."

"How many men do you think are down there?"

"I counted six the last time I was here, but there could be more," Henderson said.

"Well," Lee said, looking back down into the compound, "we're going to have to create some kind of diversion if we're going to be able to get down there and establish a beach head."

Henderson smiled. "Leave that to me."

Lee knew better than to question the wily lieutenant.

* * *

Chapter 49

Bartsow, Ca

Mei-ling put a fatigue cap on her head and looked into the mirror at the Barstow Army and Navy Surplus store.

"What do you think?" she said to Smitty, who was standing at the counter handing the clerk a list that contained everyone's sizes in shirts, hats, pants and boots.

Smitty looked over at her as she turned and cocked the hat in a jaunty tilt.

"Mei, my love, you make standard issue look like the latest Parisian fashion."

She laughed and joined him at the counter.

They had volunteered to come into town and purchase the proper attire for a military mission as Lee had put it.

"Do you have shorts?" Mei-ling asked the clerk.

Smitty's memory flashed back to Glen Ellen when she sported tight fitting camo shorts that were sexy as hell on her, but drew unwanted attention from the customers at the Jack London Inn.

"They are what I wore when we went on patrol in Vietnam," she had insisted.

"I know you like them, but I think they might be distracting. They were to me the last time you wore them. Besides, it's getting cold at night."

Mei-ling smiled. She knew exactly what she was doing. She picked out a khaki shirt and matching pants from the table indicating Women's Army Issue, and disappeared into the changing room.

"You people paintballing?" the young clerk asked, as he rummaged through the piles of clothing stacked neatly according to size. He had pimples all over his pasty white skin, and his mousey brown hairy hung haphazardly over his shoulders and down the back of the faded camo shirt he wore hanging out over blue jeans. "I try and do it every week or so. There's a group of us. It's a blast, don't you think. My boss turned me on to it. He's a Vietnam vet and still loves the action."

What was it about some veterans that still liked to play war? Smitty wondered. Most vets he knew were spending their lives running away from the memory, hiding in a maze of drugs and alcohol.

"Yes, something like that," Smitty answered. His thoughts were about Mei-ling in the tight camo shorts, and the passionate love they had made before setting out for Stover's ranch. Was it really a year ago? She was the sexiest, most desirable woman he had ever known.

"How about this?"

He looked toward the dressing room where Mei-ling stood in a pose. She still had the fatigue hat on, and she wore a khaki shirt with the top four buttons suggestively undone down to her belly button, with matching khaki pants that clung to her trim body like a second skin and the legs rolled up to reveal her shapely calves.

The clerk's jaw had dropped as he stood stupidly gaping. He finally managed to let out a low whistle. "I'd go paintballing with you anytime, miss." he said.

Smitty glared at him, but couldn't really blame him for admiring her. She was hot.

"That's fine, honey, only maybe you should button up the shirt." He turned back to the clerk. "You don't have any night vision goggles do you?"

Mei-ling went to the mirror, smiled, and then slowly buttoned up the khaki shirt.

"I never had any complaints from comrades in Vietnam," she said cheerily, as she walked back to the counter, took Smitty's arm and clung tightly to him.

"No one's complaining," Smitty said. "Goggles?"

The clerk was busy watching Mei-ling. "Huh? Night vision goggles? No, we don't carry them. You plan on paintballing at night?"

"Just total everything up."

The clerk started punching numbers into the cash register.

"That will be three hundred and fifty-eight dollars and thirty-five cents," he finally said. "Will that be cash or charge?"

Smitty pulled out a wad of bills that Lee had given him. He peeled off eight fifties."

"Don't see many General Grants these days," the clerk said, counting out the bills.

Smitty smiled to himself at the irony. Lee seemed to prefer the fifty with its picture of General Ulysses S. Grant, the man who had whipped his own grandfather in the Civil War.

The clerk shoved the bills under the cash tray and then counted out the change.

"We have a full line of paintball equipment, you know," he said.

"Just bag up the clothes if you don't mind."

The closer the raid came to being a reality, the more apprehensive Smitty had felt about it. Mei-ling, on the other hand had lit up. She was playful and happy; eager to bring closure to her mission. She had always seemed to accept the possibility of being killed in the process without a second thought. It must be a Buddhist thing, Smitty thought, wishing he could accept things as easily as she seemed to.

* * *

Chapter 50

Route 66 Motel

Nine-thirty sharp they gathered in the parking lot in front of the motel as per Lee's instructions.

They had all retired to their rooms after a dinner that only Jamal and Mei-ling seemed interested in. They had gone over the terrain one last time, and Jamal informed them that he had intercepted a call to the ranch saying the plane would be arriving around eleven that night.

Since there was no bar at the restaurant Lee had bought a bottle of Remi Martin at a nearby liquor store. It was the best Barstow seemed to have to offer. He pulled it out for the occasion and poured everyone a drink

"To our success," he said.

They clinked glasses and downed the smooth cognac.

"We'll take both vehicles," Lee said.

"What happened to Henderson?" Feinberg asked.

"The lieutenant? I suspect we'll find out when we get to the ranch," Lee said, leaving everyone wondering what he meant. The truth was, he wasn't sure himself. Henderson had said he was going back to the gun club for some things, and he would catch up to them. That was after he had dropped Lee off at three a.m. at the motel. It was the last he had seen or heard from him. For all he knew, the Lieutenant had decided the mission was too risky after scouting the lay out. Lee wouldn't blame him if he had. It looked like a hopeless situation. On the other hand, maybe Gabe was right. Maybe he had gone to the ranch and warned them—for a price—in which case they'd all be dead by the morning.

He looked at the faces of his little troop. Even in the shadowy light of the parking lot he could read each one: Gabe, the FBI man; professional concern; Jamal, hunted all his life, smiling and unconcerned; Mei-ling Wu, bursting with anticipation and hope. And then there was Smitty, the honest union man who wanted nothing more than to make his woman happy. The look on his face was one Lee had seen on men's faces who were about to be ordered on a suicide mission; that familiar look of dread and resignation. Of the whole crew, Lee felt most sorry about Smitty.

"I have to be honest with you," Lee said. "This is not going to be easy, and some of us could easily be killed. I'm giving you one last opportunity to back out. No one will think less of you if you do."

There was a moment of silence, and then Mei-ling burst out, "What are we waiting for? Who knows how long the plane will be there."

She took Jamal and Smitty by the arm and headed them to the Jeep. They obediently got in; Smitty in the driver's seat and Jamal, with his lap top, in the back. Just before Mei-ling swung into the front seat, Lee came over.

"What are you waiting for? We'll follow you."

"Just hold up a minute, Ms. Wu."

Lee went to the Caddy and opened the trunk, retrieved something and then closed it. He walked back over to the Jeep and handed Smitty a walkie-talkie. "We'll communicate over these from now on. You know how to use it?"

"I'll learn," Smitty said.

Lee gave him a quick demonstration. "Got it?"

"Copy that," Smitty said. 'That's right isn't it? I heard some cops use it while I was in the back of their squad car."

"That's right," Lee said. "Now, follow me."

* * *

Chapter 51

Mohave Desert

They pulled onto the highway from what was now called the *Historic Route Sixty-six*. The traffic was sparse aside from the caravans of trucks. Lee glanced in the mirror. The Jeep Wrangler was right behind them as if it was connected by an invisible chain.

"So, you think Henderson is going to be there waiting for us?" Feinberg asked, breaking the silence that seemed to hang over them like the stillness of the desert around them.

Lee snapped open his Zippo and ignited it, lighting up his face as he lit a cigarette.

"He'll be there," he said.

"How can you be so sure? He could just as easily have warned the Russians."

"He wouldn't do that," Lee said. "The man is Army through and through. He wouldn't sell us out. I'm sure of it."

"I hope you're right," Feinberg said, and went silent again.

Lee hoped he was right too. Henderson seemed preoccupied with money. A thousand dollars. Would he go to the Russians and see if he could do better? All Lee knew was that if he wasn't there, whether he warned the Russians or not, it could be a suicide mission. One way or the other, they would soon know.

He swung out into the left lane to avoid any passing semis that could separate him from the tailing Wrangler. Trucks had an annoying habit of trying to pass each other, and could slow the fast lane down to a crawl while they struggled to overcome the other slightly slower trucks.

They traveled south toward Mojave for about seven miles, and then took the Hinkle Road exit where a Shell station stood out like a lonely bastion of civilization in a sea of darkness. They drove down Hinkle which ran parallel to the highway for ten miles, and then Lee turned right onto an unmarked gravel road heading north.

The desert lay like a black void in front of them as they headed for the low hills in the distance standing like black silhouette cutouts. A full moon sinking in the west cast an eerie blue hue over the vast emptiness.

It seemed like they had been driving for hours, as Smitty chased behind the red tail lights of the Caddi. He was uncomfortable and out of his element. He never liked the open stillness; his senses were tuned to the constant ambient sounds of the city, and the absence of lights and landmarks threw him into confusion. Driving to an unknown destination made it all the more troubling. Their headlights caught the black shadows of the sparse Joshua Trees that stood up out of the desert like frozen guardians, and an occasional Jack Rabbit scampered off into the darkness, or the carcass of a smashed rattlesnake that had innocently squirmed onto the hot pavement. Now and then, he would glance over at Mei-ling who had her head resting on the back of the seat, staring out into the darkness. He peeked into the rear view mirror where the pale blue light of Jamal's lap top cast a surreal shadow on his dark face.

Finally Lee slowed down and stopped. The headlights of the Cadillac went off. Then the interior lights came on as Lee opened the door, and the trunk lid slowly opened on its own, lighting up its interior. The repetitive bleeting from inside the car beckoned the driver to return and remove the keys. Feinberg leaned over and remedied the situation and the noise stopped. Lee went around to the trunk and pulled out a couple of guns and a small backpack. Then he closed the trunk and came over to the driver's side of the Jeep. Smitty rolled down his window and the night air hit his face.

"Lights off from here on," Lee said and handed Smitty the AK 47, "for Ms. Wu," and the M16, "for you." Then the back pack. "Extra ammo clips."

"We got forty minutes before the plane is suppose to arrive," Jamal said from the back seat.

Lee nodded. "Keep close, we're going off the road from here on out," and then walked back to his car.

The going was slow as they bumped over the open ground, but they finally came to a stop at the foot of the low hills. Henderson's van was parked there already, but when they got out, there was no sign of the Lieutenant.

"Where do you suppose he is?" Feinberg said, still having doubts about the man.

The others got out of the Jeep and looked around into the darkness.

"He'll show himself when he's ready," Lee said. "Probably already up there." He leaned over the FBI man and opened the glove compartment.

He took out a package. "I want you to take these in case I don't make it back," he said.

"What are these?"

"CDs Malcolm gave me. They're what he called his memoirs. I have added one of my own. Give them to your reporter buddy. He'll know what to do with them."

"Why not do it yourself?"

"Just do what I ask. And make sure you stay alive. Okay."

For the first time Feinberg started to wonder if he would survive another day. He was wanted by the FBI, there were hired guns trying to kill him and his wife was going to divorce him. And now he was attacking a ranch full of Russian mafiaoso. Hell, he thought, I got nothing to lose one way or the other.

"Sure Lee. Don't worry about it."

Lee opened the trunk, handed Feinberg an M16 and took one out for himself.

"Jamal, you stay here with the vehicles," Lee said, handing him the side arm. "If you see us coming down from the hills in a hurry, start both cars so we can get out of here fast."

"I think I'll tag along if you don't mind," Jamal said. "I'd hate to miss out on the action after coming this far."

"Suit yourself," Lee said. "But keep your head down."

* * *

Chapter 52

Sokolov Ranch/Mojave

They gathered at the bottom of the hill and then started up, single file, with Lee in the lead, followed by Feinberg, then Mei-ling and Smitty, and Jamal in the rear. Smitty looked at Mei-ling ahead of him. She had her weapon slung across her back like she had been doing it all her life, looking very much like a seasoned guerrilla fighter. He felt awkward with his own weapon dangling in front of him, but he imitated Lee and Feinberg, holding the weapon with his finger near the trigger. He thought about the pimple-faced kid back at the surplus store, playing war by shooting people with paint balls, and he couldn't imagine the attraction. He wondered how the kid would react if it was live ammunition. He recalled the times he had come under live fire since he had hooked up with Mei-ling. But this was the first time he had a weapon, and would be expected to shoot back. He had been willing to face danger with Mei-ling, even be killed if that was what happened, but was he capable of shooting back, in all likelihood killing another human being? He glanced down at his hands. They were shaking. *What the fuck are you doing here? I'm a union business agent, not some goddamned commando. This is fucking insane...*

They reached the ridge overlooking the compound and took up positions. Lee, Feinberg and Mei-ling were trained in combat and fell in like it was second nature. Smitty copied what he saw the others doing, ducking low with weapons at the ready. Smitty looked down into the compound. The ranch house lights were on and several flood lights lit up the grounds around the out buildings.

Lee pulled out a pair of binoculars from his back pack and scanned the hills around them until he spotted Henderson, dug in at a low spot along the ridge about a hundred yards away. The lieutenant had come through. Lee smiled, and, for the first time since they had started out from the motel, thought perhaps there was a chance they'd make it out alive. He passed the binoculars to Feinberg and pulled out his walky-talky.

Feinberg took a look and then passed the binoculars on to Mei-ling.

"Check out the shed with all the bamboo next to the barn."

"That must be where they're keeping the panda, and look Isaac," she passed the binoculars on to Smitty. "Recognize him?"

A crew cut man was standing by the barn. "Our old friend from the Oakland Hills and Stover's."

He went to pass on the binoculars, but Jamal put up his hand. "Listen, do you hear it?"

"What?" Smitty said.

"A jet; flying low to the ground. I'd recognize those Rolls Royce engines anywhere. A Gulfstream I'll wager."

Suddenly the airstrip was lit up with two rows of edge lights running off toward the east. The moon had dropped behind the western horizon and the sky filled with stars. Armed men appeared from the ranch house and around the compound, all hurrying toward the runway. Several of them, guided by the familiar Russian, opened the doors to the large barn.

"Okay, we're going down while they're distracted." Lee said. "We'll take positions behind the ranch house."

They started to get up from their prone positions, but Lee put his hand on Jamal's shoulder. "Not you Jamal. I want you to work your way over to Henderson and see if you can be of some use."

Jamal just shrugged, "Okay boss."

They started moving as a group down from the ridge. The sound of the approaching plane's smooth engines hummed in the distance. Smitty, who was following close behind Mei-ling, stopped for a moment to look up as the landing lights of the Gulfstream II appeared in the distance, like the glowing eyes of some otherworldly creature against the black night. Smitty kept watching as the outline of the jet became silhouetted by the lights on the ground, and then touched down in a smooth, silent motion.

He looked back at his companions who were now a good twenty-five feet ahead of him and approaching the rear of the ranch house. He hurried forward to catch them and stumbled over a rock, sending him careening forward into Mei-ling.

"What are you doing, Isaac," she whispered, helping him steady himself.

Lee and Feinberg spun around, guns at the ready, to see what was the commotion.

"Sorry, I tripped."

Lee ran his finger across his throat in an angry slashing motion which Smitty interrupted as Shut the fuck up.

Jamal was also watching the jet land from his perch just above Henderson. He admired how the pilot had flown in at low altitude under the radar eyes at Edwards, with the running lights off, both serious violations of FAA rules. But these were Russian gangsters and could care less about FAA rules. Jamal figured the pilot to be a veteran of the Soviet military

www.ingramcontent.com/pod-product-compliance
Lightning Source LLC
Chambersburg PA
CBHW050921030726
47503CB00007BB/2406